WHERE WITCHES LIE

A WITCH SQUAD COZY MYSTERY

M.Z. ANDREWS

Where Witches Lie
A Witch Squad Cozy Mystery: Book #6
by
M.Z. Andrews

Copyright © M.Z. Andrews 2017

ISBN: 9781695152946
ASIN: B07Y8LD7YW
VS: 09232019.01

Second Edition
Cover Art by Arrigo Verderosa
Contact email: verderosa.arrigo@gmail.com
Editing by Donna Rich

CONTENTS

"What time did you guys get in last night?" I asked as I picked up a flat green tray from the beginning of the breakfast line and propped it up on my hip. The warmth of the steaming hot food enveloped me, and the smell of bacon and maple syrup flooded my nose. "Jax and I fell asleep waiting for you."

Alba inched forward in the line. She looked back at the rest of our friends without moving her thick torso. "What time did we get in? I didn't even look at the time," she said to Sweets.

Sweets rolled her eyes exaggeratedly. "Oh wow. It was at least one. Longest. Drive. *Ever.*"

Holly nodded and leaned on Sweets's shoulder. "It was. Oh my gosh, I'm exhausted!"

Alba puffed out her breath. "How can *you* be exhausted? You slept the entire way home from the airport! I was the one who stayed awake the whole trip to keep Sweets from nodding off at the wheel."

Holly grinned and suppressed a giggle. "True story. But it was a long vacation, and I'm jet-lagged from the flight!"

Jax's purple hair, her color of the week, brushed the tops of her shoulders as she shook her head with a smile. "You guys were so lucky that the airport rescheduled all the flights in and out of Pittsburgh after that storm. Otherwise, you might not have gotten to fly home for Christmas."

Holly's blue eyes widened as she nodded her head animatedly. "Oh, I know! Do you realize how *boring* Christmas vacation would have been if we'd have been stuck in the b&b the *whole* time."

Jax's bottom lip plumped out. She crossed her arms over her chest and shot Holly a look. "Are you saying you three didn't have fun with us on Christmas?"

Sweets shook her head in protest as the breakfast line inched forward a little more. "That's totally not what Holly is saying at all, Jax. We had a *blast* together at Christmas. I just think we all needed a break away from Aspen Falls and The Institute. We especially needed a chance to see our families. I know I did."

Jax peered up at Holly with raised eyebrows. Holly nodded somberly. "That's what I meant, Jaxie." She held up two hands when Jax's chin jutted out further. "Honest!" She giggled.

I laughed and took two steps forward as two girls at the end of the line finished filling their trays, paid, and exited through the door at the end of the line. "Oh, cut 'em some slack, Jax. They spent Christmas morning playing board games with us, and you were even able to convince them to go sledding when the storm died down. I think they deserve some credit for that."

Alba's head bobbed without turning around to face Jax. "What she said," she agreed, pointing at me with her thumb.

Jax's fake pout wore off quickly. Her bright blue eyes

twinkled as she uncrossed her arms and slid one hand into Holly's bent elbow and squeezed her arm affectionately. "I'm glad you guys got to spend at least a little of Christmas break with us. Even if it was a crazy storm – I'm glad we were together. And *flying* through a storm like that – oh man, I'll remember that forever!"

Alba and Sweets each took a green tray from the stack. "I can't believe the amount of snow left on the ground," said Alba. "I was hoping it would all be gone by the time we got back."

I shrugged as I scooped up a big glob of steaming scrambled eggs from the serving line and plopped it down in one of the squares on my tray. "How could it have melted? The temperature hasn't gotten a single degree above freezing since Christmas Eve!"

"I take it Hugh isn't back from Texas?" Sweets asked, grabbing an oversized cinnamon roll from the tray.

"He got back late last night. I haven't seen him yet, but we talked over break. We both agreed. No more messing with Mother Nature."

Holly eyed Sweets's food selection as our overweight friend moved forward in the line. "Is that the healthy choice, Sweets?"

Sweets looked down at her cinnamon roll sadly. "Does *everything* have to be healthy?"

Holly gave Sweets a sympathetic smile. "Don't you remember what Harper and Ronnie's ghosts showed us on Christmas Eve? We don't want you to die from bad eating habits. We're supposed to be keeping an eye on each other."

Sweets sighed. "I know, but changes take time. I *have* been using the fitness tracker you guys got me for Christmas, though."

"That's awesome, Sweets. Do you like it?" I asked her.

She nodded. "I do. It's been fun trying to get my steps in every day," she said, looking down at the plum-colored Fitbit we'd all chipped in and gotten her.

"If you promise to work out with me later you can have the cinnamon roll," Jax suggested brightly as she grabbed a tray and set it down on the metal serving line.

"Work out? You mean like *running*?" Sweets asked, curling her lip and scrunching up her nose as if the word *running* left a bad taste in her mouth. She shook her head resolutely. "I only run if something's chasing me."

Jax smiled. "There's still too much snow on the ground around campus to go running outside. You could come with me to my yoga class?"

Sweets sighed. "Okay. Fine. I'll do yoga with you. But I get to keep the roll, right?"

"Yes, you get to keep the roll," agreed Jax with a satisfied nod. "It's all about balance."

"I don't have a very good center of gravity, so I'm not sure how my balance will be, but yay! I get to keep the roll!" Sweets clapped her hands together excitedly.

When I had made all of my selections, I pushed my dark rimmed glasses up my nose and handed my student ID card to Brittany Hobbs to scan. She was one of Headmistress Stone's lackeys. She usually worked in the front office doing secretarial work for Stone, but at breakfast and lunch, she also worked as the cashier in the cafeteria. "Welcome back, Mercy," the young woman said cheerfully. "How was your Christmas break?"

I looked at her with contempt. As it had done on the first day of school, her cheerfulness still made my skin crawl. "Peachy," I said without making eye contact with her. I waited at the end of the line for the rest of the girls to fill up their trays. The clanging sound of a metal serving tray being changed caused me to look up. For the first time since entering the cafeteria that morning, I noticed Denise, the cafeteria lady. Her eyes were red and swollen, and she was fighting back tears. The Institute employed two cafeteria ladies. Denise and Midge. Of the two, Denise was my favorite.

"Denise!" I said louder than I had intended. "What's the matter?"

Immediately the rest of the girls looked up at Denise. She was an amazonian woman with wide hips and broad shoulders. Her brown hair was pulled back into a tight bun, highlighting the fact that she was graying at her temples. In that moment of looking at her closely, I became aware of the fact that I'd never seen her hair out of its net nor had I ever noticed the crow's feet that adorned her face like an unwelcomed badge of time.

Sweets sucked in a breath at the sight of Denise's puffy-eyed, haggard appearance. "Denise! What's wrong?" she asked, stopping dead in her tracks.

The girl standing behind Jax groaned as the extraordinarily slow line stopped moving again. She threw her hand on her hip and cocked it out.

Denise glanced at the girl behind Jax, tucked her thumb into the collar of her shirt and used the material to blot her eyes. "Oh, it's nothing, girls."

Jax shook her head with resolve. "This isn't *nothing*. You're a mess! What's the matter?"

Denise's eyes filled with tears as she looked out at the five of us. "Really, girls. Thanks for the concern, but I'm okay. How was Christmas break?" she asked, attempting to change the subject.

Sweets and Jax exchanged worried glances, but before they could turn the subject back to Denise's obvious problem, the girl behind Jax shoved her tray into Jax's, moving the convoy of trays ahead in a jerky fashion.

"Can you losers host this pity party in your room or something? The rest of us back here are starving," said the girl.

Jax, Sweets, Holly, Alba, and I all made a face, as our eyes narrowed to pinpricks looking down the line. I was sure I'd never seen the girl before. She was a tad shorter than my 5'10" height with a slender, athletic build. Her long brown hair was swept up into a ponytail, and she wore an oversized taupe cardigan over a plain white t-shirt, skinny jeans, and a pair of UGG boots.

Alba lifted her tray off the end of the serving line. "*Excuse me*," she grumbled angrily.

The girl rolled her eyes. "There *is* no excuse for you. Oh, and the 80's called. They want their sweatsuit back."

My jaw dropped. I'd never heard anyone speak to Alba like that before. Except maybe Holly, but only when Alba deserved it.

Alba's face flushed red, and her posture straightened. She took a defensive step towards the girl. If Alba hadn't been holding a tray of food, I was sure she would have been grinding that girl's face with her fist by now.

Holly put a hand out against Alba's stomach, to gently hold her back. Then she whipped around to face the new girl. "I'm sorry. Who are you?" Holly asked angrily as she stirred the air near her head with her hand.

The girl let out a chortle as she looked Holly up and down. "You're right about one thing. You *are* sorry. And it's none of your business who I am."

Holly's face filled with red and her nostrils flared as she stomped her foot down on the floor angrily.

"Let's go, Holly," I commanded. The new girl was

apparently looking for a fight, and I for one didn't have the energy or the desire to give it to her on our first day back at the Paranormal Institute for Witches.

Holly picked up her tray as she glared at the girl.

Sweets looked up at Denise, ignoring everything else. "Are you sure you're going to be okay, Denise? Is there anything we can do to help?"

Denise smiled at Sweets gratefully, but before she could get a word in, the new girl interjected. "I'm not kidding. Either keep your personal problems to yourself or deal with them somewhere else. This is the breakfast line, not the counselor's office," growled the beastly girl.

Sweets furrowed her eyebrows at the girl. "You're rude!"

The girl closed her eyes and raised her eyebrows as she shrugged. "You're fat."

Jax's mouth dropped open as she turned towards the offender. "Uh!"

"What's with the witch hat, Shorty?" the girl asked, looking down her nose at Jax disdainfully. "Is it dress up day in kindergarten?"

That was the last straw with Alba. Catching me off guard, she thrust her tray into my chest. I tried to balance both hers and mine without letting her food squish mine. She plunged herself forward and rushed the new girl, pushing back the sleeves of her oversized black crewneck sweatshirt. "That's it. I've had enough out of you. Now we're going to settle this like witches," Alba said gruffly, tilting her head from side to side, cracking her neck.

Jax placed her body between Alba and the new girl worriedly. "It's okay, Alba. Sorceress Stone is going to flip if you start a fight in the cafeteria," said Jax nervously.

Alba shook her head. "Alright then, let's take it outside."

The girl laughed. "You really think you'd win, don't you?"

With her shoulders pulled back, Alba pressed her chest into the other girl's chest. "Oh I don't *think*, I *know*."

The girl shrugged. "Fine. Let's do this."

At the end of the line, Brittany Hobbs stood up nervously. She'd taken in the whole scene quietly, but now that things were getting intense, she knew she needed to intercede. "Alba, please don't," she said, her voice trembling.

Alba turned around, not to acknowledge Brittany, but to leave the line and take the fight elsewhere. With Alba's back turned, the new girl took the opportunity to grab an empty tray off the line. With two hands she held it over her shoulder, then with one even, steady, powerful move; she whacked Alba over the back of her head and shoulders with the tray, making a loud thudding noise.

I sucked in my breath as I watched Alba's expression change from anger to rage. In a split second, she whipped back around to face the girl. "Jax. Holly. Sweets. Clear out."

"Alba, I don't think you should—" Jax began, her eyes filled with fear for Alba's safety.

"Clear out!" Alba roared as the new girl turned around, laughing wildly with the girl behind her.

Jax, Holly, and Sweets scampered to the end of the line next to Brittany and me.

"Alba, don't do it," Brittany hollered at her. "It's not worth you getting in trouble too."

"Alba, please!" Sweets cried. "Don't do it!"

But Alba didn't wait. Once the girls were safely out of range, Alba unleashed a torrent of energy at the girl. Crackling, the bolt of green and blue energy tossed the girl against the stone wall behind her like a rag doll.

Brittany bolted then. I groaned. I knew where she was going – to find Stone. "Alba, Brittany is getting Stone. Don't do this. Let it go. We'll deal with her another way," I assured her. But I knew Alba wouldn't stop.

Alba moved quickly towards the girl, pouncing before she had a chance to recover from the fall and get to her feet. With her left hand, she gripped the girl's sweater and pulled her up to her feet. Her right hand balled into a fist and pulled back, but before she could strike, Denise came out of nowhere and grabbed Alba's arm, stopping the punch before it could land.

The diversion was enough for the new girl's friend to pull her out of the line and through the doorway into the dining hall.

"Lemme go!" insisted Alba with wild eyes. Her chest heaved as she growled, "I'm gonna crush her face!"

Denise continued to hold Alba's arms pinned behind her back until Sorceress Stone showed up.

Sorceress SaraLynn Stone's long thin face was beet red. The contrast of her red face against her long white hair gave her the illusion of steam coming out of her ears. "What's going on?" she demanded, looking at Denise and Alba with shock and horror.

"That new girl struck her over the head with a lunch tray," said Denise. "Alba tried to punch her, but I was able to restrain her."

Sorceress Stone nodded, looking relieved. "Very impressive, Denise. Thank you for restraining her. What started the fight?"

"She insulted us!" Jax hollered out from the other end of the line.

"We were going to take it outside," Alba hollered angrily as Denise slowly released her arms. Alba reached back and rubbed the back of her head. "But out of nowhere, she smacked me with a tray. I want her expelled!"

Sorceress Stone puffed air out of her nose. "You just said. You were going to take it outside. Looks like she got the best of you before you could get the best of her."

Alba's eyes widened. "You're going to let her get away with that?!"

"I'll have a talk with her," Sorceress Stone assured us. She looked down her nose at Alba and with one long, bony finger pointing at her she muttered with tight lips, "No fighting in my school. Understand?"

Alba spun on her heels and walked towards me. "Whatever," she grumbled before taking her tray from my arms. "Let's go, girls."

CHAPTER 2

Mumbling under her breath, Alba led us to a table in the dining hall. Snow covered the courtyard with drifts up to our elbows, so there would be no more eating outside until springtime. I looked around as I set my tray down. The dreary cafeteria had so much less to look at, but we had no other choice. Alba slammed her tray down on one of the rectangular tables near the far corner of the room.

"Can I get you some ibuprofen, Alba?" Jax asked as she sat her tray down opposite of Alba's tray.

"Yeah, is your head alright?" Sweets asked, her voice filled with concern.

Alba looked up, snarling at both of them. "I'm fine. That witch hits like a girl."

"She is a girl," said Jax. A tiny smile curled the edges of her mouth.

Alba's angry glare wiped the smile off of her face immediately.

"Sorry," Jax mouthed as she took a seat in front of her tray.

I climbed over the bench seat and sat down in front of Jax. "Calm down, Alba," I suggested. "At least Stone didn't lock you in the tower."

"I wish she had! I wish she'd locked me up with that… that…THING! Then I'd have gotten to smash her ugly face in!"

"Then you'd have gotten expelled," said Holly calmly as she buttered her piece of toast.

"I don't care!" Alba growled, bouncing on her feet. She was too wound up to sit down.

"You do care," I assured her. "Your family would have been upset if you'd have gotten sent home without your diploma. Now take a deep breath and relax. Then sit down. Let's eat. We have to get to class." I unrolled the silverware wound up in my napkin as Holly and Sweets joined Jax and me at the table. Jax and Sweets both kept a close eye on Alba. Holly, on the other hand, didn't seem to mind that Alba was worked up. She slid down the smooth bench and grabbed the salt and pepper from the middle of the table.

Without looking up, Holly patiently addressed Alba while she salted her eggs. "Your food is going to get cold. Then *she* wins because you had to eat cold food. You don't want to let her win, do you?"

"She hasn't won anything!" Alba growled.

Holly shrugged calmly. "Then sit down and let's eat. We'll figure out how to get her back in a way that won't get you in trouble."

Alba looked around at the girls filling up the rest of the chairs. "Where did she go?"

"She took off with her friend before my mom showed up," said Jax. "I saw them head for the stairs; they must have gone back to their rooms."

Alba closed her eyes and blew out the deep breath she'd been holding. She leaned her head from side to side, cracking her neck. Wordlessly, she slid in next to me and opened her carton of chocolate milk.

We sat for what seemed like an entire minute of silence before Sweets decided to try and broach a new conversation. "What classes are you guys taking this semester?"

"I'm taking Ghost Science," said Jax. "And I'm *so excited!*"

"Alba and I took that last semester. It's pretty easy," I said with a mouthful of scrambled eggs. "I'm taking the advanced class this semester. I'm thinking about majoring in Mediumship after all." I had given my "special gift" a lot of consideration over the course of the last semester and the holiday break. Upon beginning my time at the Paranormal Institute for Witches, I'd wanted to major in something new – in fact at the beginning of the first-semester I would have considered majoring in *anything* besides Mediumship.

Growing up, my mother was a medium, and I was sure that wasn't the life I wanted to live. Helping people talk to their dead family members seemed like a depressing sort of life. But the more the girls and I used my "gift" to help the Aspen Falls Police Department solve crimes, the more interesting the field became. I was starting to think I'd found my calling. Of course, I'd yet to tell my mother that. While she'd be ecstatic that I was finally considering going into the "family business," I didn't think she'd be happy to know that I was thinking about more of a career working with law enforcement than with grieving widows.

"I have to take History of Witchcraft this semester," said Holly sadly. "I didn't want to take it at all, but my advisor said it was a requirement for graduation. I hate history."

"We all took that last semester," said Sweets. "It's not that bad. Sorceress Edmonton teaches it. She's old, but she's way nicer than Sorceress Stone."

"What are you taking this semester, Alba?" Jax asked sweetly.

Alba shrugged. "I don't know. A bunch of stuff," she said. She was still fuming over what had happened minutes earlier, but Jax could tell she was trying to let it go.

"We're all taking a bunch of stuff, but what class are you *most* looking forward to?"

Alba shrugged and thought about it for a moment. "Mmm, probably Intro to Mind Control."

Jax's jaw dropped. "You're taking Intro to Mind Control? With Benson? I heard that was super hard!"

Sweets looked at Jax and nodded. "Yeah, I heard that was hard too. I thought you had to be a second year to take that class."

Alba shook her head. "Not for the Intro class. For the advanced one, you have to be a second year. I'm taking that next year. I'm also taking Mind Reading this semester."

I leaned over and pinched the underside of Alba's arm playfully, causing her to jump. "You'll be excited. I'm taking Kinetic Energy this semester," I revealed.

"With Hahn or Edmonton?"

"Hahn."

Alba winced. "Oooh. Hahn is rough. You're going to wish you had taken it with Edmonton. She's, like, way easier."

"I didn't have a choice," I pouted. "I'm taking Chants and Spells at the same time that Edmonton teaches the class and I have to get that general class done this semester before I can take Advanced Spells next year."

"Why didn't you take Chants and Spells first-semester

like the rest of us did?" Sweets asked. "I thought that was a first-semester class."

I sighed. "I took Incantations first-semester because my advisor told me it was good for people without much chanting experience. I'm glad I took that first because learning the breathing techniques and body mechanics of doing spells has really helped me a lot. It was sort of like learning how to meditate. I am a lot more calm and confident. I think I'll do better in Chants and Spells because of it."

Sweets looked up with a big smile on her face. "I get to start my internship today," she revealed excitedly. "I talked to Mr. Bailey over break, and he said he already worked it out with Sorceress Stone! It counts for six credits, and I get to go to his bakery Monday, Wednesday, and Friday from nine to noon."

I looked up at Sweets and gave her a wide smile. "Sweets! That's really great!"

"Yeah, Sweets, that's awesome," agreed Holly.

"Does this mean you're going to be bringing us treats now?" I asked.

Sweets giggled. "I'm afraid I'll eat them if I bring them home."

"Willpower," said Jax with a wink.

"I'll do my best."

"Are you excited?" Holly asked her.

Her eyes were wide as she nodded somberly. "Excited, but terrified! I've never had a real job before. What if I'm terrible?"

"Sweets, you'll be amazing, don't worry. Baking is your *jam*. There's no way you're going to mess up working at a bakery, especially one that makes potions," I assured her.

Holly looked her up and down. "And you *look amazing*."

Sweets looked down at her new coral colored blouse. "You like it? My sister Peach gave it to me for Christmas. She got it when she was in Milan for work."

Holly nodded. "It's super cute. You could unbutton the top button, though. You never know, you might meet a cute boy. A little cleavage never hurts."

I rolled my eyes. Cute boys were always on Holly's mind.

"Speaking of cute boys," said Jax excitedly. "Tristan told me about a big welcome back party one of the girls is throwing this weekend."

I'd already heard about the party. It was all Jax could talk about the day before. I hadn't considered going until Hugh told me that one of his buddies had invited him and he'd already told them he was going, so by default, I was going.

"Who's throwing it?" asked Sweets.

"Darcie Larson. Her grandpa lives in Aspen Falls, and he has an old building on his property that they just cleaned out. He said she could use it for the night," said Jax, clapping her hands together excitedly.

Holly's face lit up. "Well, that sounds promising. I assume all the wiz kids got invited?" she asked, referring to the boys in the Paranormal Institute for Wizards.

"Darcie said she invited everyone at The Institute."

My eyes widened. "She invited *everyone*? That could be a *huge* party."

"Fingers crossed," said Jax with a smile as wide as the Grand Canyon.

"I hope that new girl's not going to be there," said Alba, crossing her arms across her chest with a loud harrumph.

"So what if she is? You're not going to allow her to chase you away from a party, are you?" I asked with surprise.

"Of course not. We just don't go to many parties. If we're going to this one, I want to be able to enjoy myself. If she's there, there's no way I'm going to enjoy myself."

"You'll enjoy yourself, Alba. We'll all have fun. Who cares what she's doing? This party is about us, not her," said Holly.

Jax scrunched up her nose. "Where did she come from anyway? I've never seen her before."

"Me either," agreed Sweets. "She's got to be new."

I was just about to put my two cents in about the party when I heard the low rumble in the dining hall turn up a notch. I looked up to see none other than Houston Brooks strutting across the cafeteria and drawing an array of appreciative eyes. "Hugh!" I cheered excitedly, leaping out of my seat. I hadn't laid eyes on him since the morning of Christmas Eve.

As he approached me, his cowboy hat tilted back slowly, revealing his gorgeous hazel eyes and that sexy little smile that made my heart flutter. I lunged at him. He wrapped his muscular arms around my waist and spun me around, planting a kiss on my lips in front of the whole cafeteria, before he sat me down on my feet.

"Hey, darlin', I missed that pretty face of yours," he said. He lifted his cowboy hat and nodded at my friends. "Ladies."

"Hey, Hugh. How'd you get over to Winston Hall? The quad's completely covered in snow!" observed Holly curiously.

I narrowed my eyes and looked up at him inquisitively. "Yeah! How'd you get over here?"

"A cowboy never tells," he said, shooting the girls a wink.

Jax giggled. "I bet he took the tunnels."

"Wait. Tunnels? What tunnels?" I asked with surprise.

"Winston Hall and Warner Hall have tunnels connecting them. They also connect all the other buildings too," explained Jax.

Sweets's eyes widened. "No way? That's so cool."

"Yeah, I can't believe we've never heard about them," agreed Holly.

Jax nodded hesitantly. "Yeah, but they freak me out. They are super scary. I always think someone is going to come out of nowhere. There are a lot of shadows and the lighting isn't very good."

Hugh laughed. "They aren't scary. I heard that's how most people are getting to classes, though. They got so much snow they ran out of places to push it. All of the side-walks on campus are still blocked."

"Thanks for *that* by the way," Alba said to Hugh pointedly. "We just about missed Christmas break with our families because of you."

Hugh's cheeks pinked up as a slow smile spread across his face. "Oh, yeah. About that," he said, slowly taking his hat off of his head and holding it over his chest. "I'm really sorry ladies. I had *no idea* that would happen when I left town. If I had, I would have never left town. Or I wouldn't have messed with Mother Nature in the first place. I can assure you all that I will *not* make any drastic changes to the weather in the future."

"I'm holding you to that, Cowboy," said Alba pointing at Hugh.

I rolled my eyes and linked arms with him, pulling him away from my friends. "Come on," I said quietly to him. "Alba's in a mood. You don't want to be around her right now."

"I noticed," he whispered back. Before we walked away completely, he turned around and waved at my friends. "Bye, ladies, I'll see y'all later."

"Bye, Huey," called Jax.

"So what's up with grumpy pants?" Hugh asked as we walked back towards the lobby.

"She got into a fight with a new girl," I explained hastily. "She hit Alba over the back of the head with a lunch tray."

"Doh!" Hugh stopped walked and covered his mouth. His eyes crunched up in the corners as he smiled down at me. "You're joking."

"No, I wish I was. The girl started throwing insults at all of us and then Alba told her they should take it outside and she turned her back to the girl for, like, a second and *wham* – the girl cracked a tray over her head. They were both lucky Stone didn't toss them out on their rears. That's totally something I could see Stone doing."

"Wow. Exciting stuff is always happening to you girls," said Hugh with a bewildered smile as he threw his arm around my shoulders. "I guess you're just a magnet for trouble, aren't you?"

I playfully punched him in the ribs. "I wasn't a magnet for trouble until I met you," I quipped back. "Ever stop to think that maybe all of this is *your* fault?"

He put a hand on his stomach, threw his head back and laughed heartily. When his laughter had subsided, he looked at me with twinkling eyes. "Oh man, I've sure missed you. When do we get to hang out?"

I looked down at my Batman watch. "I wish we could hang out right now, but I've got to get to class."

He nodded. "Yeah, I do too. I've got a full schedule this

semester, and my first class starts in ten, so I have to get going. I just wanted to come give you a quick kiss before I started my week."

Under the weight of his arm, I curled myself into his body. "Aww, that's sweet," I said happily.

"So what do you think? Supper tonight?"

I nodded excitedly, my eyes brightening. "Sure!"

His mouth brushed against mine softly before he wrapped his arms around me one last time. Squeezing me tightly, his aftershave filled my nose. I unconsciously melded against him. When we parted, he planted one final kiss on my lips and then slowly pulled away. He turned on the heel of his boot and squeezed my hand before letting it go. "I'll text you the details for tonight," he said as he moved towards the hallway to the basement stairs.

"Bye, Hugh."

"Bye, darlin'," he called back then turned his back to me.

I watched as he left. Giddy with excitement over getting to see him again and our upcoming dinner date. Then, seemingly out of nowhere, the girl who had started the fight in the breakfast line, appeared from a doorway. I watched as her expression changed when she caught sight of Hugh. Her body switched directions, and she caught up to him in the hallway. When she linked arms with him, my jaw dropped and my adrenaline spiked.

"What the?" I whispered to myself as the two of them disappeared down the hallway. Taking only a second to process what I'd just seen, I darted over to the hallway just in time to see them turning the corner to the next hallway which would lead to the basement.

I looked at my watch again. I only had seven minutes to finish my breakfast and grab my books for class and then figure out how to navigate the school's tunnel system. While I fully trusted my boyfriend of just over three months, I most certainly *did not* trust the new girl.

"Ugh," I groaned before heading back to the cafeteria with my temper now dialed to a low simmer.

CHAPTER 3

Jax hadn't been exaggerating when she described the underground tunnel system as creepy. The stone walls sloped up into rounded ceilings where electrical lines and heating pipes were anchored. The lighting was bad, and in some places, it cast weird shadows across the dirt floors.

"This is incredible," I said to Jax as we walked the length of the tunnel together. Sweets had left campus to start her internship, and Holly and Alba had gone on ahead of us. Jax decided to wait for me so she could show me how to use the tunnel system.

"Eww, spider web!" she squealed, high-kneeing herself away from me. Bouncing off the balls of her feet, she swatted at her arms crazily as if a spider had just landed on her.

"Was that you showing off your ninja moves?" I asked her with a chuckle.

"I thought I felt a spider on my arm!"

I rolled my eyes. "Seriously, Jax? You're scared of

spiders? We're witches. Witches are supposed to like spiders."

She furrowed her eyebrows and scrunched up her nose. "In case you've forgotten, let me remind you. I'm not a witch."

"Yeah, what are we going to do about that anyway?" I asked her curiously.

"What do you mean?"

"You can't keep wasting your time studying to be a witch if you're never actually going to *be a witch*. You might as well be going to a normal college then. You could go to, like, nursing school or something. I could see you as a nurse."

"Are you trying to get rid of me?" she asked, narrowing her eyes and peering at me suspiciously.

I laughed and threw my arm around her shoulders. "Don't be silly. I just don't understand the point of you studying to be a witch if you don't have powers."

Jax looked down at the grey Converse sneakers I'd bought her for Christmas. She looked so much cuter in them than the usual pointy-toed black boots she used to wear, though she still insisted on wearing her striped leggings and offbeat witch outfits. "I'm still hoping that I'll get my powers. Maybe when I turn eighteen."

"Your birthday's in May, right?"

Jax nodded. "May 14th. I was born on Mother's Day."

My eyes widened as I looked ahead. "Oh…how…lovely," I said with a stifled groan.

"I know what you're thinking," Jax chirped as we walked along. "You're thinking my mother should be a better mother especially since she *became* a mother on Mother's Day. Yeah, I don't know what happened. I just don't think she really wanted to be a mom. Some people just aren't cut out to be mothers I think."

"Do you know who your dad is?" I asked her. It was something I'd never asked before, but I'd always been curious.

Jax shook her head. "Not a clue. I've tried talking to her about it, but you know how she is."

I nodded. I certainly did know how Sorceress Stone was. She was a hard nut to crack. I couldn't possibly imagine what it was like for Jax to be her daughter.

The tunnel came to a fork in the road. There was a big black sign with white lettering on it. Warner Hall was to our left and campus classrooms were to our right. Jax and I hung a right and were soon confronted with another black sign with white lettering.

"Canterbury Building, that's me," I told her taking a left.

"Okay. I'm this way. I'll see you at lunch," said Jax as she kept walking straight.

I gave her a short wave and then picked up the pace to head to the third floor of the Canterbury building to see Sorceress Hahn for Kinetic Energy 101.

I glanced down at my watch. I had less than a minute to make it to class without being late. I sprinted up the stairs at the end of the tunnel and found myself in the lobby of the over-sized stone building. I darted over to the wide staircase where I took the stairs two at a time. By the time I got to the third floor, I was wheezing and found myself wishing once again that I'd brought my inhaler with me to college. I took three big deep breaths and tried to relax before walking to the end of the hallway and letting myself into Sorceress Hahn's classroom.

Entering, I immediately became aware of the fact that class had already started. A short, stocky woman with black hair was standing in front of the class. She looked up at me sharply as I entered the room, as did the rest of the students in the small class.

"You're late," she said, her tone sharp.

"I'm sorry, Sorceress Hahn," I said, still puffing a bit for air. "I'm not used to using the tunnels."

She nodded. "Please don't make it a habit. Find a seat. We're just getting started."

There were less than ten students in the classroom. One of the things The Institute prided itself on were small class sizes and individualized instruction. I found a seat beside a girl I'd had in Incantations class last semester. I appreciated the fact that she wasn't much of a talker.

"Hey, Jamie," I whispered as I slid into the desk beside her.

"Hey, Mercy," she whispered back.

I pulled my backpack off my shoulder and dropped it to the ground. The classroom door opened once again. I glanced up sharply, thankful that I hadn't been the second student late as that was sure to annoy Hahn even more. The sight of the late student immediately made my blood run faster. It was the new girl.

She breezed into the room haughtily, like she owned the place, and took a seat on the far right side of the classroom where there was a front row seat still available. I had intentionally passed up that seat. Avoiding front row seats like the plague was a personal decision I made, despite the fact that my mother had specifically suggested that I *always* sit in the front row of classes, *"Just so the teachers know you're there to learn."*

Sorceress Hahn looked at the new girl sharply. "You're late," she said to her as she had said to me less than a minute before.

The girl glared at Sorceress Hahn unapologetically. "I'm a new student. Today is my first day at this school. I had no idea where I was going."

Sorceress Hahn nodded. "I heard I was getting a new student today. Why don't you stand up and tell us a little bit about yourself."

The girl put her backpack down on the ground and then stood up. "Sure. My name is Victoria Decker. Everyone can call me Tori. I'm eighteen. I'm from Norwalk, Iowa. I graduated high school in December at semester, and my parents wanted me to get started with witch school right away."

"What's your magical specialty?" Sorceress Hahn asked her.

"Oh. I'm an illusion caster, but I'm also getting really good at spells," she said matter-of-factly.

"I see. Well, welcome to The Institute. Please let me know if you have any questions about how we do things here."

Tori gave Sorceress Hahn a thumbs up signal and then plopped down in her seat and reached down to unzip her backpack and pull out her book.

"Alright. We're going to go ahead and get started. Welcome to Kinetic Energy 101. As I said earlier, I'm Sorceress Hahn. In this class, we are going to learn about all the different types of kinetic energy, and I like to start the first day of class by talking a little bit about what the different types are. Who can name a type of kinetic energy?"

Hands shot up around the room. Almost everyone's hand but mine. I wasn't a big fan of answering questions in class. Instead, I suddenly discovered how extraordinarily interesting the cover of my purple notebook was.

"Mercy Habernackle," said Sorceress Hahn, looking

down at a roster in front of her. "Do we have a Mercy Habernackle?"

I groaned to myself then quietly raised my hand. "I'm Mercy."

She nodded. "Very good, Mercy. Can you name a type of kinetic energy?"

"Telekinetic?" I said, unsure if that was what she was talking about.

"Puh!" laughed Tori from across the room.

"Is something funny, Tori?" asked Sorceress Hahn curiously.

All eyes turned towards the new girl. She shrugged unapologetically, flipping her long brown ponytail over her shoulder. "I just think that's the most unimaginative answer. I mean aren't we here to challenge ourselves from the obvious and look outside the box a little?"

I furrowed my eyebrows at her and felt my temperature rising again. "She just asked for an *example*. She didn't ask for creativity."

"Right, well you'd think *that* would go without saying," she mocked, rolling her eyes. "This *is* essentially *college* after all."

Sorceress Hahn looked intrigued listening to our conversation. "Perhaps telekinesis *is* where everyone's mind goes to when they hear the words kinetic energy. Mercy, can you think of another example of kinetic energy?"

Being put on the spot in such a way made my mind go blank. This was Alba's field of study, not mine. "Um, well – uh," I stuttered as my face heated up.

Tori rolled her eyes and turned around in her seat to face the front of the room. "Sorceress Hahn, obviously Mercy doesn't have an answer."

"Does anyone else know any other kinds of kinetic energy?" Hahn asked the class.

Only Tori's hand went up in the air.

Sorceress Hahn nodded at Tori to answer her question.

"Obviously there are just tons. Hydrokinesis comes to mind first, aerokinesis, umm geokinesis, oh! And atmokinesis."

Sorceress Hahn looked impressed. "Atmokinesis, now there's an interesting one. I'm surprised you mentioned it. Would you like to explain to the class what atmokinesis is Tori?"

Tori nodded, turned around in her seat to face the group, and began gesturing with her hands as if she was the one teaching the class. "Atmokinesis is the manipulation of weather. There are several subsets of atmokinesis such as air manipulation, electricity manipulation, thermal manipulation and water manipulation. It's really an interesting subject. In fact, just this morning I met a fascinating man from the wizard's school, and he is an atmokinesis major. Handsome fella too," she said with a smirk.

My temperature shot through the roof. I knew she was talking about Hugh. I wanted to lunge across the desks and wring her scrawny little neck. I'd never heard Hugh refer to his weather manipulation skill as atmokinesis, and he'd certainly never told me that was the name of his major. Whether I should be mad at Hugh for omitting that or Tori for knowing something about *my boyfriend* that I didn't was currently weighing on my mind. I felt my face burn red as I heard *that girl's* voice ringing in my ears, "*handsome fella too.*" The nerve!

CHAPTER 4

SWEETS

My heart pounded excitedly in my chest as I pulled up to Mr. Bailey's Bakery and Sweets and parked the car. I peeked at myself in my rearview mirror and gently patted the little brown bun I'd bundled my hair up into on top of my head. I smoothed out my bangs, pulling a few longer pieces loose to frame my face and shot myself an encouraging wink. Watching my reflection closely in the mirror, I opened my eyes wide, took a deep breath, and blew it out slowly. The nerves just weren't dissipating. I blew out a few more puffs of air and shook my shoulders and arms. Finally, I let out a tiny squeal and then grabbed my purse from the passenger's seat of my car.

I climbed out of my four-door Ford Taurus and onto the sidewalk. Turning to slam my door shut, I caught sight of my reflection in the car window. I straightened the new coral blouse my sister Peach had given me for Christmas and took a long pause looking at my top button. Had Holly been right? Should I unbutton the top button? What if I did meet a cute boy while I was working my three-hour shift? Holly's specific instructions were to lead with my best assets. My lips swished to the side of my face as I debated. I fingered the button but then felt silly. This was a job. Not a dating service. I shook my head as I decided against Holly's advice. "You look good, Sweets," I whispered to myself with a small motivational nod.

I fought back the squeal wanting to escape my throat as I pulled open the heavy glass bakery door. Immediately the warm, inviting smell of fresh bread baking in the brick hearth oven behind the counter engulfed me. I approached the glass display counter tentatively. The sight of all the candies, cakes, and pies filling it made my stomach rumble immediately. It was going to be *extra* hard fighting the battle of the bulge while working here. I was going to have to work on my willpower if I didn't want to end up with blocked arteries by the time I was in my forties.

A tall, thin man of about thirty rounded the corner when the door bell chimed. The dark haired man's posture was slightly stooped, and the lack of meat on his frame made the bones in his shoulders and elbows very prominent. His high cheekbones and pale skin accentuated the hollowed darkness of his cheeks. While there were days that the over-abundance of meat on my frame frustrated me, I was more than thrilled not to be *that* gaunt.

"May I help you?"

"I'm here to see Mr. Bailey," I explained nervously.

The man looked at me inquisitively then turned towards the kitchen and hollered, "Vic! There's a lady here to see you." He turned back towards me again. "Can I get you anything?"

I put a hand nervously over my mouth and shook my head.

He nodded and was just about to turn around and return to the kitchen when Mr. Bailey made an appearance.

His bushy white eyebrows sprung up animatedly when he saw me and immediately his arms shot out wide. "Sweets! I'm so happy you're here! I almost forgot what day it was."

"Mr. Bailey. It's so good to see you."

He waddled around the counter to greet me, throwing his arms around me like I was a member of his family. "How was your Christmas vacation?" he asked me, the lights from the bakery reflected off the top of his shiny, smooth head.

The tall man behind the counter continued to watch me curiously. His surprise seemed to indicate that Mr. Bailey hadn't mentioned to him that I was coming.

"It was good," I said. My face lit up as my mind went back to my trip home to Georgia. "I got to see my new nephew, William, for the first time."

Mr. Bailey clasped his hands together in front of his round belly. "Oh, I'm so glad to hear it. There's nothing like spending time with family to put a smile on your face."

"How was your Christmas?"

Mr. Bailey's face got serious, and his eyebrows went up again. "Oh. I've got some exciting news for you," he said, pointing his finger towards the ceiling. "I proposed to my Char on Christmas Eve!"

My jaw dropped. Excitement welled up inside my chest, and my heart felt like it might burst. "Mr. Bailey!" I exclaimed. "I'm speechless. That was so fast!"

"Love at my age is like trying to scoop water with your hands while it's spiraling down the drain. You must be thankful to catch anything before it's gone," he said with a chuckle.

I giggled. "That's one way to look at it."

Mr. Bailey looked up at the dark-haired man behind the counter and then pointed at me. "Louis. This is Sweets

Porter. She's the one that matched my Charlotte and me together!"

Louis pulled his head back and his raised eyebrows, setting deep wrinkles into his forehead. "I see," he acknowledged, unimpressed.

I sucked in my breath. "Mr. Bailey! You knew?!"

He touched his chest and tilted his head sideways, his eyes closed. "Hey, I'm a potion maker myself. I know a spiked strawberry chocolate mousse cake when I taste it."

"But you let Charlotte have a bite anyway?" I asked him in surprise.

He elbowed me with an ornery smile and a wink. "I know a good catch when I see one, too."

I giggled.

"Besides, it was love at first sight anyway. I told her later it was spiked and do you know what she said to me? She said 'if it was meant to be, it was meant to be.' When she accepted my proposal, I knew it was meant to be."

"When is the wedding?" I asked him.

"Soon. Soon. This Sunday in fact! No time to waste at our age. I hope you and the girls will come and join us on our happy day? I was also hoping you'd consider making us a cake for the wedding."

Louis interrupted quickly. "Vic, I can make you a wedding cake!"

Mr. Bailey shook his head and waved a hand in the air. "Nonsense, nonsense. Sweets is the one who matched my Char and me. If she's willing, she'll make the cake."

My heart leapt in my chest. "What an honor! Of course, I'll make the cake for your wedding! And yes, the girls and I would *love* to come. I'll invite them all at lunch today!" I shook my head, unable to remove the broad smile from my face. "This just makes me so happy. I wish I could make matches every day."

He nodded. "I know how you feel. I feel the same way when my customers get pain relief from one of my herbal remedies. It just makes my heart feel twelve times bigger!"

"That's exactly how I feel," I chirped. It was nice to know someone else felt the way I felt about helping people.

"Now," he said with a more serious expression. "On to business! Sweets, this is Louis Albertson. Louis is my right-hand man. He's done everything I've ever asked of him and more."

Louis beamed as Mr. Bailey bragged about him.

"And, Louis, Sweets is a first-year student at the Paranormal Institute for Witches. She will be doing an internship here this semester, maybe longer if things go well," he shrugged. "So. Treat her like a queen."

I giggled at Mr. Bailey's words. I'd never had anyone tell someone to treat me like a queen before. It was kind of flattering. I peered up at Louis. Something about his glaring dark eyes wiped the smile right off of my face. I shifted my weight to my right leg. "It's nice to meet you, Louis," I said uncomfortably.

Louis nodded at me but kept his thin lips in a straight line.

Mr. Bailey didn't seem to notice Louis's snub, and he wasted no time in getting to work. He motioned for me to follow him. "Come, come. This way. Let's get you settled in."

CHAPTER 5

Holly, Alba, Jax, and I waited in the lobby for Sweets to get back from her internship before we headed to the dining hall for lunch. It had been a long morning of classes. Not only had I had Victoria Decker in my Kinetic Energy class, but I'd also had her in my Chants and Spells class. She'd used every opportunity she had to argue with me in both classes. I was ready to get to lunch and do some serious vengeance planning with the Witch Squad.

"What's taking Sweets so long?" I asked, tapping the toe of my hi-top Converse sneaker on the ground.

"She gets done at noon," said Alba looking at her watch. "It's only twelve-fifteen. She has to drive back to campus."

I sighed. I *needed* to vent about the morning I'd had, or I was going to burst. I wasn't waiting any longer. I'd fill Sweets in when she got here. "I had the new girl in two of my morning classes," I said in a hush to the group as I pulled my zip-up hoodie tighter around me, plunging my hands deep inside the pockets.

Alba looked up sharply. "Did you find out her name?"

I shivered. "Is the heater broken again? It's freezing in here!"

The girls exchanged glances. "I think it feels normal," said Jax.

Holly nodded. "Yeah, me too."

Alba sighed impatiently. "Well, what's her name?"

"Oh. Yeah. Her name is Victoria Decker. She goes by Tori. She graduated high school at semester, so her parents sent her on to witch school early. She's eighteen and from Iowa. She's unbelievably annoying. After breakfast she totally grabbed Hugh's arm and drug him off into the tunnels with her. And then she tried to show me up in both of the classes we had together," I huffed angrily. The mere thought of that girl again was riling me up even more.

"What was it you said to me before, Red?" Alba asked snidely. "Oh yeah. Just take a deep breath and relax."

"Ugh," I growled. "That was before she was making a play for *my man*!"

"But that was *after* she hit one of your best friends over the back of the head with a lunch tray! Where's your loyalty?" asked Alba incredulously.

I sighed. "You have my loyalty. I swear. We just needed to get you calmed down so you'd eat your breakfast."

Alba glared at me menacingly.

I pulled my hands out of my pockets and held my palms out. "What? We were going to be late for class!"

"Whatever," said Alba, turning her head away from me.

I let out a deep breath, trying to release the tension from my shoulders. I bounced around a little on my toes, like a boxer prepping for a fight. "I'm serious. Now I'm ready to make a plan to get back at that witch."

Holly looked up sharply. "Hey, quit calling her that. You'll give witches a bad name."

"What's taking Sweets so long?" Jax asked, rubbing her stomach anxiously. "I am *starving!*"

Holly glanced out into the parking lot. "Here she comes."

"*Finally!*" cheered Jax, rushing towards the door to open it for Sweets.

"Doesn't Jax look adorable in her new sneakers?" I asked Alba and Holly when Jax was out of earshot.

Holly's head bounced from side to side. "I haven't gotten used to them yet. I'm so used to seeing her in those little pointy-toed witchy *things*, that seeing her in Converse and striped leggings is messing with the whole witch vibe she's going for."

Alba shrugged her shoulders and put her hands on her hips. "I don't know. I'm feelin' it. Now if only we can get her to lose the hat and the weird outfits."

Holly's eyes widened as she shook her head. "Jax wouldn't be Jax without the weird outfits."

"I'm used to the outfits. I'd settle for her losing the hat," I said.

With her arm locked into Sweets's, Jax rushed her back over to us. Having run in from her car in the parking lot, Sweets was out of breath. Her hair was bundled up into a bun on top of her head, and her straight bangs touched the top of her eyebrows. Her cheeks, nose, and the tips of her ears were flushed red from the cold.

"I'm loving the new haircut, Sweets," said Holly, looking up from her phone.

I nodded. "Me too. Bangs are definitely flattering on you."

Sweets smiled. "Aww, thanks, girls. I needed that after the morning I had," she sighed.

Jax shot her a concerned look. "You didn't have fun with Mr. Bailey?"

Alba began moving towards the dining hall on the other side of the lobby. "Can we walk while we talk?" she asked. "We're so late for lunch we'll never find a place to sit."

Sweets nodded as she pulled her mittens off of her hands and shoved them into the pockets of her puffy raspberry colored coat. "It wasn't that I didn't have fun with Mr. Bailey, I did. He's going to be such an awesome boss, and I'm really going to learn a lot from him, but..."

"But what?" Jax prodded.

"There's this other guy that works there. His name is Louis Albertson. And I don't think he likes me very much."

I made a face as I walked backwards towards the cafeteria so I could hear Sweets's story. "Not possible, Sweets. You're one of the most likable people there is."

"Aww, thanks, Mercy. I appreciate that."

"So why don't you think he liked you?" asked Holly.

Sweets shrugged as we got to the doorway of the cafeteria. "I don't know. I just felt like he was giving me the evil eye the whole time I was there. It was creepy."

"Maybe you won't have to work with him very often," suggested Jax.

As we entered the cafeteria, we found the lunch line longer than it had ever been before. It extended from the kitchen door, down the length of the dining hall and ended at the door to the lobby. "What's up with this line?" I asked, poking my head around the other girls in line.

Alba groaned. "Ugh. Next time we aren't waiting for you, Sweets. We'll just save you a spot at the table."

Sweets's shoulders crumpled. "I'm sorry, girls. You really didn't have to wait for me. You're right, next time just save me a place at the table, but get your food without me."

Alba poked her head out of the line too. "This is ridiculous. We're never going to get done eating in time to make our next class."

I looked down at my watch. Alba wasn't exaggerating; it was getting really late. Something didn't feel right. "I'm going to go see what's going on," I said as I rubbed my hands on my arms. The skin on my legs prickled, alerting me that something was amuck.

I made my way to the front of the line with Alba by my side. Two of our friends, Libby and Cinder, were about three-fourths of the way to the front of the line. "What's going on? How long have you been waiting?" I asked them.

Libby rolled her ice-blue eyes. "I have no idea what's going on. We've been waiting for at least ten minutes."

Cinder nodded towards the kitchen. "They haven't even opened the doors yet."

Alba frowned. "The door to the lunch line isn't open, and you're all just standing here? Why didn't someone just open it?" she asked like they were all a bunch of idiots.

Cinder and Libby shrugged.

"I just assumed the food wasn't ready yet," said Libby.

In a huff, Alba moved further up the line to the kitchen doors. A girl in my first-semester Animal Spirits class was the first in line.

"Hey, Cami. Have you tried the door?" I asked her.

The short, sandy blond haired girl nodded. "Yeah, we've been banging on it. No one answers. I don't know what's going on."

"Did anyone go to the office?" Alba asked her.

Cami looked at the girl next to her, unsure. "I have no idea. *We* didn't."

As the goose bumps skidding across my flesh prickled more intensely, I looked up at Alba. "Something doesn't feel right, Alba. I'm going to go have someone in the office unlock the door."

Alba nodded, her face filled with concern too. "I'm coming with you."

"What should *we* do?" Cami asked as Alba and I walked away.

"Nothing. Just hang tight. We'll be back in a few," I hollered back at her.

We rushed back to the end of the line where the rest of the girls were waiting for us.

"What did you find out?" Jax asked. "I am *so hungry*."

"Me too!" said Sweets, her eyes wide. "I think my blood sugar is dropping."

"Don't you carry a snack with you or something?" I asked her.

"Usually. I'm trying to watch what I eat, though. I didn't think I'd need to bring a snack to the lunch line!"

"Okay, well. We're going to go check with the office and see what's going on. You guys stay here and hold our place in line," I said as I spotted a pair of girls in the lobby heading towards the cafeteria.

Jax sighed. "Okay. Hurry up please."

Alba and I rushed towards the back hallway where Sorceress Stone's office was located.

Brittany Hobbs, Sorceress Stone's secretary, was sitting behind her desk typing with a set of earbuds stuffed in her ears when we arrived. She nearly jumped out of her skin when we entered the office.

"Brittany, why aren't you in the lunch room?" I asked immediately. "No one has unlocked the doors, and the line is like a mile long."

Brittany threw her hand over her heart as she pulled the earbuds out of her ears. "Oh my gosh, you two scared me!"

"You need to come unlock it right now," Alba insisted. "The girls have been pounding on the door and no one is opening it up."

"Oh no! What time is it?" she asked in a panic. Her eyes flew to the clock on the wall.

"Twelve-thirty!"

"Crap!" she exclaimed as she jumped up hastily. "I didn't even realize what time it was! I was re-doing some schedules for this semester. Sorceress Stone wanted them done by lunch. I totally lost track of time. Why didn't anyone come and get me sooner?" Her hands trembled as she pulled open her desk drawer and grabbed a set of keys.

"I don't know. We were late for lunch and everyone was just standing around waiting. I guess they weren't thinking."

"Why wouldn't Denise or the other lunch lady open the door?" asked Alba. "What *is* the other lady's name anyway? The short one that looks like Edna from *The Incredibles*."

"That's Midge. I think she only works part-time. Maybe she doesn't work today," I suggested.

Alba and I had to hustle to keep up with Brittany who was leading us down a back hallway.

I looked over my shoulder as we walked. We weren't headed towards the cafeteria. "Why are we going this way?" I asked. "The lunch line is that way."

Brittany's eyes opened wide. "Oh, I-I don't know," she stammered. "I always go this way."

"I didn't even realize there was another door to the lunchroom this way," said Alba as we followed her down the hallway and stopped at a pair of doors.

Brittany tried the handle, but it was locked. Alba glanced up at me as Brittany fumbled with her keys.

Finally, she found the right one and pushed it into the door handle on the left.

"What's in this door?" I asked her, pointing at the door on the right.

"It's just storage."

"For the kitchen?"

She nodded. "Yeah, mostly." The door handle clicked, and the door opened. All the lights in the kitchen were on and there was food in different stages of completion scattered around the room.

"Where are Denise and Midge?" Alba asked as the three of us pushed our way inside.

Brittany looked around curiously. "Midge called in sick today. I don't know where Denise is. Denise?" she called out.

Alba rolled her eyes. "Well obviously she's not *in here*."

"Where else would she be?" I asked as I walked around the kitchen. Denise had already put out the lettuce salad and the pasta and potato salads into the salad bar. The hot bar was in various stages of completion. There was one metal container that had hamburgers in it, but the place where the French fries usually sat was empty. "She didn't finish setting up the hot bar. Maybe she's in the storage room," I suggested.

Alba nodded. "Let's go check."

Brittany led us out of the kitchen. She tried the storage room door to find it locked also. The kitchen door slammed shut behind us as Brittany fumbled with her keys again. "They usually leave these doors unlocked," she said as she tried to figure out which key worked in the lock.

Once she had the door unlocked, she threw it open. Tall metal shelves lined the walls and two back to back rows of metal shelves filled the center of the room also.

"Denise?" Brittany called out from the doorway. "It doesn't look like she's in here either."

The skin on my arms and legs prickled. I took a step into the storage room and looked to my right. Everything looked to be in order. There were commercial sized containers of mustard, ketchup, and ranch dressing on the shelving to the right. In the middle of the room the shelves were packed full with paper products, like napkins, paper towels, plastic cups, silverware, and toilet paper. I walked further into the room.

I could feel my pulse quickening. I turned around and looked at Alba. "I'm getting a funny feeling," I told her nervously.

She nodded. "I can tell. I'm right behind you."

I swallowed hard and together, the two of us slowly crept forward, to the end of the middle shelving unit. We saw the blood before we saw the body. Our eyes immediately met.

Alba turned to look at Brittany. "Go get Sorceress Stone and call 911. Now."

Brittany's eyes widened. "What is it? What's wrong?" she asked, her hand flew to her mouth nervously.

Alba and I took two more steps forward, to confirm our suspicions. My eyes narrowed at the sight. "It's Denise. I think she's dead."

CHAPTER 6

W hat happened after that was nothing short of chaos. Detective Whitman made it to The Institute in less than fifteen minutes, and within minutes of being on the scene, he had the whole kitchen and dining hall cordoned off with police tape. His officers were on the job too, photographing the scene, searching for clues, and interviewing potential witnesses.

Sorceress Stone gathered all of the witches from The Institute into the Clara Mason Memorial Gymnasium in the east wing of Winston Hall. She'd been forced to order pizza from the local pizza shop when Detective Whitman refused to allow the students access to the food Denise had almost finished cooking. Even though the murder had taken place in the storage room and not the kitchen, the fact remained that the murderer could have entered the kitchen, possibly even tampering with the food.

A long row of folding tables had been set up in the gym, and when the three pizza delivery guys arrived, the girls cheered then practically tackled them before they could unload the stacks of pizzas they carried.

When everyone had gone through the line, including the five of us, we all found seats on the wooden bleachers on one side of the gym. The Witch Squad congregated near the top of the bleachers. Libby and Cinder sat a few rows below us with some of the other second-year students. Tori and her single cohort sat all the way at the bottom of the bleachers right in the middle. Sorceress Stone stood in front of us with Brittany Hobbs by her side.

"We've had a tragically gruesome event happen inside of our school today. Our hearts go out to the dearly departed soul of Denise Whiting and to her husband and children. May her soul forever rest in eternal peace," said Sorceress Stone reverently with her hands clasped together in front of her body.

I pressed the palm of my hand against my chest. Sucking in a deep breath, I fought to keep myself calm. The sight of Denise's body, lying on the ground with a knife lodged in her lower spine, continued to haunt me. Still trembling, I doubled over. I felt the need to vomit again, but my body was empty – I'd already tossed what was left of my breakfast after seeing her in the pool of blood. Despite my previously overwhelming hunger, I couldn't even fathom consuming the pizza Jax had put on a plate for me.

Alba looked over at me, her face pale. "You gonna be okay, Red?"

"I can't believe Denise is dead," I whispered. I felt like I was in shock.

"Maybe you two should go lie down," suggested Sweets, looking around nervously. "I – I can ask Sorceress Stone to excuse you."

Alba shook her head. "Detective Whitman told us not to leave. He's going to come interview us soon."

Sweets nodded sadly with downcast eyes.

Sorceress Stone sucked in a deep breath. "The police are here, and they are going to find out who could have committed such an evil deed, but I am going to ask each and every one of you to report anything out of the ordinary. Did any of you *see anything*? Did you *hear anything*? Anything even *remotely* out of order needs to be reported to me *immediately!* Do we all understand?" she asked sternly, looking around the bleachers of girls. Her eyes stopped and rested on me and the rest of the Witch Squad. She was talking to us. We were to go to her with any information we had, not to Detective Whitman.

Alba raised her hand. "It seems odd to me that the part-time cafeteria lady, Midge, didn't show up for work today. She's always here for lunch," she shouted. Her voice reverberated off of the walls and wooden floor of the gym and carried down to Sorceress Stone and Brittany.

Sorceress Stone's face expressed the validity of Alba's concern. "That's a very legitimate point. Thank you. I will make sure that Detective Whitman is informed that Denise's co-worker did not show up for work today."

Brittany Hobbs leaned over and whispered something in Sorceress Stone's ear. While they spoke in hushed tones, I noticed Tori Decker turn around in her seat to face us. Her venomous eyes had narrowed into tiny slits, and her mouth had contorted into an angry pout.

Sorceress Stone raised up two hands as whispers began to fly around the room. "Now. That's not to say that Midge didn't have a very valid reason for not being at work today. We *will not* make assumptions based on that fact. We also *will not* spread rumors nor gossip about that or any other information that comes to light during the investigation. This is a very serious matter and will be treated as such."

From the front row, Tori Decker raised her hand.

"Should we be concerned about our safety, Sorceress Stone?"

Our Headmistress sighed. She closed her eyes with her hands still clasped in front of her long grey dress. She took a deep breath in through her nose and then opened her eyes. "I wish I could answer that. But we don't know who did this. We don't know *why* they did it. And until we do, we all need to be vigilant. You all have roommates. You need to stay with your roommates or someone else at all times. No one should be alone until we get some answers from the police."

Sweets's hand flew up into the air. "Sorceress Stone! I don't have a roommate," she said nervously.

"Put your hand down, Sweets," hissed Jax. "You can stay with us!"

Sweets put her hand down. "Never mind. Jax said I could stay with her and Mercy."

"Thank you, ladies," said Sorceress Stone. "Now, finish your lunches. I've canceled classes for the rest of the day. I will send out an email later in the day as to whether or not we'll have classes tomorrow. Please make sure to check your messages. You are all remanded to your dorm rooms for the rest of the day. No one leaves campus unless they've gotten permission from me. I will dismiss everyone from the gymnasium when Detective Whitman gives me the authorization to do so."

With that, Sorceress Stone spun on her heel and headed towards the gym exit. Brittany turned and followed her. The second they were gone the gym erupted into loud chatter.

"Now what do we do?" Holly asked, settling her rear into the groove of the bleachers and leaning against the bleacher behind her.

"We wait," said Alba. "Whitman will be here to interview us soon."

My trembling had subsided, but I still didn't think I
could eat a thing. I blew out a few long heavy breaths.
Groaning, I leaned back into the bleachers as Holly had
done. I needed to get the sight of Denise out of my mind. I
needed to talk about something else. "We can't leave our
dorm rooms. Now I have to cancel my date with Hugh.
That really stinks."

Holly rolled her eyes. "What stinks is the fact that *you*
had a date planned for the first day back at school and I'm
not even talking to any boys right now."

Jax smiled at her. "You'll meet someone at the party on
Friday."

Holly looked down at her nails and fidgeted with her
cuticles. "I hope so. College is so boring without a
boyfriend."

Sweets sucked in her breath as if she'd just thought of
something exciting. We all looked up at her. "Oh! I almost
forgot. I have big news."

"Is it good news?" Jax asked trepidatiously.

Sweets's head bobbed up and down rapidly.

"Spill," said Alba gruffly.

"Mr. Bailey and Char are getting married this weekend!
And we're invited to the wedding."

My eyes widened. "*This* weekend?"

She nodded. "Yeah. He proposed on Christmas Eve, and
they didn't want a long engagement."

"Boy, they don't waste any time," said Holly.

"I don't blame 'em," said Alba. "Engagements are
stupid."

Jax shot Alba a face. "No they aren't! I can't wait to be
engaged!"

I curled one lip. "Really? Why? What's so great about being engaged?"

Jax's jaw dropped. "Seriously? I thought *you'd* understand."

My eyes swiveled from left to right. "Why would *I* understand?" I asked, confused.

"Because of Hugh."

I shook my head. "What does that have to do with Hugh? We're never getting engaged!"

Jax, Holly, and Sweets looked at me as if I were nuts.

"You might *someday*," countered Jax.

I let out a half laugh. "I'm too young to get engaged. I'm only nineteen for crying out loud. I'm not looking for a husband."

"So? Hugh's twenty-three. Don't you think he might be looking for a wife?" asked Sweets.

That thought had never occurred to me. I sat looking at the girls, with my mouth hanging open. It was as if someone had taken the wind out of my sails.

"What's the matter, Red? Cat got your tongue?" Alba asked with a half smile.

I closed my eyes and shook my head, bewildered. "No. I just – well, I hadn't thought of that. He's never said anything about wanting to get married. I'm not ready for marriage." The realization that I really didn't know where Hugh stood on marriage hit me hard. Just this morning I'd found out that I didn't even know what my boyfriend's major was. Were Hugh and I really as close as I'd once thought? The idea bothered me. And now, we weren't able to go out on our date so I could pose some of these weird questions to him.

I groaned. I didn't know which thought made me more uncomfortable. My suddenly weird relationship with Hugh or the fact that I'd just discovered a murder. "Ugh. I can't think about any of this right now," I said, shaking my head.

"Yeah," said Sweets sadly, hanging her head. "Poor Denise. She was my favorite lunch lady."

"That's so weird that Midge called in sick on the day Denise was stabbed to death," said Alba. "It really raises a red flag in my mind."

Holly nodded. "You have to assume that's the first place Detective Whitman will check."

I turned towards the door and as if on cue, I noticed a dark figure looming in the doorway of the gym. He was tall with broad shoulders that filled out his brown corduroy blazer. He had dark curly hair and a matching dark mustache.

"Whitman's here," said Alba, looking up also.

Detective Mark Whitman scanned the faces in the auditorium. I assumed he was looking for us. I held up a hand and waved at him tentatively. When he saw it, he lifted his head and walked towards us.

"Finally," I said, balling up my napkin and setting it on top of my uneaten pizza. "I just want to get this over with."

"Does he want to talk to us, too?" Sweets asked nervously.

"Doubt it. You weren't the one who found the body," I told her with a sigh. I stood up, as did Alba. "Here. Can you throw my pizza away for me?"

Sweets looked down at the slice of cheese pizza I was handing her. "Well that's wasteful," she chastised.

Jax plucked the pizza out of my hands. "I don't like the way you're looking at that, Sweets."

Sweets stuck out her bottom lip. "I do have self-control you know. Besides, I've already gotten almost half of my ten thousand steps in for the day," she said and looked down at the Fitbit on her wrist. "Look!" Sweets pushed a button on her watch and held it up to show us proudly.

"I'll be impressed when you hit ten thousand," said Jax.

Detective Whitman was now standing at the bottom of the bleachers. "Mercy, Alba, may I have a word with the two of you?"

"We're coming," I called down to him.

Holly gave us a little wave as we passed her on the way down the stairs. "Good luck."

"Thanks," I said. From the corner of my eye, I could see Tori Decker watching us intently with a scowl on her face.

CHAPTER 7

"Okay. So let's go over this one last time," said Detective Whitman, seated behind Sorceress Stone's desk with a notepad in his hands. Alba and I sat across from him. "The lunchroom door was locked, so the two of you went and got Ms. Hobbs from her office to unlock the door."

I nodded. "Yes."

"You said she was supposed to have been in the kitchen at that time?"

Alba shrugged. "She usually is."

"Do you recall what time you went to get her?"

"Yeah, it was twelve-thirty."

He nodded and jotted something down in his notebook. "What is it that she does in the kitchen?"

"She scans our ID badges. That's how we pay for our meals," I explained and held up the ID badge that was hanging around my neck.

"Did she say *why* she wasn't in the cafeteria when she was supposed to be?"

"She told us that she was trying to finish up some schedules that Sorceress Stone wanted her to have done before lunch," I explained.

"Did she seem *normal* to the two of you?" he asked, looking from Alba to me.

Alba and I looked at each other and then back at Detective Whitman.

My head snapped back as my mind reeled. His tone implied he was looking closely at Brittany as a suspect. "Are you trying to say you think *Brittany* killed Denise?!" I asked incredulously.

Detective Whitman looked up from his notepad. His mouth was set in a straight line, and his eyes were dark. "The position and angle of the knife in her back suggests that it was done by someone, uhh....vertically challenged."

"Vertically challenged?" I asked.

"Short," said Alba.

My eyebrows knitted together. "Why would Brittany want to kill Denise?"

"I didn't say she did it. I just want to make sure I'm covering all of my bases here. So, I'll ask again. Was Ms. Hobbs acting normally to you?"

I looked down at my hands. I didn't want to admit to Detective Whitman that Brittany had appeared to be a little jumpy in my opinion.

"I would say she was jittery." Alba's voice rang out before I could speak. My head snapped up nervously to stare at Alba.

Detective Whitman's face tilted slightly to the side. "Jittery, you say. How so?"

Alba shrugged. "She seemed nervous. Right, Red?" she asked, looking at me pointedly.

I opened my mouth, but nothing came out.

Detective Whitman watched me for a moment. "Mercy, what was your opinion of Ms. Hobbs?"

I looked down at my hands again. "She seemed a bit jumpy," I agreed with a sigh and a tiny bob of the head.

He nodded. "I see."

I looked up quickly. "But that doesn't mean that I think she's guilty. She could have just been worried about Sorceress Stone finding out she wasn't in the cafeteria when she was supposed to be."

He gave me a tight smile and looked down at his notepad again. "Possibly."

We sat in silence as Detective Whitman made some notes on his pad. Finally, he looked up at the two of us. "Do you mind showing me what happened after you retrieved Brittany?"

"Showing you?" I asked.

He stood up and motioned for us to move towards the door. "If you don't mind."

Alba stood up quickly. "Sure. She got the keys from her drawer and then took us down the back hallway."

The two of them looked at me, waiting for me to stand up. I hesitated and then finally stood. It just seemed wrong for him to suspect that Brittany had done this. While I couldn't say that I particularly *liked* Brittany Hobbs, I'd be the first to admit that she just didn't seem to be the murdering type.

Alba led us out of Sorceress Stone's office and into the reception area, just outside Stone's door.

"Where did she keep the keys?" he asked.

Alba walked around Brittany's desk and pointed to her top desk drawer.

He nodded and jotted that down on his notepad. "And then what?"

Alba stepped out of Brittany's office. "Then she led us down this hallway. Which we thought was a little strange."

He followed Alba. "You thought that was strange? In what way?" he asked.

"Well, usually we go in through that door," said Alba, pointing back towards the dining hall door.

He nodded. "I see. Did you ask her about it?"

"Yeah, she said this is the way she always goes."

Detective Whitman made another note as he followed us down the hallway. "I see. So you came this way and then what?"

"She got out her keys," said Alba.

"She didn't try the door handle first?"

Alba furrowed her eyebrows as if she had to think about that.

I shook my head. "She tried the door handle to the kitchen first. Then she used her keys."

"She *fumbled* with her keys," specified Alba.

"Sure. Then we came in the kitchen and all the lights were on, but there was no Denise or Midge."

"Midge is the part-time cook?" he asked.

I nodded. "We asked where she was and Brittany said she called in sick."

"Okay. And then what?"

"Then we left the kitchen and tried the storage room," I said. "That's when we found Denise."

"Was the door to the storage room locked?" he asked.

Alba nodded. "Yes, because I remember she said that these doors usually aren't locked."

Detective Whitman rose an eyebrow. "I see."

"So then we went in. Denise called her name and of course got no answer, but Mercy immediately got a weird vibe, so we looked around and then we saw the blood."

Detective Whitman looked at me curiously. "Did you look for her ghost?" he asked.

I shook my head. That hadn't been my first instinct. "No. We told Brittany to go tell Stone and call 911."

I sighed and cast my eyes towards the floor. I felt bad for not making that my first instinct. Maybe if I were going to pursue a career in law enforcement assistance, I would need to start making that my first instinct. In this particular case, I had been too shocked and sick over finding the dead body to even think about looking for her ghost. Maybe Denise's murder would have been solved by now if I had.

He nodded. "That's okay," he said softly. "I was just asking. You don't have to feel bad about that. If you're okay with it, I'll have my officers give you some time alone in this area. I don't want you to touch anything, but just in case Denise's ghost decides to come back, I'd like to give her the opportunity to come back without all the officers around."

I smiled at him thankfully. "Yeah, I'm okay with that. Can Alba stay?"

He nodded. "Absolutely. Again, I just don't want either of you messing with my crime scene. You're only going to see if you can coax her ghost out."

"We understand," I said quietly.

He put a hand on my shoulder. "Are you two alright? That was a pretty gruesome scene."

Alba looked at me. She was handling it better than I was.

"Yeah, we're fine," I said hoarsely.

"Okay. Well, I am going to let Sorceress Stone know that unless someone else has something they want to come forward with, we are going to dismiss all students back to their dorm rooms."

"Now?"

He nodded. "Yes. I don't see any reason to keep all those girls locked up in the gym."

"Okay."

"Come find me if you come up with any new information, okay?" he asked.

Alba and I nodded. "We will."

Detective Whitman nodded at the three police officers standing in the hallway to follow him. Alba and I looked around. Both the storage room door and the kitchen door had been propped open with small wooden wedges.

"I can't go in there," I said to Alba uneasily.

"Come on, Red. We have to find Denise's spirit."

"I know. I'm not sure that I'm ready to see her body again, though."

"Then let's not start in there. Let's start in the kitchen," she suggested.

I nodded and together we began in the kitchen. We looked around, using only our eyes, careful not to touch anything as Detective Whitman had asked.

When we'd been in the kitchen for a long minute or two, Alba looked at me. "We could do a spell. I think we have had enough practice to figure out how to summon a ghost on our own now."

"She's had a rough day. She should want to come to us on her own," I whispered.

I heard a rustling outside the door.

"Did you hear that?" asked Alba as both of our heads swiveled to listen more carefully.

I nodded silently.

Alba motioned for me to follow her. Quietly she tiptoed to the doorway and peeked outside. I followed her and peered around her shoulder just in time to catch a glimpse of a shadow disappearing down the hallway that led to the basement.

Alba and I left the kitchen and headed in the direction of the shadow. When we got around the corner, I saw a tall ghostly figure with a green glowing aura around it.

"Hello?" I whispered into the hallway.

The apparition slowly turned around to face us. Her eyes were filled with terror, and her hands were covered in blood. It was Denise.

My hand went up and instinctively covered my open mouth as I sucked in a breath. "Denise!" I said, stunned.

Alba's jaw dropped. "Oh my God, I can see her too!"

"You can?" I asked, shocked. I was the only medium in the group and aside from a few group spells that we had cast and of course the whole Christmas debacle, thus far I was the only one of my friends who could see and talk to ghosts.

Alba nodded and leaned over towards me. "Do the dead bodies always glow like that?" she asked out of the side of her mouth.

I shook my head slowly. "No. I don't know why she looks like that," I whispered back. Then I put my hands up in front of me in an "I won't hurt you" sort of way and slowly moved towards Denise. I didn't want to spook her.

"Mercy?" asked Denise hesitantly.

I nodded and kept moving closer to her. "Oh, Denise, I'm so sorry!"

She furrowed her eyebrows at me. "I'm dead!" she said, the words catching in her throat.

I nodded my head as my eyes clouded over with tears. "I know. I'm so sorry."

Denise looked down at her bloody hands and then looked up at me. "She killed me!" she hollered.

I stopped moving. "You know who did it?" I looked back at Alba, frozen in her place several feet behind me. She nodded me forward and stayed, her feet stuck to the ground. "Who killed you?" I asked fearfully, holding my breath, scared to hear her answer.

Her eyes were wild and crazy as she sucked in a ragged, fearful breath. "It was Brittany. Brittany killed me!"

CHAPTER 8

My heart stopped beating then. My breath caught in my throat as I spun around to face Alba. Had I just heard her right? Had she just said that Brittany killed her? I turned back around to face Denise. I squinted my eyes as I looked at her. The bright glow of green burned my eyes, and it was hard to look at her with all that blood on her. "What did you just say?" I asked her.

"Brittany killed me," she repeated.

"You're sure?"

She nodded. "Of course I'm sure," she snapped.

"Brittany Hobbs?"

"Yes, Brittany Hobbs," she said, repeating my words. She was understandably upset.

"I don't understand. Why would Brittany kill you?" I asked her.

She shrugged her shoulders and lifted her eyebrows as if that was a stupid question. "That's what you're going to have to figure out."

I was stunned. I didn't even know where to start. "Okay. So, you *saw* Brittany stab you. With your own eyes?"

"Of course I did. That's how I know she killed me!"

I nodded. "Yeah. I'm so sorry, Denise. Of course. Wow. I'm just surprised. Brittany doesn't seem like the killer type."

Denise nodded. "Well, she is!"

"Okay. I need to tell Detective Whitman and Sorceress Stone. This will be such a relief to them to have figured this out so quickly. I'm glad we found you," I said. "We're all going to miss you, Denise."

She gave me a tight smile. "I'll be fine. I've got to go now," she assured us.

"So that's it? You're not going to stick around?"

Denise made a face. "For what? I'm dead. And I know who did it. Why would I stick around?"

I turned and looked at Alba over my shoulder. She shrugged. "I don't know. To tell your husband and kids that you love them?"

"You can do that for me. Tell my husband I love him and give my kids a hug for me. Tell them I love them too," she said.

I was surprised at how cavalier she was being about her death. I peered at her more closely. "Denise, you're acting strangely. Is everything alright?"

She rose up both hands to show me the blood on them. "Of course everything isn't alright! I'm dead for Pete's sake! Someone just killed me!"

I nodded. "You're right. I'm so sorry," I said, shaking my head. *I guess everyone handles their deaths differently.* "I'll tell your family that you love them, I promise."

"Thank you, Mercy. I'll see you on the other side," she said crassly and then just like that, she disappeared.

The second she was gone, my eyes widened. I couldn't

believe what we'd just seen. I spun around and raced back to Alba. Alba's jaw was nearly down to her navel.

"Did we seriously just see Denise Whiting's ghost? Unreal!" Alba gushed, almost excitedly.

"That. Was. Weird." I said, my eyes still wide as I looked around the hallway slowly.

"What was weird about it?" Alba asked curiously.

I pulled my head back. "You didn't think she was acting strangely?"

Alba looked at me, confused. "The woman was just *stabbed* to death. Of course she's acting strangely."

Maybe Alba was right. Maybe my overactive imagination was just making something out of nothing. I gave her a tight smile. "You're probably right. We should go talk to Stone and Whitman."

Alba nodded. "Let's go," she said and turned around.

We walked quietly for about ten or fifteen paces and then she looked at me. "Are you alright?"

I swallowed hard as I looked up at her. "No. But I will be. Thanks."

When we got back to Sorceress Stone's office, we found it empty. Even Brittany was gone.

"They're probably dismissing people back to their rooms," said Alba, taking a seat in one of the chairs out in front of Stone's door.

Unconsciously, I found myself pacing the length of Brittany's office. The thought of having to turn her into the cops was making me anxious. "Maybe we should think about this."

Alba looked up at me from her chair. She raised one eyebrow. "Think about what?"

"Turning Brittany in. It just doesn't feel right."

"She killed Denise. We can't have a killer running

around campus. What if she kills someone else while we're *thinking about it*?"

I sighed. She was probably right. And yet...I felt very unsettled. "Can we go back to our room? Just for a few minutes? I need to clear my head."

Alba stood up and took a step towards me. "We're telling Stone and Whitman about this."

I closed my eyes and nodded, holding up a hand. "Yeah, yeah. I know. I just need a minute before we go back into witness mode with Whitman."

Alba sighed and then threw an arm over my shoulder. "Yeah, that's fine. You're probably just hungry. You didn't eat your pizza."

Together Alba and I walked back to our dorm room. There were no other girls around yet, so we had to assume that they were still in the gym. I opened the door of my room and was shocked to see a black cat on the window sill outside my room. Jax and I had stopped leaving the window open for Sneaks after the weather had shifted so dramatically. "Sneaks!" I said as I entered the room and rushed to open the window.

"What in the world is Sneaks doing here?" asked Alba.

Sneaks leapt through the window and onto my desk. It had been *ages* since I'd seen the black cat. I had actually been wondering if she'd gotten caught in the winter storm we'd had at Christmas time or if she'd found somewhere to take cover.

"*Finally* you're back," said my mother's familiar voice from Sneaks's mouth. "I've been waiting out here all afternoon!"

"Mom! What are you doing here?" I asked.

"I've been trying to call you. You don't answer your phone!" she chastised.

I pulled my phone out of my back pocket and pressed the home button to find at least a dozen missed calls from my mother and my brother, Reign. None of the calls had been there when I'd texted Hugh to cancel our date an hour or so ago.

"Huh," I said casually.

My mother growled at me. "What's the point in me paying for a phone for you if you don't answer it in emergency situations?" she demanded.

I looked up at her sharply. "Emergency situations? Did something happen to you or Reign?"

She put a paw to her forehead. "Nothing happened to *us*. Word is all over downtown Aspen Falls that there was a murder at the college. Reign and I have been worried sick!"

I fell onto the bottom bunk of my bed. I didn't have the energy to deal with my mother, of all people . "You could have just walked around campus and eavesdropped," I told her with a sigh.

The cat rolled her green eyes at me. "Oh yeah, *that* wouldn't have been noticeable at all. A black cat just wandering through the hallways? They would have called animal control on me!"

I shrugged.

"So what happened?" she demanded. "Are all of your friends alright? Where have you been?"

I looked up at Alba who was still standing in the doorway. She couldn't hear my mother talking. She could only hear Sneaks meowing.

"What's she saying?" asked Alba.

"She and Reign heard about the murder in town," I explained. "She's been trying to call."

Alba leaned her back against the closed door. "Tell her we've been busy."

"Busy doing what?" Mom asked. I could hear the frustration in her voice. "Who was killed?"

"Denise Whiting," I told her. A lump formed in my throat as my eyes got cloudy again. "She was our lunch lady."

Alba walked towards the desks and grabbed a tissue from Jax's side. She handed it to me without saying a word.

"Thanks," I whispered as I blotted my eyes. I didn't know what was wrong with me. It wasn't like I hadn't seen a dead body before. In fact, it seemed it was becoming a habit. But this one felt a little different. I'd seen Denise three times a day since September. She had kind of become a second mother to us girls at The Institute.

Just then we heard a commotion coming from the hallway.

"Girls must be back," said Alba, opening the door.

All of our neighboring girls were making their way back to their dorm rooms. Jax, Holly, and Sweets were in the middle of the large group. Alba stuck her head out into the hallway. "We're in here," she said when she spotted our friends.

"What happened?" Jax asked in her usual excitable voice as she came inside with Sweets and Holly right behind her.

"We gave our stories to Whitman," said Alba. "And then he wanted Red to see if Denise's ghost would appear to her."

Everyone looked at me.

"Well, did it?" Mom asked.

Everyone's eyes turned towards Sneaks.

"What's your mom doing here?" Holly asked, pointing at the cat.

"She's being nosy," I said and shot my mother an annoyed glance.

"Mercy Mae Habernackle! Answer the question. Did you see the poor woman's spirit?"

I leapt off the bed, frustrated. I still didn't have a handle on my emotions and having my mom here was not helping me feel better. If anything, it was making me more tense. "Yes!" I hollered at the group. "I saw her ghost. Alba saw her too."

All the eyes were on Alba now.

"You saw her ghost?!" Sweets asked in awe.

A slow smile spread across Alba's mouth, even though she tried not to let it, she couldn't help it. I could tell she thought it was pretty cool that she was able to see ghosts now too. "Yeah. I saw her."

"Well, did she have anything important to say?" asked Holly as she scrambled up to sit cross-legged on Jax's desk.

Alba and I exchanged a look. She might as well tell everyone. I knew I couldn't.

"She told us who killed her," said Alba, tipping her head slightly to the left.

Jax's eyes widened. "She told you who killed her? Oh my gosh! Who was it?"

Alba hesitated. I could tell she didn't feel good about saying it either. She looked down at the floor as her toe made tiny circles in the grey carpet. Finally, she looked up. "It was Brittany."

Holly leapt off of the desk and onto the balls of her feet. "Stop it!"

Sweets's jaw dropped, and she looked around the room, unsure of what to say.

Jax shook her head in shock. "I don't believe it!"

"Who's Brittany," asked my mom from the desk.

I looked over at her. "You remember Brittany. She was the cheerful one we met on move-in day. She gave us my room key and my ID badge?"

Sneaks's eyes widened. "*That girl* killed your lunch lady? Why?"

I shrugged.

"Why would *Brittany* want to kill Denise?" Sweets asked, plopping herself down on my desk chair.

"We don't know. Denise didn't know. She said that was for us to figure out," I said quietly.

"Well then we better figure it out!" said Jax. "Because I don't believe it. Brittany is like one of the most cheerful people in the world. I just love her!"

Alba rolled her eyes. "Of course you do."

"I do! I've been around this school longer than all of you combined! Even though I went to boarding school, I still lived at the school on holiday breaks and during summers and stuff. Brittany was like my big sister when she first started. I used to play in her office while my mom was working. She's my friend!" said Jax. Her face began to drop as the reality of the situation started to hit her. Her friend was being accused of *murder*!

Alba shrugged uncaringly. "Well, sorry to tell you, Shorty. Your bff is a murderer."

Jax shook her head wildly. "I truly don't believe it," she retorted angrily. She turned and looked at me. "Mercy, tell me what Denise actually said."

I let out a sigh. "She said '*Brittany killed me.*' I'm sorry. I don't want to believe it either. Brittany is not my favorite person, but I agree with you. It's hard to imagine Brittany doing something like that. But we *saw* Denise's ghost. That's what she told us!"

Alba looked at me again. This time the patience that had

once been in her eyes was gone. "Come on, Red. We have to go tell Whitman and Stone about what we know."

I hung my head. I still wasn't feeling better. In fact, hearing Jax's testimonial made me feel even worse. I didn't know what to do. I looked at Sneaks. Suddenly the room felt too small. I wished that everyone was gone and I could just talk to my mom alone without all of them around. I tried to suck in a deep breath, but my lungs suddenly felt two sizes too small.

Sweets put her hand on my back as I leaned over, trying to catch my breath. "Are you alright, Mercy?"

I put a hand on the desk next to me and shook my head. "Not really. Can I have a minute alone with my mom?"

Sweets nodded. "Absolutely. We'll wait for you in the hallway." She turned towards the rest of the girls. "Mercy wants to talk to her mom alone. Let's wait for her out here."

Alba let out a frustrated sigh and opened the door to the hallway. "If you're not out here in five minutes, Red. I'm going to Whitman and Stone without you," she promised me.

I pretended like I didn't hear her.

"We'll be right out here if you need us, Mercy," Jax said sweetly as she followed the rest of the girls out into the hallway, shutting the door behind her.

Sneaks put her soft black paw on my hand and rubbed it gently. "Mercy Bear, are you alright? Do you need me to drive up to The Institute in person?"

Doubled over, I continued to wheeze heavily. "I just need to catch my breath, Mom. This morning has been *so* overwhelming."

"I understand," she said softly. She looked around. "Where's your inhaler?"

"I didn't bring it."

"Mercy!" she began. She thought better of it and instead whispered, "I'm sorry about Denise."

I looked up and gave her a tight smile. "Me too."

Then my mom sat down and curled her tail around her bottom. "Mercy, sweetheart, I know this is hard for you, but I think you're missing the point of your involvement in this."

I tilted my head to the side and gave her a curious glance. "What do you mean?" I breathed heavily.

"I mean, you're not the judge here. Or the executioner. Or the detective, for that matter. You're simply a witness with a piece of the puzzle."

"I know Mom, but—"

Sneaks shook her head firmly. "No buts, Mercy. As a medium, you have to be completely honest with authorities. You have to tell them what you know to be the truth. It's up to them to figure out if it *is* the truth."

"Denise said it was up to us to figure out why Brittany killed her," I said sadly.

"But it's not. It's up to Mark and his guys. He'll figure it out. Have faith. He's a very smart man," she said.

I looked up at her curiously but kept my mouth shut. I didn't have it in me to inquire about my mother's dating situation at the moment. I'd save that for later. Right now, I needed to figure out how to handle what I knew.

"What if they find out that Brittany did it?" I asked her.

My mother sighed. "Then she did it. You can't go around blindly trusting people, Mercy. I thought you were more street smart than that."

"I'm not trusting people blindly, Mom. I just have a gut feeling here. And my gut feeling is telling me that Brittany didn't do this."

"Has your gut feeling ever been wrong before?" she asked me.

I looked down at my shoes. The memories of me being wrong about Morgan Hartford's killer came rushing back to me. For awhile I'd thought that her uncle Seymour had killed her. In Harper Bradshaw's murder, the girls and I were convinced that her boyfriend Vaughn was the killer and in Ronnie Edwards's murder, I was *sure* that Merrick Stone had done it. I groaned and let my head fall into my hands. Mom was right. My gut instincts really sucked.

"Let Mark handle it. Go. Go tell him what you know and then leave the rest to the professionals," she said.

I looked up at her and gave her a tight smile. She was right. In that moment, I was thankful she'd come when she did. I felt better. "Thanks, Mom."

"You're welcome," she said with a smile. "Now go. But the next time you and the girls drive into town, come to the b&b. I could use a hug."

I nodded. "Sure thing, Mom," I said as I rushed out of the room to meet the girls in the hallway. I gave Alba a brave smile. "I'm ready."

"Good," she said. "This is for the best."

"I know. I feel better about things."

The five of us raced down the wide stone staircase and took a right at the Paranormally Delicious Coffee Shop underneath the stairs. Turning the corner, we went down the hallway and stopped in front of Brittany's door. I could hear Detective Whitman's deep voice coming from inside Sorceress Stone's office.

I held a finger up to my lips for a moment, silencing the chatter from the girls.

"SaraLynn, I can't," he said. His deep voice carried easily out into the hallway. From where we stood at the doorway of Brittany's office, we could see directly into Sorceress Stone's office and the back of Detective Whitman's jacket. He sat in the chair in front of her desk.

"Is it because of *that woman*?" Sorceress Stone asked.

Detective Whitman paused and then I saw his body shift slightly in his seat. "Linda's part of the reason, yes. But you're a larger part of the reason. You aren't the person that I thought you were."

"I'm sorry, Mark. There's family history there. She brings out the worst in me," her voice was tight, but there was a tinge of regret present in there, humanizing her if only slightly.

Without moving my feet, I stuck my head into Brittany's office and peered to the left to see if she was listening to their conversation. Her desk was empty.

"I'm sorry that you don't like her, SaraLynn, but I do. And that's really all that matters. Now, like I said before, I'm here to solve a murder, not discuss my personal life with you. Can we discuss the matter at hand?"

"I don't understand why you just can't say you'll go with me. It's only a wedding for crying out loud. I can't show up by myself. It's just – *uncouth*," she hissed. "We don't have to be *dating* for you to be my escort."

"It would look like we were dating if I took you. Now, back to Denise Whiting. Where are those girls of yours?" he asked, giving us only a momentary heads up before he leaned back in his chair to peer out of Sorceress Stone's office door. His eyebrows rose as he spotted us, taking steps through Brittany's office. His eyes caught mine momentarily. I could tell the thought of possibly having his last conversation overheard by me concerned him. I tried to play it cool and not let on to what I'd heard. "Oh, there you are!" he said with a slight smile.

"We need to talk to you," said Alba forcefully. "It's important."

His face sobered to reflect Alba's serious expression. "Did you see Denise's ghost?"

Our heads nodded as the five of us stood in Brittany's office. My stomach rolled around nervously, making me slightly nauseous.

He stood up and left Stone's office, meeting us in the reception area. His wide frame towered over Jax as he stood next to her. His eyes never left mine. "What do you know?"

"Denise knew who killed her," I told him blankly.

In a huff, Sorceress Stone left her office. Her long flowing grey dress swept the floor lightly as she walked. "Tell us. Who did she say it was?"

"Denise said Brittany killed her," said Alba from behind me.

Suddenly there was a loud noise at the door. We all turned around to see Brittany standing in the doorway. The stack of files that she had been carrying were now scattered around her feet in disarray. "What? Denise said – *I killed her?*"

CHAPTER 9

The revelation of Denise's words chased shock and fear into Brittany's eyes and caused her face to fade to a ghastly white. She appeared stunned and not in the least bit guilty of the murder. Even though my mother had convinced me to look at this like it was Detective Whitman's case to solve, it didn't feel that way. I suddenly felt like Alba and I had made a huge mistake and regret washed over me like a cold shower, prickling my flesh into tiny pimples.

Sorceress Stone sucked in her breath as her hand flitted to cover her mouth. "Brittany!" she gasped.

"Sorceress Stone! I didn't! I would *never!*" cried Brittany, holding her hands out in protest.

"Then why would Denise say that you did?" Alba asked curiously. It was the question I wanted to have answered too.

Brittany shook her head furiously. "I – I – I don't know! Denise and I got along great! I'm devastated that she's gone!"

"Devastated because you got caught?" Detective Whitman asked her.

Tears shimmered in her eyes as what was happening rained down on her. Her head shook vigorously from side to side. "I didn't do it! You've got to believe me!" she asserted.

Detective Whitman looked at me. "What *exactly* happened when you went to see Denise?"

"Alba and I started in the kitchen, and then we heard something out in the hallway. So we went out there to see what the noise was. That's when we saw a shadow turn down the corridor to the basement. We followed it, and that's when we saw Denise's ghost."

"We?" he asked, looking up from the notepad he was writing on.

I nodded. "Alba saw her too."

Detective Whitman rose one eyebrow as he looked at Alba curiously. "You can see ghosts now too?"

Alba shrugged and curled one lip. "Apparently. I mean, I saw her. I heard her speak too."

"What did she say?"

"She said she knew who killed her."

I nodded encouragingly and then interjected, "And then I said, who did it? And she said, Brittany. Brittany killed me. We asked her why Brittany killed her and she said that was for us to figure out. And then she said we should give hugs to her family and tell them that she loved them and then she just left."

Brittany's eyes were wide, and her bottom lip trembled. "I don't know why she would say that! I swear! I didn't do it! Sorceress Stone, you *have* to believe me!" the petite blond woman begged.

Sorceress Stone lifted her chin, raising her nose higher in

the air. She closed her eyes and turned her head slightly as if the sight of Brittany would make her ill. "Take her away, Detective."

~

I PACED THE LENGTH OF MY ROOM MINUTES LATER, BITING ON the inside of my lip nervously. Sweets and Jax were sitting on my bed, Holly was curled up on top of Jax's desk, and Alba sat on my chair, leaned back on two legs, watching me pace.

"I can't believe we just did that," I said as I walked. Tension mounted on my shoulders as the weight of the day set in and caused my head to throb. "I really don't think that Brittany did this. I feel like we just fed her to the wolves."

"Well, then you're not going to like what I have to say," said Alba trepidatiously.

My pacing stopped as if I'd hit a brick wall and I stared at her. The rest of the girls turned their eyes to her also.

"Now don't get mad at me for not saying anything right away," she said, stiff arming me so I wouldn't tackle her when I decided I didn't like whatever was coming next.

I furrowed my eyebrows anxiously. "What? Why would I get mad? What are you talking about?"

She scratched the top of her head and studied the pile of clothes on the futon behind me. "You know I can read minds sometimes, right?"

"Yeah?" I asked her testily.

"Well, usually it comes and goes, and I don't have much control over it. But this morning I had my first Mind Reading class, and my professor began to talk about how our brains work and how to be able to control our mind reading abilities we must focus our attention on the energy signals others omit."

I let out a breath of annoyance. "Yeah? So…long story short?"

Alba sighed. "My point was, it takes a lot of focus, but while you were talking to Detective Whitman, I was trying to read Brittany's mind."

"Did it work?"

Alba smiled. "Yeah, I think it did."

I pulled up Jax's desk chair and sat down, across from Alba.

"Don't keep us in suspense!" cried Holly, leaning forward. "What did you get?"

"She really thinks she's innocent," said Alba, leaning back against the seat rest.

Jax stood up and pumped the air with her tiny fist. "*I knew it!*" she cheered. "There was *no way* Brittany did it! We've got to go tell Detective Whitman!"

I jumped off my chair. "You're right! We need to leave!"

Sweets lifted both hands up to slow us down. "Whoa, whoa, whoa. Sorceress Stone put everyone in the no-traveling ban," she said. "We can't just leave."

I sat back down. Sweets had a point. Until the ban was lifted, if we so much as stepped foot off campus and Stone found out, we'd be goners.

"We could call Detective Whitman," Jax suggested with a small shrug.

Alba shook her head. "We're going to have a hard enough time convincing him that Brittany's innocent in person. There's no way we'll convince him over the phone."

"As much as I don't want to just sit on this information, I don't think we can just leave right now," I said hesitantly.

Alba looked at me in shock. "Are you serious right now?

Is that boyfriend of yours making you soft? Since when are you scared of Stone?"

The rest of the girls giggled.

I stood up. "I'm not scared. Are you scared?"

Alba stood up too. "I'm from Jersey. Nothing scares me."

The girls giggled again as Jax stood up confidently. "My mom can't hurt me too badly; she's my mom after all, and it's to help Brittany so I would think she could understand that. I'm in."

We turned and looked at Sweets and Holly.

Holly shrugged and stood up casually. "Fine. Let me go put on a different shirt. I didn't know we were going *out*."

Alba rolled her eyes but surprisingly kept her mouth shut. Considering that I hadn't heard her cracking on Holly since they got back, I silently wondered if her New Year's resolution was to quit making fun of Holly and her boobs.

All that was left was Sweets, and *she* was the one that had brought up the restriction in the first place. She looked at the four of us nervously. "What if she banishes us to the room in the tower again? I can't go that long without eating. I'm on a diet, and I haven't eaten much lately."

"You're not on a diet," I told her dryly. "You had a huge cinnamon roll for breakfast and two slices of cheese pizza for lunch. That's not what I would consider a diet."

"Most people would not consider that a diet," agreed Holly.

Sweets sighed. "I'm starting slow. I don't want my body to go into hypoglycemic shock or something."

"Fine, Holly, go change your shirt. Sweets, go pack a snack pack just in case we get busted and have to go to witch jail," I ordered. I looked down at my watch. "We're leaving in five minutes."

THE POLICE STATION WAS PACKED WHEN WE WALKED IN. Officers were all over the place, and there were even some news reporters waiting in the lobby. As usual, Officer Vargas sat at his desk behind the plexiglass window. As the first of the girls to enter the building, I gave him a tiny wave. I thought I saw the smallest glimmer of a smile when he saw me, but I couldn't be sure. I was going to win that man over yet.

When we approached the window, I pulled a small wrapped package out from behind my back. "Merry Belated Christmas, Officer Vargas," I said with a smile. I had promised myself for months that for Christmas I was going to get Officer Vargas an eyebrow groomer to take care of the oversized black bushes atop his eyes, but I'd eventually decided against it. I hadn't wanted him to take my gesture the wrong way.

With a startled expression, he buzzed us back. I handed him his gift. "It's from all of us," I said with a smile.

"You got me a gift?" he asked us curiously. "Why are you girls giving me a gift?" His voice quickly changed from surprise to suspicion.

"Because you're so sweet, letting us see Detective Whitman all the time. We wanted to express our gratitude. It's just chocolate, don't get too excited," I told him with a wink.

He shot us a genuine smile and then gestured with his head towards Detective Whitman's office. "He's back there, go ahead."

"Thanks, Officer Vargas," chirped Jax.

"Thanks for the chocolate!" he called out after us.

I knocked on the frame of Detective Whitman's office.

He was on the phone, but he looked up and waved us in. Jax and Holly took a seat while Alba, Sweets, and I just leaned against the wood paneled wall behind them. His office reeked of stale coffee and burnt tobacco. The poor guy needed a window and an air freshener.

"Yeah, I'll check into it. Yup. Okay. Thanks," he said. He looked up at us curiously when he'd hung up the phone. "What are you girls doing down here? I thought Sorceress Stone issued a lock-down until we could confirm the details of the murder investigation."

Alba nodded. "Yeah, about that. We're gonna need you to keep this visit on the down low."

"The down low?"

Sweets nodded. "If you tell on us, we'll get in big trouble. So, can you, like, not tell on us?"

"Please?" Jax added.

He shook his head, trying to wash away the confusion. "I'm sorry. I just want to know *why* you're down here."

"We don't think Brittany did it," I said point blank.

The way his jaw hung open and his eyes bugged out slightly, made me wonder if he thought we were crazy. "But you said…"

I raised one side of my mouth, pinching my cheek up into my eye, making my eye squinty. "Yeah, I know what we said, but forget about that. I don't think Denise was thinking very clearly."

He closed the folder sitting in front of him and leaned back in his chair. It creaked heavily with the shifting of his weight. "So I should just let Brittany Hobbs go because you don't *think* a ghost was thinking clearly? Can you hear how ridiculous that sounds?"

Alba pushed herself away from the wall and held out her hand. "Look, Detective. I've been working on my mind reading abilities, and I'm pretty sure that Brittany was thinking that she didn't do this, that she wasn't guilty."

"Pretty sure, huh?" His question made a mockery of us coming down to the station.

Alba stiffened. "Yeah, pretty sure. You'd think if I were reading her mind and she was guilty, she'd have thought something like, *'oh no, they caught me.'* Wouldn't you think?"

His laughter erupted, echoing off the walls of his office. "You girls. You should have your own reality TV show. You're funny."

Alba's nostrils flared, and her cheeks flushed. "I'm not trying to be funny. I really think she's innocent."

He shoved his chair backwards. "Fine. Let's just go let her out then."

Jax stood up happily. "Well, that was easier than I thought it was going to be!"

I put my hand on her shoulder and pressed her down towards the chair. "He's being sarcastic, Jax. He's not letting her out," I grumped.

"Of course I'm not letting her out! You said that Denise's *ghost* said she did it. Who better to know that than the victim herself?"

I sighed. "Detective Whitman. We just don't think Brittany is capable of murder."

"Look. I'm not just going to take the word of a ghost. I'm still going to investigate the murder, okay?"

"You are?" I asked him.

He nodded. "You seriously just thought I was going to arrest Ms. Hobbs and throw away the key without even finding evidence that she did it? I still have to make a case to a jury!"

Alba and I looked at each other. "So you'll keep investigating other leads?"

"Of course I will!"

I leaned back against the wall in relief. "Good. Thanks, Detective Whitman. That makes me feel better."

"Alright. Now, if you don't mind. I've got some work to do. That knife we found in Mrs. Whiting's back didn't come from the school's kitchen like we initially thought. The handles are different. I'm working on finding out who sells that particular brand of knife, and I need to make a few phone calls. So. If you'll excuse me…"

Jax and Holly stood up.

"Thanks, Detective Whitman," said Sweets as we left the room. "Don't forget, you shouldn't mention to anyone that we were here."

He smiled slyly. "You girls should be getting back to campus."

"Let us know if you find out anything new?" I asked him when the rest of the girls had gone.

He nodded. "I'll tell you what I can."

"Hey, by the way, thanks for not going out on a date with Sorceress Stone," I said with a conspiring wink.

One of his eyebrows immediately shot up. "So you *did* hear that discussion. I wondered. Maybe you'll promise to keep that information between the two of us?"

I smiled broadly. "Sure. If you promise not to tell Sorceress Stone we came down here today."

He nodded. "You've got a deal."

CHAPTER 10

I was able to convince Sweets and the rest of the girls to take five minutes before heading back to campus to stop by Habernackle's Bed, Breakfast, and Beyond to reassure my mom and brother that we were all okay. Holly didn't need much convincing, and as usual, when going to see my brother, she'd primped the few blocks it took to get there.

As we breezed in through the front door, Jax immediately ran directly for Reign, bumping past Holly on her way. By now he was used to her youthful spirit, and when she ran for him, he scooped her up and gave her a big hug, spinning her around in a dizzying circle. The attention always made Jax's day.

"I've missed you, Cuz," said Reign, setting her down on her feet. His dark onyx eyes glinted in the light as he smiled.

Jax laced her arm through his and hugged his bicep happily. "I've missed you, too," chirped Jax.

Reign looked up at the rest of us and ran a hand through his dark, wavy hair. He wore a red and black plaid flannel shirt, denim jeans, and beige Army boots and it looked like he hadn't shaved in a week.

I poked his ribs as I passed him. "Looking a bit grungy today, bro. Ever heard of a razor?"

He caught hold of my arm and pulled me into him, enveloping my shoulders in a bear hug. "Good to see you too, sis." He leaned over and nuzzled the prickly stubble of his beard against the smoothness of my forehead.

I pressed my flattened palms against his chest and shoved as I giggled. "Reign!" I hollered.

"You like my beard, don't you," he said playfully.

"Not even a little bit," I teased. He poked into the side of my ribs as I skipped out of his reach.

"Oh, come on. Say you like it!"

I shook my head and bit my lips between my teeth.

"I like it, Reign," said Jax happily.

Sweets nodded. "Me too."

"Why thank you, ladies, I'm so glad *you* like it." He rubbed his hand against his jaw. "I think I'm going to keep it."

Holly gave him a little flirtatious wink. "I think you look hot, Reign. Definitely keep the beard."

Reign glanced up at Holly who as usual, was leading with her breasts in a white, v-neck, mohair sweater and black Aztec print leggings and boots. Her long blond hair lay around her shoulders in smooth, sexy waves and her blue eyes sparkled mischievously. Reign coughed nervously. Holly's flirtation always seemed to make Reign uncomfortable. "Thanks, Holly, I think I will," he said, smiling back at her.

My voice alerted Chesney, our chestnut colored Cavapoo puppy, of my arrival. He came galloping out of the kitchen on his short little legs and plopped down in front of me then immediately rolled onto his back. I squatted next to him and gave him a quick scratch on his belly. "Hey, lil buddy, I missed you too."

I stood back up again. "Where's Mom?" I asked my brother, looking around.

He jerked his head towards the kitchen. "She's prepping for the dinner rush," he said. Then he leaned backwards, held a hand aside of his mouth, and hollered. "MOM! Mercy and the girls are here!"

In seconds my mother burst out of the double swinging doors behind the bar. "Oh! I'm so glad you all decided to come out to see me!" she gushed. She hurried around the counter to throw her arms around my shoulders. "I was so worried!"

I rolled my eyes at her dramatics but hugged her back. It had been a rough morning, and as much as I didn't like to admit it, I welcomed the hug. I squeezed her back and then let go, not wanting to seem too eager in front of my friends. "Sorry to burst your bubble, Mom. We didn't leave campus to see you."

Her back stiffened. "Oh, well, then why did you leave school?"

"When we told Detective Whitman and Sorceress Stone about what Denise said, Brittany immediately said she didn't do it," I told her.

Mom nodded her head as if to say *tell me more.* "Well, did you expect her just to fess up?"

I sighed and plopped down on the bar stool next to Alba. "No."

"So why did that make a difference to you?" Mom asked, walking around the counter.

"Alba read her mind," I admitted.

Mom looked at Alba in surprise. "You can read minds?"

Alba shrugged. "Sometimes. I'm working on my skill right now."

My mother nodded. "It certainly would be a handy skill to have as a witch."

"I'm thinking about majoring in mind studies," Alba admitted.

My mother smiled broadly. "I'm so glad you girls are finally starting to figure out what you want to do with your lives! I only wish my daughter could figure out what she wants to major in," she declared.

I rolled my eyes again. "Quit it, Mom."

She ignored me and looked at Sweets. "No. I'm serious. Sweets knows what she wants to do, too. Right, Sweets?"

Sweets nodded excitedly. "Yeah, pretty much."

"When do you start your internship at Mr. Bailey's Bakery?"

"Oh, I started today, actually."

Mom's smile widened. "Oh, did you really? How did it go?" she asked, leaning onto her elbow on the bar.

"It was pretty exciting."

"Did Mr. Bailey tell you that he got engaged to Char over Christmas?" Mom asked.

Sweets' eyes widened. "Yes, he did! He told you too? Isn't that exciting!"

Mom pulled the towel from over her shoulder and began wiping the counter while she talked. "It's very exciting."

"The wedding is on Sunday," said Sweets. "We're all invited."

My mother nodded. The look on her face told me that she'd been invited too, but she didn't say anything.

I looked at her curiously. "Were you invited to the wedding, Mom?"

Mom glanced up nervously at Reign who was smiling from ear to ear.

"Mom?" I prompted again.

She dried a mug that was sitting at the end of the bar, even though it didn't look wet. Then she put both hands on the counter. "Yes, I was invited," she admitted.

The girls and I were all curious now. I furrowed my eyebrows together and looked at my brother. "What's going on?"

"Mr. Bailey and Char weren't the ones that invited Mom," said my brother.

My head pivoted back towards my mother. "Who invited you, Mom?" My mind raced, trying to think of who else could have invited her to Mr. Bailey and Char's wedding. A slow smile spread across my face as Detective Whitman popped into my mind. I prepared myself to squeal when she announced he was her date to the wedding.

"Merrick invited me," she admitted. "He knows the couple somehow and well; he asked me to be his date."

It felt as if my heart dropped onto the floor and Mom danced all over it. My smile vanished. "Mom! You can't possibly tell me you're going to *go* with him?"

Reign scowled at me from across the room. "Leave her alone, Merc. She's a grown woman and can do what she wants."

I furrowed my eyebrows together and pursed my lips at him. "You just want them back together because he's your *dad!*"

Reign pointed a finger at me. "First of all, he's not *my dad*. He's my *father*. There's a difference in my opinion. And second of all, what's so wrong with wanting my *mother* to give my *father* a chance?"

"He's a disaster, that's what's wrong with it!" I hollered at him.

"Can you honestly stand there and tell me that if your father came into the picture and he wanted to get back together with Mom, that you wouldn't be excited about the possibility?" Reign demanded.

My skin prickled as I leapt off my stool. "I can *honestly* say that. My sperm donor *abandoned me*, and he *abandoned Mom*. Why would I want that creep in Mom's life?"

Reign sighed, trying to calm himself. "Well, my father didn't abandon our mother or me intentionally. Our grandmother forced him out of her life, and he didn't even know about me. So maybe he still deserves a chance."

My mother sighed. "I knew this would happen. I wasn't going to tell you about Merrick's invitation. I should have just kept that to myself until I knew what I was going to do."

My heart perked up. "You mean you haven't said yes?"

"I told him I'd have to think about it. He knows I haven't had time for dating. The b&b and restaurant have been a time suck, and then there was the trip back to Dubbsburg before Christmas and then the big storm."

"So it's not too late to say no then?" I asked happily.

Reign growled in frustration.

"I think you should give him another shot," said Jax from across the room.

I pointed at her angrily. "You stay out of this, Jax Stone. He's your uncle, and that's nepotism."

Sweets looked at me with disappointment. "Mercy, don't be mean to Jax. This isn't her fault."

"Don't start with me, Sweets. I've had a very bad day, and now I'm hearing that my mom might be going on a date with the evilest man in Aspen Falls."

Alba sighed. "This again? Red, I don't like the man any more than you do, but just let your mom figure this out on her own. If she wants to date Merrick Stone, then let her. If she wants to date Detective Whitman, then that's her choice. You wouldn't want *her* to be poking her nose into *your* dating life."

"Ugh!" I growled at Alba. "What was that you asked me this morning, Alba? Where's your *loyalty?* How about where's *yours*?" I shoved my barstool under the counter roughly and headed for the door in a huff. "I've heard enough. I'm outta here."

Alba shrugged. "Come on, girls. We need to go before Stone finds out we left campus."

CHAPTER 11

That evening I was both surprised and happy to find out that Sorceress Stone had arranged for us to have our evening meal at the Paranormal Institute for Wizards. Typically The Institute preferred to keep the two schools separate with the exception of the occasional social event on Friday nights. In this case, however, I think Sorceress Stone and her brother, Sorcerer Merrick Stone, must have decided that they needed a way to feed us.

After having had to cancel my date with Hugh, I was very pleased to find out that I was going to get to see him after all.

The girls and I marched through the tunnels with a big group of girls from Winston Hall and when we came to the fork in the road, veered left.

Hugh and Jax's boyfriend, Tristan, were waiting for us in the lobby when we arrived. "Hi, Hugh," I said happily, giving him a hug. "Hey, darlin'," said Hugh as he lifted me off my feet in a bear hug. "I'm glad we get to have supper together after all."

I smiled up at him as he sat me down. "Me too. It's been a horrible day. I needed to see you."

Holding onto Hugh's hand tightly, I looked up at my friends. "Do you guys mind going ahead without us? I want to have a few minutes to talk to Hugh alone."

Holly winked at me. "Of course you do."

I rolled my eyes. "It's not like that, Holly."

Sweets giggled. "Of course it's not."

"Do you mind?" I asked again, this time a little more firmly. My patience was starting to wear thin. It had been a long day, and I was exhausted, hungry, and determined to have a talk with my boyfriend.

The group left with small smiles and tiny waves, leaving the two of us alone in the lobby.

"Save us a seat," I called out to Jax, who gave me a little wink while her boyfriend pulled her away.

"What's up, darlin'? I thought you said you were starving?" Hugh asked as he took me to sit on one of the lounge chairs in the lobby.

"I *am* starving, but I wanted to talk to you about some things that have been bothering me all day."

Hugh looked at me with concern. "What's the matter?"

I looked down at my hands. The idea of him sharing the fact that he was an atmokinesis major with Tori Decker and not me, bothered me. But every way I tried to think to say it sounded dumb in my head. It made me sound like a stupid, jealous girlfriend. I didn't want to think of myself as a stupid, jealous girlfriend. I wasn't like that. I'd never been like that. Why was I like that suddenly? *Ugh*, the thought frustrated me.

I looked up from my hands and smiled at him, trying to think of the right words to say. "You being able to control the weather. That's called atmokinesis?" I asked him.

With his eyebrows furrowed together, he nodded. "Yeah. Why?"

"How come you never told me about that before?"

He looked confused. "I told you I could control the weather on our first date. What do you mean?"

"You never told me that your major had a name," I explained slowly. It sounded stupid coming out of my mouth, but it was like a train wreck I saw happening but couldn't figure out how to stop before it derailed.

He sat up a little straighter. "Well, I guess I just never thought of it," he said. "You never asked. I didn't realize that was something you wanted to know. I would have gladly told you if I knew it was going to bother you."

I squeezed his hand. He was right. I was being silly. I had never asked him. He certainly hadn't told Tori that intentionally to upset me. What was I doing? I was getting in my own head, and it was ridiculous. I gave him a tight smile. "You're right, Hugh. I'm being silly. I had Kinetic Energy 101 today, and we learned about atmokinesis and I didn't know what that was and it just made me feel stupid that I didn't even know what my own boyfriend's major was." I laughed nervously, trying to play it off like I wasn't a complete moron for pulling him aside and trying to make him feel bad for not telling me something I'd never asked about.

He shot me his dazzling smile. "I'm sorry, darlin', I hadn't even thought that might catch you up one day." He pulled me a little closer to him on the sofa. "I'd be happy to make it up to you."

I allowed a little giggle to escape my lips before he kissed me, erasing all doubt about his intentions towards me. When we came up for air another thought struck me. The girls had been teasing me about engagements earlier, and Hugh's intentions were called into question. Was he looking for a *permanent* relationship or just having a good time, like I was? I struggled to smile when he looked at me closely again.

"That didn't make it better?" he asked, concern colored his hazel eyes.

I tilted my head to the side as I looked down at my hands again. "No, that made it better."

"Well, then where's that million dollar smile I've fallen for?"

Should I just ask him? Will it make me sound silly? I didn't know what to do. I forced all of the air of my lungs in frustration. Why was talking about this serious stuff so hard?

"Just say whatever's on your mind, darlin'."

"The girls just put a stupid idea in my head," I said slowly.

"I hear that's what happens when girls get together sometimes," he admitted with an impish grin.

"They just have me a little paranoid."

"Let me make you unparanoid, darlin'. What are they worried about?"

"Fine," I said. *Just rip off the Band-Aid.* "They think because you're twenty-three that you're looking for a wife, not just a girlfriend," I said. *Wow, did that just sound as ridiculous to him as it did to me?* I flushed at the sound of my own words.

He blinked three or four times and then looked up at me with a strange expression on his face. "I mean, I'm not looking for a wife *tomorrow*," he answered honestly. "But I do want to get married someday."

"But you're not looking at us as like *marriage* material, right?"

Hugh shrugged. "I haven't *not* thought about us as marriage material."

My mind reeled. What was he trying to say? "Right, but you know I'm too young for marriage?"

"You're too young, *now*, a-course I know that!" He smiled at me as if he'd just solved the problem weighing on me.

I furrowed my eyebrows at him. "I'm too young now? I'm going to be too young for awhile, Hugh."

"Right. But someday you'll be old enough."

I let a rigid laugh escape my lips. "Yeah, maybe when I'm thirty!"

Hugh patted my hand. "Oh, darlin'. Why are you worrying about this now? I'm not thinking about it now. You don't need to be thinking about it now."

I nodded. The worry still lingered, but my immediate hunger outweighed Hugh's marital intentions. I pasted a stiff smile on my face. "You're right. We should go eat now."

He pulled me towards the cafeteria. "I'm starvin' too. I could eat a whole side-a-beef. Let's go."

Before we could even take a step forward, the sound of chatter and laughter emerged from the stairwell to the basement. We watched as two figures became visible. It was Tori Decker and her friend. They were both dressed as if they were going out to a nightclub or on a fancy date. Tori had on a long-sleeve crimson shirt dress, belted at the waist. She had a killer body, and even I had to admit that her legs were killer in her black high heels and that short dress. She'd let her smooth brown hair out of its ponytail holder, and it glided silkily around her shoulders.

Out of the corner of my eye, I watched Hugh's reaction. He seemed to be taking her and her friend all in. I glanced down at my ratty old Red Hot Chili Peppers sweatshirt, jeans, and sneakers. I had been so busy during the day chasing down a murderer that I hadn't even taken the time to brush my hair before supper. I was a mess. Seeing Tori looking so hot made me suddenly very self-conscious.

I pulled on Hugh's arm as he tried to keep walking forward. I didn't want to stand behind those girls in line.

Hugh turned and looked at me as he felt me tugging on his arm. "What's the matter, darlin'?" he asked curiously.

"Oh, nothing," I lied. "I just wanted to give you one last hug."

He beamed at me and wasted no time throwing his strong arms around my shoulders.

When another group of students passed through the lobby on their way to the dining hall, I felt like it was safe enough to eat. I squeezed him around the waist and then let go. "Okay, we can go eat now," I said happily.

He led me to the cafeteria where the line was now quite long. Jax and the rest of the girls had already gotten their trays of food and were exiting the kitchen line and looking for a place to sit that would fit all of us.

I squeezed Hugh's hand. "Hold my place for me, Hugh? I need to go talk to the girls quickly."

"Sure thing, darlin'," he said with a broad smile.

I quickly caught up with the girls and grabbed Holly's free arm. "Holl, I need your help."

She looked at me curiously. "Now? I just got my food."

I shook my head. "Not now. But soon. I need you to make me hot."

Holly's eyes widened. "Well, it's about time! You've come to the right place!"

CHAPTER 12

The next morning Jax held me to my promise and woke me up at the crack of dawn to go to yoga class with her. I'd slept in her and Mercy's room the night before because even though Detective Whitman had arrested Brittany for Denise's murder, Alba and Mercy were convinced that she was innocent which meant there was still a killer on the loose.

When Jax shook me awake, I opened one eye and peered around. For a long moment, I didn't remember where I was. I thought Jax had somehow slipped into my room and she caught me off guard.

"What are you doing here?" I asked her in shock, pulling my fuzzy blanket up around my face.

"It's time for yoga class," she whispered back to me. She held up a finger in front of her face. "Shh, we can't wake up Mercy, she'll kill us."

I craned my neck back and caught sight of the alarm clock on Mercy's desk. The time, 5:45, glowed bright red in the dim room. I stretched both arms over my head and yawned. My back ached in places I didn't know could ache from the night on Mercy and Jax's incredibly uncomfortable futon. I had almost forgotten that they even had a futon. No one ever sat on it because it was always covered with mountains of clothes.

I reached an arm around and rubbed my lower back. "My body is sore from yesterday and this stupid futon. I don't wanna go."

Jax gave me a silly little smile. "Oh, Sweets. Don't be silly. You're just tired. You'll be happy once you're there. The first step is to get up," she whispered.

I rolled over and pulled the blanket with me. "But I don't want to get up," I said louder than intended.

I heard a noise come from the bunk beds across from me. "Jaaax!" cried Mercy from her bottom bunk. "It's too early! Be quiet!"

Jax turned around and looked at me. "See!" she hissed quietly. "Come on, Sweets! You promised."

I sighed and flipped the blanket off of me. My friends were taking the whole "get Sweets healthy" thing pretty seriously. My first indication that they were *really* serious was when they all pitched in and got me a Fitbit for Christmas. I hated to admit it, but it was actually kind of fun challenging myself to get in my ten-thousand steps for the day. Since I'd voluntarily taken away almost all unnecessary sweets from my diet, I had decided to reward myself with small treats when I'd hit my steps for the day. Jax complained that that defeated the purpose of getting in my extra steps every day, but I told her that I needed motivation and she grudgingly agreed. The app on my phone also tracked my daily calories, my heart rate, and if I wore it to bed, my sleep pattern. I looked down at it. I suddenly wondered what kind of sleep it would say I had for last night. I must have tossed and turned all night. *I bet it says I didn't sleep a wink*, I thought grudgingly.

Standing up, I grabbed my sneakers from underneath the futon and the workout clothes I'd brought from my room. "I'll meet you in the gym," I whispered to Jax. "I need to go change."

She nodded and bounced away. That girl had so much energy. I just didn't know where she stored it. She was such a tiny thing, and she ate like a bird most of the time, so I really didn't understand where all the energy came from.

Minutes later, I was dressed and ready. I'd bundled my hair up into a ponytail on the top of my head. I slipped my student ID badge and room key attached to my lanyard around my neck. After leaving the communal dorm bathroom, I took the back staircase down to the first floor slowly. I was busy watching the stair counter on my fitness tracker, and I didn't want to go too fast lest I take a tumble down the stairs. I wasn't the most coordinated girl at The Institute that was for certain.

When I emerged from the stairwell, I was in the back hallway of the school. There was another stairwell just across from me that would take me down to the basement and the tunnels. To my left, the hallway went about ten feet and turned left, leading me to the kitchen entrance and the storage room where Denise's body was discovered, and further down the hallway it would take me to Sorceress Stone's office. I was just about to hang a right and head to the gym when I heard a noise coming from my left. It was coming from the hallway to the kitchen.

I looked down at my fitness tracker and pressed a button again. It was 5:55. The gym wasn't far away, and yoga class started at six. I had a minute or two to spare. I took a left and slowly crept forward along the ten feet or so until I got to the mouth of the next corridor. I heard the noise again. It sounded as if someone was kicking a door. I stopped and took a deep, silent breath. My heart was pounding wildly in my chest. I debated on whether or not I should just turn around and high-tail it back to the gym or be brave and check out what was going on.

I took another deep breath and tried to calm the sudden adrenaline rush I was feeling. I knew if it were Mercy or Alba or even Jax, they'd just fearlessly leap forward and see who was making the noise. I also knew I wasn't as brave as they were. That was part of the reason why I'd decided to go to witch college – to gain some confidence. *You can do this, Sweets*, I thought. I nodded my head as if to punctuate my thought and surged forward. Slinking back against the stone wall, I slowly let my head fall around the bend.

I was shocked at what I saw. The new girl that had picked a fight with Alba in the lunch line on the first day of school was standing in front of the storage room door. She had a pry bar in her hands and was wedging it in between the door and the jam. I watched her curiously for a moment as she used her body to pull the crowbar back, trying to force open the door. When it wouldn't budge, she read-justed it, jamming it into the crack, then took a step back-wards and slammed her foot onto the lever, resulting in the noise that had originally drawn me to the hallway.

Immediately, I shrank back before she could see me. I couldn't wait to tell the girls what I had seen. I turned around and raced down the hallway in the direction I'd just come to the gym. "Jax! Come quick!" I hollered at her as I flew around the corner of the gym.

She was kneeling on a blue mat with her head tucked between her knees, and her arms stretched out over her head touching the floor. She pulled her body up slowly as she heard her name. The rest of the girls around the room looked at me sharply. "Calm down, Sweets. That energy is too much for yoga."

When she saw the crazed look on my face, she stood up and looked at me curiously. "What is it?"

I motioned for her to follow me. I didn't want to announce to the class what I had just witnessed. Out in the hall, we stopped just outside the door. "I saw the new girl trying to break into the storage room! Where Denise was murdered!" I told her excitedly.

Jax sucked in a breath. "Did you ask her what she was doing?"

I shook my head. "No! I was too scared. What if she's the killer?"

"Is she still there?" Jax asked.

"It was only a minute or two ago; she might be."

Jax nodded. Hesitantly she looked back into the gym at the yoga class.

"We'll be right back, I swear," I begged.

She nodded and sighed. "Alright, let's go check it out."

Together the two of us ran back down the hallway on the balls of our feet, trying to be as quiet as possible. When we got to the intersection of the two corridors, we stopped. I pointed towards the hallway, signaling Jax to look first. Her short, newly dyed purple hair was bound on top of her head in two spry pigtails that bounced animatedly when she nodded. Carefully, she dipped her head around the corner. She looked for only a moment and then pulled her head back around the corner to look at me.

"There's no one there," she said, as her body eased up.

My shoulders relaxed a little too, and I poked my head around the corner to see an empty hallway. "Oh. She's gone."

"You're sure you saw Tori breaking into the storage room?" Jax asked, her face told me she didn't believe me.

I nodded. "Absolutely. One hundred percent, I saw Tori breaking into the storage room." Then a thought occurred to me. My eyes widened. "Maybe she got in!"

Jax tipped her head to the right and stared at me. I could tell she was wondering if I was going crazy or not.

"What?!" I asked her when she didn't speak.

"Are you just trying to get out of yoga class right now?" Jax asked suspiciously.

My jaw dropped. "Would I do something like that?" I asked her, offended.

Jax put a hand on either of her tiny hips and looked up at me closely with a wrinkled nose. Finally, she nodded. "Yes. Yes, I think you would."

I rolled my eyes at her. "Fine. Don't believe me. Mercy and Alba are going to want to know why we didn't go check the storage room, though."

Jax shifted her weight onto her right leg. "You *really* saw Tori trying to break in?"

I nodded and with my finger drew a cross on my heart. "Swear. Hope to die if I lie."

"Alright, let's go check," said Jax grudgingly. She took a step towards the storage room.

I didn't move. The thought of opening the door where Denise's dead body was found didn't set right in my stomach.

Jax stopped and looked back at me. "Sweets! Come on! We have to get to yoga class. We need to get this over with."

My heart was still beating wildly in my chest. I winced. "I'm scared," I admitted.

Jax came back to me and linked her arm in mine and

pulled me forward with her. "Don't be scared," she whispered.

I clung to her arm as we rounded the corner; even though I wasn't sure what good Jax was going to do in case of an emergency. I had eaten snacks bigger than her, and on top of that, she wasn't even a witch. I wished I could do cool electrical magic like Alba could. That would keep us safe if Tori was in there.

Standing in front of the storage room, Jax put her hand on the doorknob and tried it. "It's locked," she whispered.

I pointed to a dent in the door where the crowbar had bent the metal frame. "Jax! Look! See, I told you I was telling the truth," I said, happy that I had proof.

Jax smiled at me and squeezed my arm. "Sorry I didn't believe you."

I nodded. "It's okay."

"So what do we do now?" Jax asked, looking up and down the hallway.

I shrugged. "I don't think there is anything we can do now. We tell the girls at breakfast and see what they make of it."

Jax nodded. "Alright. Now, let's get to yoga class!"

CHAPTER 13

Sorceress Stone lifted the travel restriction and canceled classes the next morning as she'd suggested and neither the dining hall or the kitchen were re-opened yet. I wasn't sure if it was because we didn't have a full-time lunch lady or if it was because the police were still considering the kitchen part of the crime scene.

Instead, Sorceress Stone had boxes of donuts brought in and placed in the gymnasium on tables like she'd done with the pizza the day before. My stomach rumbled as I plucked two glazed donuts out of the boxes and put them on my paper plate and followed Alba to the bleachers. Holly and Sweets weren't far behind. Jax was running late and had told me to go ahead without her.

The four of us sat high up in the bleachers in the same spot we'd sat the day before for the assembly. I sighed and leaned back against the bleacher behind me with my butt dangling in between the bleacher rows. "I hate this," I groaned.

Sweets looked over at my donut with interest. "Oh, I'll have it if you don't like it."

I looked at her and rolled my eyes. "I wasn't talking about my donut, Sweets."

She let out a little nervous titter and then looked down at her food. "Oh, hehe."

"I was talking about this situation. Our favorite cafeteria lady is dead. The not-possibly-guilty-secretary is in jail. We can't use our cafeteria. And once again, nothing is normal on the first week of a new semester. It feels like *last semester* all over again."

Alba nodded. "I hadn't thought of it like that," she said with a wry smile.

Holly furrowed her eyebrows as she pulled a piece of dough off of her donut and popped it in her mouth. "Thought of it like what?"

"There was a murder on the first day of first semester too. Now there's been a murder on the first day of second semester. I'm sensing a trend," explained Alba.

Holly shook her head. "Twice is a coincidence. Three times would be a trend."

"They say that bad things happen in threes," said Sweets with a convincing nod.

"There *were* three murders last semester," Holly rationalized.

"And, there's plenty of the semester left for two more," Sweets predicted sadly.

I shook my head and then clarified. "There were four murders last semester."

Holly looked confused again. "Four? Morgan, Harper, and Ronnie. That's three."

"You forgot Jimmy," said Alba.

"Oh yeah. I almost forgot about Jimmy. But does he count? He was a bad guy," she asked.

I let out a chortle as I took a bite of my glazed donut.

"Of course he counts, Holly. He was a *person,* and he was *murdered.*"

She shrugged and turned her attention back to the cream filled long john she'd selected.

"You guys know what all those murders had in common?" Alba asked from her side of our group.

We all turned to look at her.

Holly shook her head and took a guess. "They were all young?"

Sweets eyes widened, and she sucked in a breath. "Oh! And Denise is old. So you think this is the semester of the old people dying?"

I palmed my forehead. "Denise isn't old. She's probably only in her forties or fifties."

Holly made a face. "That's not old?"

"Not old enough to *die*! She had a lot of life left in her! She probably had a family at home."

The thought of Denise's family grieving for their wife or mother made us all quiet for a moment.

Finally, Alba broke the silence. "I suppose they all had that in common, but that wasn't what I was thinking."

We all looked up at her curiously. No one made a guess this time.

"*We* solved all of their murders," she stated simply.

I rolled that detail around in my head a little bit. She was right. Five students from witch college had solved those murders. And now there was a new murder and a potentially innocent woman sitting in jail. While we were eating donuts. The idea didn't sit well with me.

"So you're saying we need to solve this murder too?" I asked, pulling myself out of my slumped position on the bleachers.

Alba lifted one shoulder to her ear and closed her eyes for a brief moment as if to say, *that's up to you.*

Sweets sucked in her breath and sat up straighter, holding up a finger as if she had something important to say.

"What?" I asked her.

She put her finger down and looked around. "What's taking Jax so long?" she asked impatiently.

I shrugged. "She'll be here any minute. She was fixing her hair."

"So what do you think?" Alba asked. "Are we going to solve this murder and put the right person behind bars?"

Holly shrugged. "Sure, why not. No classes today. What else are we going to do?"

We all looked at Sweets. She was biting her lip and bouncing on her bottom anxiously.

Alba gave her a funny face. "Do you need to use the bathroom, Sweets?"

Sweets stopped bouncing and scowled at Alba. She turned her head to watch the door and seconds later we all witnessed Jax come rushing around the corner. Sweets threw both of her hands into the air in relief. "Oh, thank goodness she's finally here!"

As Jax selected her donut, I looked at Sweets curiously. "You're acting weird this morning. What's going on with you, Sweets?"

She held up a finger as Jax climbed the bleachers.

"Did you tell them yet?" Jax asked as she sat down just below Alba.

Sweets shook her head. "No, you said to wait!"

"Oh wow, you actually waited. Good job, Sweets! Okay, tell 'em," Jax prodded.

Sweets smiled at all of us nervously. "I saw something this morning. On my way to yoga class."

I looked at Jax curiously. I was surprised she hadn't told me the big secret when we saw each other earlier. "What did you see?"

She took a deep breath. "I saw Tori Decker trying to break into the storage room that Denise was killed in."

"What?!" I asked in shock.

Sweets nodded. "She had a crowbar and was prying the door open."

Holly shook her head with her mouth agape. "Did she get in?"

Jax shrugged. "We don't know. Sweets came back to get me, and when we went back, she was gone. The door was locked, so we don't know if she was in there or if she left."

"Why would Tori be trying to get into the storage room?" I wondered aloud. The thought just didn't make sense to me.

Jax shrugged. "Maybe *she* killed Denise."

I looked out into the gym. Tori sat with one friend further down the bleachers. She didn't look like she'd just been up to no good, but I couldn't get a good read. I leaned over to Alba. "What do you think, Alba? Can you get a read on her?"

Alba took another bite of her donut and followed my gaze towards Tori. She shook her head. "Not really. I'm not getting the vibe that she's thinking about the murder right now. I feel like they are talking about the party on Friday."

I sighed and sat back up straight.

"Speaking of the party on Friday, what are we wearing?" Holly asked, looking around.

I furrowed my eyebrows at her. "What do you mean

what are we wearing? I was planning on clothes, how about you girls?"

Alba nodded. "Yeah. Clothes, definitely clothes."

Holly rolled her eyes and picked another piece of dough off of her long john. "Okay, knock it off. I meant what kind of clothes. Are we wearing dresses? There's three to four feet of snow everywhere we go, so I wasn't sure if heels went with snow or not. I'm from California; they never have snow, so I don't know how you mountain people dress for parties in the winter."

Jax giggled. "Us mountain people?"

Alba held her hands up in the air. "I'm from Jersey. There are no mountains in Jersey."

"I'm from *southern* Georgia," said Sweets. "I don't know how mountain people dress for parties either."

I shrugged. "Obviously I don't know anything about mountain people or dressing for parties, so I think you're asking the wrong bunch of witches."

Holly scowled. "Fine. I'll ask Darcie Larson. It's her party. She should be able to tell us what kind of dress is appropriate."

"Anywho, back to the issue at hand," I said. I looked at Jax. "We're trying to decide whether or not we should investigate Denise's murder ourselves."

Jax pulled her black witch hat down tighter on her head. "Oh, that was a question? I assumed we'd try and figure it out. I'm all about proving to Detective Whitman that Brittany is innocent."

I nodded. "I agree. I'm in too."

Sweets sat her donut down and sat up straighter. "I think since we knew Denise, we should pay our respects to the family first. I can make a casserole to take to them. I'll call Mr. Bailey and ask him if he's got any ideas for an herbal grief relieving potion I can bake into it."

A light bulb turned on in my head. "Sweets, that's a great idea!"

She nodded and reached back into her pocket to pull her cell phone out. "Okay. I'll call Mr. Bailey for a recipe now!" she said excitedly.

I reached out and touched her hand. "No, not about the potion. About visiting the family."

A smile spread across Alba's face. "I get where you're going with that, Red. That's where we start investigating her murder."

"Oh," said Sweets with disappointment heavy in her voice. "I see."

I squeezed Sweets's arm. "A casserole is still a great idea, though. It will give us a reason to just show up on the family's doorstep. How soon can you have something ready?"

Sweets looked down at the time on her fitness tracker. "I don't have any groceries. And since I can't use the school's kitchen anymore, we'll have to go into town and use the b&b's kitchen."

Alba shook her head firmly. "We don't have time for that. Let's just stop at the grocery store and grab them a frozen lasagna."

"Isn't that sort of tacky?" Sweets asked the group as a hand flew up to her heart in true southern fashion.

I shrugged my shoulders. I didn't know the first thing about funeral protocol.

"That's not tacky. The Whiting's are probably getting all kinds of fresh baked casseroles. They can put a frozen lasagna in the freezer and then cook it when they run out of all the hot stuff. It's totally acceptable. When my Aunt Angela passed away, my family got all kinds of frozen casseroles. We probably got half a dozen frozen lasagnas," said Alba.

"Were they store bought?" Sweets asked.

"Why does that matter?"

She shrugged. "I don't know. I'm from the south. We cook everything from scratch there. Store bought seems tacky."

I groaned. "It's the thought that counts and we should really get moving. We're burning daylight and who knows if we'll have classes tomorrow. We need to do what we can now."

Sweets crossed her arms across her chest. "Fine."

"Sorry, Sweets. You can cook for the next memorial we go to, okay?"

She shot me an annoyed glare. I was thankful Sweets was too sweet to stay mad for long.

CHAPTER 14

After picking up a family-size Stouffer's frozen lasagna from Schmidt's, the local mom and pop grocery store on Cherry Street, we headed over to the Whiting family house. The street out in front of their modest two-story house was lined with cars and a woman wearing pot holders carried a casserole dish up the front walk.

"See, people are taking hot dishes. This is so embar-rassing that we're giving them a *store bought* frozen lasagna!" Sweets cried as she parallel parked in front of a car a block away from the house. "Grandma Wilhelmina is probably rolling over in her grave right now."

"If everyone brought hot food how would they ever eat it all? And what are they supposed to eat in a few days when the hot food is all gone? They need stuff for their freezer too," said Holly rationally. "I don't think it's stupid that we brought a frozen lasagna. I mean, I don't cook. If I were ever to go to a funeral by myself, I'd probably take a store bought casserole too."

Jax nodded. "You're over thinking this, Sweets."

Sweets took a breath like she was going to say something else and then thought better of it and snapped her mouth shut. Instead, she turned off the ignition and unlocked her doors.

The five of us piled out of the car and made our way to the sidewalk. Walking towards the Whiting house, I felt suddenly awkward. I wasn't the best person in social situations, nor was Alba. I poked Jax in the waist. "You go first," I said to her, shoving her ahead of me on the sidewalk as we walked towards the house.

"Why me?!" she demanded, stopping and moving to the back of the line.

"Because I'm awkward in social situations," I hissed back.

"So am I," agreed Alba, moving to the back of the line, leaving Holly up front.

Holly scooted around to the back of the line too. "I don't want to go first!" she complained in a panic.

This left Sweets in the front. I handed her the lasagna. "Thanks, Sweets," I said with a smile.

She looked down at it. "Ugh. *Fine*," she said with a sigh. "But if they ask whose idea it was to take a store bought lasagna, I'm not taking the credit."

"Totally fair," I agreed as she took the lead.

We each climbed the two small wooden steps to the front door and stood on their deck. I peered inside. The place was full of people. I wasn't sure how warm of a reception a few students from The Institute were going to get. Sweets knocked on the door. A teenage girl about Jax's age answered. She wore a long black cardigan over a black top and black leggings. Her sandy-blond hair was combed over one shoulder, and her eyeliner and mascara were smudged around her eyes. It was obvious this had to be one of Denise's daughters. She looked just like her.

"Hi. Are you Denise's daughter?" Sweets asked.

The girl nodded as she took a step out the door and looked out at the five of us curiously. I was thankful that we had been able to convince Jax that her black hat was not appropriate for a memorial. "Yes, I am. Who are you?"

"I'm Sweets Porter. I was a student at the school your mother worked at," said Sweets somberly.

The girl's eyes brightened up a little. "You're Sweets?" she asked.

Sweets nodded and looked at Alba and me who were on either side of her now. "You've heard of me?"

The girl gave us a little shy smile. "Yeah. My mom used to talk about you. She talked about a lot of the students at The Institute. But she especially seemed to like you because you used to come to the cafeteria and use her kitchen to cook once in awhile."

Sweets blushed as she nodded. "Yeah. I spent some time with your mom. She was such a great woman. We are all so sad to lose her."

The girl nodded as tears filled her eyes again.

"Oh, I'm so sorry," said Sweets. She reached forward and engulfed the girl in a hug. Denise's daughter seemed to welcome the embrace. She even laid her head on Sweets's shoulder as she cried.

We all looked at her with our hearts full of sadness. We had decided to pay our respects with the additional motive of investigating the murder, but I hadn't considered how hard seeing the family in such agony would be on us. My eyes clouded over. I looked back and saw Jax wiping away tears from her face. Even usually self-absorbed Holly was batting at her eyes.

The girl let go of Sweets and stood up. She held the door

open wider. "Would you like to come in and meet the family?" she asked.

Sweets nodded. "Yes, that'd be great." She handed her the lasagna. "Here, we brought you supper. It's frozen, but we didn't have a kitchen to cook in—"

The girl shook her head. "This is perfect. We have a lot of hot food; we couldn't possibly eat it all right now. Thank you."

I squeezed Sweets's hand as we followed the girl into the house. Denise's daughter stopped in the entryway and turned to us. "I'm Danielle, by the way."

I gave Danielle a smile and pressed my fingers into my collarbone. "I'm Mercy," I said moving aside so she could see the rest of the girls.

We made the rest of the introductions and then followed Danielle to the kitchen where she put the lasagna into the freezer. She turned around and led us back through the dining room where crowds of people had gathered, mourning the loss of Danielle's mother.

"I'll let you meet my dad," she said as she led us into the living room where a man with brown hair was sitting on a faded blue sofa with his head in his hands. Two women were sitting on either side of him comforting him softly, one of them I immediately recognized as Midge, Denise's co-worker at the school.

"Dad," said Danielle tentatively.

He seemed to stop crying almost immediately. He used the sleeves of his shirt to blot his eyes before he looked up at his daughter. His eyes were bloodshot and his face puffy. "Yeah, sweetheart?" he asked.

"These girls are students at mom's school. They brought some food. I thought maybe you'd like to meet them."

The man unfolded his long legs from his seat and stood

up. When he did the two women comforting him stood up too. He took a step around Midge's knees and then around the wooden coffee table and stepped towards us, extending his hand to Alba who was the closest. "I'm Cal," he said.

Alba shook his hand. "I'm Alba. This is Mercy, Jax, Sweets, and Holly."

Cal made a sad face. "I've heard a lot of those names from Denise," he said sadly.

"I told them that Mom mainly talked about Sweets because they used to cook together," said Danielle.

Cal nodded. "She loved all the girls at The Institute. It was very kind of you girls to come."

Sweets bowed her head. "We're so sorry for your loss. We all loved Denise."

The group of us nodded politely, but inside my heart wrenched in my chest. The memory of Denise's corpse had come rushing back to me. I stifled a sob; I had to keep it together. This was so hard. I couldn't imagine the pain the family must be feeling.

"Thank you," he whispered.

Next, our eyes swung to Midge. She looked shorter than usual in her solemn black suit jacket and skirt. Maybe it was because she was standing next to Cal who dwarfed her by two feet. Her black hair, which was usually pulled back into a hair net except for her blunt bangs, had been freed and hung simply next to her jaw line in a smooth pageboy bob.

"Hi, Midge," said Sweets sadly.

Midge reached out and grabbed Sweets's hand and squeezed it. "Hi, girls. It's so nice of you to come today."

Finally, our eyes turned to the woman on the other side of Cal. She was taller than Midge, but still, she only stood about as high as Cal's shoulder. Her smooth strawberry blond hair shone under the living room lights and curled gracefully at her shoulders. She was a slim woman and wore a simple black sheath dress and black heels.

Cal made a face. "Oh, this is Tish Thomas. She's a dear friend of the family and works in my office."

The woman gave us all a little congenial wave and a tight smile. "Hello, girls. It's very nice to meet you."

Danielle rocked back on her heels and swung her arms out in front of her. "Dad, I'm going to take them up to meet Aaron and Rachel. I think they'd like to meet some of the girls Mom knew too."

He nodded and sat back down. "That's fine, sweetheart. It was nice to meet you, girls."

We all shot Cal and the two women our best sympathetic smiles and then followed Danielle to the stairs. She went first and talked as she moved. "They *were* down here, but they've taken it really hard. All the mourning was really getting to them, so they went upstairs awhile ago."

"We don't have to meet them if they're too upset," said Sweets, ahead of me on the stairs.

Danielle waved a hand. "Oh, they'll be happy to meet you." She knocked on a wooden door at the end of a hallway and then opened it to reveal who we assumed were Denise's other children. "Guys, these girls go to the school where Mom worked." She turned to us and pointed to the teenage girl lying on the bed. "This is Rachel, and that is Aaron." Aaron, who looked to be a little older than Danielle and Rachel, was sitting on a chair next to the bed. He looked more like his dad than Denise, but Rachel looked a lot like her sister and her mom.

Aaron stood up. He was impressively tall, but then both of his parents were pretty tall as well. "So the five of you go to The Institute?" he asked somberly.

We all nodded.

"Does that mean you're all witches?"

I looked at Jax and then at Aaron. "Yup, we're all witches," I said with a little smile.

"Mom told us about a group of witches at The Institute that solved some of those murders that happened in town this past fall. She said the other girls call them the Witch Squad. Do you know those girls?"

Danielle looked at her siblings curiously as if something had just occurred to her. "Wait. Didn't Mom say there was a girl named Sweets in the Witch Squad?"

Aaron nodded. "Yeah. She talked about them a lot. Why?"

Sweets put a hand over her mouth, trying to hide a giggle.

Danielle's head swiveled to stare at us.

"Why do you want to know if we know the Witch Squad?" I asked with an amused smiled on my face before Danielle could rat us out.

"It's personal," said Aaron. "We just need their help."

Danielle shut the door and pointed at Sweets whose face was fire engine red by now. "Aaron. *This* is Sweets."

Sweets lifted one hand and waved awkwardly. "Hello."

"So – are you – one of the members of the Witch Squad?" he asked Sweets with surprise, cocking his head to the side. Rachel sat up on the bed and looked at Danielle curiously.

Sweets looked at us. I could tell she felt extremely uncomfortable. "I – uh, well…"

Alba took a step forward. "We're the Witch Squad," she said matter-of-factly. "We didn't invent the name, but that's what people call us."

He looked at his sisters. Tears gathered in the corners of

his eyes. He cleared his throat before he spoke. "We'd like help solving our mother's murder."

I let out the breath that I'd been holding. "Haven't you heard the police arrested someone from the school?"

Rachel nodded. "Yeah, Brittany Hobbs. My mom was friends with Brittany. We've had her at our house before. I know Brittany – there's no way she did this. It's just not in her nature. What would she have had to gain?"

"Do you have any suspicions of your own?" I asked.

Danielle's head tipped from side to side. "Not really *suspicions,* more like concerns."

"What do you mean, *concerns*?" Jax asked.

"Our mom was *really* upset the other day. She and our dad got into a *huge* fight Sunday night and then she stormed out of the house. We didn't know what to make of it. Then she came home late and went to school Monday morning and…" she said, trailing off.

"And then she never came home," I whispered.

She nodded and wiped a tear from her eye. "Yeah."

I nodded sadly. "Denise was a mess when we went through the breakfast line Monday morning. She was crying, but she wouldn't tell us what happened," I admitted. I had a sudden pang of guilt for not trying harder to have figured out what was wrong. Then my mind raced back to Tori Decker and the breakfast line antics that she pulled while we were trying to talk to Denise.

Aaron nodded. "Can you help us?"

Holly, who had been standing in the back of the group and leaning against the closed door, wiped away a tear and then pushed her way forward. She walked up to Aaron and took hold of his hand with both of her hands. She lifted it up to her bosom and squeezed it tightly in her grasp.

"Aaron. We are going to do our absolute best to find your mother's killer. You have my word on it."

I looked at Alba. I wanted to smile, to break the tension, but I knew it wasn't the time or the place. Instead, I nodded. "Holly's right. We're going to help you figure this out. We owe it to Denise. But we're going to need your help."

Aaron looked down at Holly curiously. He casually pulled his hand away from her grasp and smiled at us. "Thank you. Just tell us what you need from us, and we're happy to help."

Holly beamed at him.

"Well, first of all. We need to know what your parents were fighting about," said Alba.

The trio of siblings looked at each other curiously. "We really aren't sure. If we had known what was going to happen, maybe we would have been paying closer attention, but we didn't know. I was working on my homework, so when they started raising their voices, I just drowned it out with my headphones," said Rachel.

Danielle nodded. "I did too."

All eyes turned towards Aaron. He glanced at his sisters anxiously. "I really didn't want my sisters to have to know this, but the word *divorce* was tossed around."

Rachel stood up and walked to her brother's side. He threw his arm over her shoulder, and she buried her head in his side. "I heard that word too, Aaron. That's why I put my headphones on," she admitted.

"I hate to suggest this, but—" I began. I didn't know if I could even say what I was thinking out loud.

Aaron held up a hand. "Don't even say it. He would *never*."

"He's the most obvious," interjected Alba.

"He was at work on Monday," Rachel protested.

I lifted one shoulder. "He could have snuck out."

"Where does your dad work?" Jax asked curiously.

"He's an engineer. He owns his own engineering company," said Aaron.

"So he owns his own company. How can we prove he was actually at work yesterday?" I asked.

Aaron shrugged. "Easy. He has tons of employees. There are several here right now."

"Tish?" asked Holly.

"Yeah, that's his secretary. She would be the one to ask if he was there like he said he was."

"Okay, we'll ask her. But first – before we start asking people questions, what about her things. Did your mom keep a diary or a journal?"

The girls shook their heads. "Doubtful," said Rachel. "But I guess you never know."

"Can we search her room?"

Danielle opened the bedroom door and peered out into the hallway. "Yeah. We should do it now before anyone comes up here. Come on," she said and waved us forward.

CHAPTER 15

We followed Danielle to the end of the hall where she quietly opened the door. Aaron and Rachel followed. "You two keep watch at the bottom of the stairs," she whispered. "I'll keep watch at the door. Holler at me if Dad decides he needs to come up here for some reason."

Aaron nodded at us. "Better hurry. He could come up here any minute."

"We will," I said confidently. "We'll just look around."

"Good luck," he said before he and Rachel descended the stairs.

Danielle shut the door behind the five of us, enclosing us in the silent tomb. The curtains were drawn making the room very dark. Jax flipped the light switch. It was an average sized room. Nothing immediately jumped out at us. The queen size bed hadn't been made, and the amber colored quilt was twisted in the center of the bed as if Cal had tossed and turned in the night. A chair in the corner had some of Denise's clothes thrown over the arm.

I looked around, holding my arms out by my sides. "I don't even know where to start."

Alba shrugged. "Everyone spread out. Jax, you check the bathroom. Holly, you've got the walk in closet. Sweets, you check those shelves over there. Make sure you look through all the books. You never know, Denise might have stuck a note inside one of them. I'll check this nightstand. Mercy, you check that one."

We all nodded, satisfied with our assignments. Before we separated, Jax looked back at us. "What are we looking for exactly?"

"I don't know, anything that is a clue. Find out why Cal and Denise were fighting," suggested Alba.

I rounded the corner at the foot of the bed and had barely reached her nightstand when Holly shrieked. "What?" I yelled. I was already on edge, and her shriek had done little to settle my nerves.

"Oh my gosh! Look at this jacket! Isn't this adorable!" she said excitedly. She held it up and slowly spun it around. "I can't believe Denise had such great taste!"

We all shot her unhappy groans. "Focus on the task at hand, Cosmo," Alba growled. "No shopping in Denise's closet!"

Holly went back to work as did I. I looked down at her nightstand. Pictures of her and the kids and Cal covered it. I lifted one picture and looked at it closely. She and her two daughters were smiling brightly on a sandy beach some-where. Seeing Denise's bright, smiling face made me suddenly angry. It just wasn't right that such a great lady was dead. For what? Who could have done this to her?

I picked up another picture frame. Aaron and his two sisters were standing together. He was in a cap and gown, proudly holding his diploma. Rachel and Danielle looked quite a bit younger in the picture. Maybe twelve or thirteen.

The last picture on the nightstand was a snapshot of

Denise and Cal. They were both dressed up. Denise was wearing a long blue floral dress and Cal was wearing khaki trousers, a black sports coat, and a tie. The balloons in the background made me wonder if the picture had been taken at Aaron's graduation. The huge smiles on their faces told the story of a happy couple. I wondered what could have happened in the last few years to change Denise and Cal from happily married to being on the precipice of divorce.

I sat the last picture back down on the nightstand and opened the top drawer. There was a bottle of hand lotion in it, a nail file and fingernail clippers, some lip balm, and a small book of daily devotions. I flipped through the book, hoping that a secret letter would fall out, explaining what had happened. No such luck.

I opened the next drawer. There were several books inside. The top one was a hardcover mystery book. I took it out and flipped through the pages quickly. Then I looked down at the next book. It was also a hardcover. The title of it shocked me.

Slowly I pulled it out. My jaw hung open. I looked up at Alba. "Alba, check this out."

She looked up. Sweets, who was looking through all the books on the shelf, looked up too. I lifted the book up and showed them the cover. In big bold letters, it read, *After the Affair*.

Alba's eyes widened. "He was having an affair?"

"One of them was," I said sadly. I couldn't believe it. Cal and Denise seemed so happy in the pictures. And now to find out that one of them was having an affair? It just didn't seem right.

Jax came out of the bathroom. "I didn't find anything. Denise didn't wear much makeup. Her drawers were pretty empty."

I tossed her the book. "Look what was inside her night-stand," I said.

Jax caught the book and read the cover. "Is this why they were getting a divorce?"

"Looks like a great place to start the investigation, don't you think?"

"I think we have to assume since the book was in *her* nightstand he was the one having the affair, right?" Alba pointed out.

"I would think so. I mean, why would Denise be reading a book about how to get over an affair if *she* was the one that was having the affair?" I asked. That didn't make any sense to me.

Danielle poked her head in the room. "Are you guys almost done? I'm worried my dad is going to come up here any minute."

"Yeah, we'll be done in a minute," I assured her. I looked up at Sweets. "Find anything in her books over there?"

Sweets shook her head. "Nothing. She likes mystery books, though."

I held up the J.D. Robb book I found in her drawer. "Yeah, I noticed that. Did you find anything, Alba?" I asked.

Alba shook her head. "I found business cards and golf tees in the top drawer. The rest of the drawers are Cal's underwear and socks. I even checked in the back of the drawer, and there isn't anything hidden away."

"Keep the business cards. You never know if one of them will come in handy," I suggested.

"Holly, you find anything?"

Holly came out of the closet. "No, but Denise was a

much better dresser than I would have ever guessed. She's got some cute clothes in there – for a mom!"

I rolled my eyes. "Alright, lights off. Let's go."

Silently, we retreated out the door we'd come in through, shutting the door behind us. Danielle's slender frame leaned against the hall wall, keeping watch. Rachel was standing at the top of the stairs, and Aaron was still at the bottom.

"Can we talk?" I asked Danielle.

She nodded and pointed at the room on the other end of the hallway. "Yeah, let's go back to Rachel's room."

I led the girls down the hallway to the room we'd been in earlier. Danielle and Rachel motioned to Aaron that the coast was clear and he could come back upstairs.

Once we were all inside, he looked at us with interest. "Find anything helpful?"

It wasn't going to be easy to suggest, and the words seemed to clog in the back of my throat. I wasn't sure if I would be able to get it out.

Alba took the bull by the horns. "Is it possible your father was having an affair?"

The siblings all looked at each other. Rachel and Danielle's eyes were wide. "No, what makes you think that?" Rachel asked hesitantly.

"Your mother has a book in her second drawer called *After the Affair*," I explained. I felt bad having to tell them. It wasn't something anyone wanted to know about their parents, but if we were going to make any headway into solving this mystery, we had to get to the truth.

Aaron's jaw dropped. "What?!" He shook his head vigorously. "No way. I don't believe it."

"Why would she have the book?" I asked.

Danielle shook her head as if she were trying to get the

cobwebs out. "Maybe she… maybe…" she trailed off. She couldn't think of a reason that her mother would have had a book entitled *After the Affair* if they weren't dealing with an affair.

"Unless Denise was the one having the affair," I suggested.

The girls looked at each other immediately. In unison both of their heads began shaking from side to side. "There's no way," Danielle insisted.

Rachel nodded in agreement. "Not our mom."

Aaron let his head drop into his hands. His russet-colored hair slid between his fingers in little bunches. My heart leapt into my chest. Not only had they lost their mother, but now there was an affair to consider.

"I'm sorry," I whispered. "Maybe we shouldn't have told you."

Aaron looked up sharply. A dark shadow covered his eyes. "No. We needed to know. It's the only way we're going to solve our mother's murder. I still don't think my father could have done this."

Alba winced. "I hate to point this out right now, but you also didn't think your father would have cheated on your mother. Maybe there's more that you don't know about your father?"

They were quiet for several long moments. I looked at my friends, unsure of what to do or say next.

Holly broke the silence. "Who would've he cheated with?"

"He didn't have time to cheat!" said Rachel, her voice catching in her throat. "He was either at work, or he was at home. He was a very devoted husband and father."

I smiled tightly. "His secretary is very pretty."

Rachel and Danielle's eyes widened. Danielle shook her

head. "Nuh-uh. Tish would never. She's too good of a friend of the family. She got along great with our mom!"

"Maybe your mom didn't know," Holly suggested.

It made sense. Tish was being awfully supportive of Cal when we arrived. "I could see it," I whispered.

Rachel scoffed at the thought. "Tish is too sweet of a person to cheat with my dad. She's the assistant track coach at the high school, and she volunteers at our church's food pantry."

"Is she married?" I asked them.

"Well, no," Rachel admitted.

"How old is she?" Alba asked. "She looks like she's in her thirties at least."

Rachel and Danielle looked at each other and shrugged. "I don't know, maybe thirty-five," said Rachel.

"And she's never been married?" Holly asked.

"She was married before she moved to Aspen Falls, but that was when she was younger, like in her twenties. She moved here after her divorce, which was maybe ten years ago."

"So, she moved to Aspen Falls and started working for your dad?" I asked.

Aaron nodded. "Yeah, he was just starting his company. She's been amazing. I've worked there for two summers now. I've never noticed anything inappropriate going on between them."

"Doesn't it seem weird that she's down there comforting your dad though?" Holly asked.

Rachel shook her head. "No, she's a very close friend of the family. Mom and Dad have had her over for dinner at least once a week since I can remember. She's single and doesn't have any family in town. She has a few girlfriends, but mostly just work friends."

"Does she date?" I asked.

"Yeah, she dates. In fact, I think one of the guys she dated is downstairs!" said Rachel.

Danielle nodded. "Dad's whole office is down there. It's totally not weird that she's here. She used to date Doug, one of the junior engineers in Dad's office."

"But she doesn't date him anymore?" Sweets clarified.

Rachel shook her head. "No, they broke up a while back. I don't know why, though."

"Okay, but you really don't have any reason to think that your dad was cheating with Tish?" Holly asked again.

I knew what she was thinking because I was pretty sure we were all thinking the same thing. Who else would Cal be having an affair with if the only place he ever went was to work?

CHAPTER 16

Back at school, we sat at one of the many folding tables and chairs that Seymour, the school custodian, had set up in the gym. It was lunchtime, and Sorceress Stone had had more pizzas brought in for lunch. She assured us that she was working closely with Detective Whitman to get our cafeteria service up and running again, but we had to wonder how soon that would be if tables and chairs were being brought in instead of just having us sit on the bleachers for one more day.

"Do you think Midge will be the full-time cafeteria lady now that Denise is gone?" Sweets wondered aloud.

I shrugged as I bit off a piece of rubbery cheese pizza. "I don't know, but this pizza is horrible."

Jax picked at the cheese on top as she looked at her slice skeptically. "Maybe if we'd gotten back on time, it would have been warm."

"I suppose." I let out a heavy sigh and then took another big bite. Despite the fact that the pizza was cold and rubbery, I had to eat it. The churning in my stomach was overpowering. It seemed like forever since we'd last eaten.

"So, are we going to talk about the investigation?" Alba asked, ignoring my complaints.

"Sure," I groaned absentmindedly.

"Okay. So, what do we know?" Sweets asked, looking around.

"Well, we know that Denise and Cal were arguing and possibly throwing out the idea of a divorce," said Holly.

Alba held up a finger and scanned our faces. "I looked through those business cards I found in his top drawer. One of the cards is from a lawyer."

"So he was talking to a lawyer. That's interesting. Maybe we should go question the lawyer?" Jax suggested.

I made a face. "Lawyer's have to keep everything confidential. There's no way a lawyer is going to talk to a handful of college kids."

We were all silent for a second. Finally, Alba nodded. "What else do we know?"

I thought for a moment and then added, "Well, we know that Cal was probably having an affair with someone."

The girls all nodded in agreement.

"How did you guys feel about Tish? Could it be her?" Alba asked.

I scanned the faces of everyone at the table. Four pairs of eyes blinked in unison. No one wanted to say they thought it was Tish. "Fine. I'll just say it. She was the one comforting Cal on the couch. It seems the most logical that she was the one having an affair with him."

"Midge was comforting him too," Sweets pointed out.

"Really? You think *Midge and Cal*?" Holly asked disdainfully.

Midge wasn't what I'd call *un*attractive, but she was like the polar opposite of Cal. She was cartoonishly short, and he was tall. If I had to guess, I'd guess Midge to be in her mid fifties and Cal to be at least ten years her junior. I just couldn't see the two together. "I don't see it."

"I don't either," Holly agreed.

"Well, Denise's kids don't think it's Tish," said Jax.

"They also didn't think their father had it in him to have an affair!" I argued.

"Denise's kids are grieving right now. They have their father up on a pedestal, and they're thinking with their hearts. We can't think with our hearts," said Alba. She was addressing the table, but her eyes were focused on Jax. "We have to think with our heads."

I looked at Holly. "We especially can't think with our emotions when it comes to Denise's kids."

"Why are you looking at me?" Holly demanded indignantly.

I shrugged as I bit off another piece of pizza.

"She's looking at you because of that whole flirting thing you were doing with Aaron," chirped Jax.

"I wasn't flirting!" Holly disagreed.

"You were totally flirting," said Jax with a laugh. "Oh, Aaron, we'll do whatever we have to do to solve your mother's murder," Jax said, mocking Holly's voice.

Sweets giggled. "He *is* cute."

"I was just trying to make him feel better."

I rolled my eyes. "Sure you were."

"Alright. So we know that Denise and Cal were talking divorce," said Alba in an attempt to right the conversation. "He was having an affair. Maybe he was having an affair with Tish. We don't know. Put that on our list of things to find out. We know that Midge was not at school on the day of the murder. We know that Tori was seen breaking into the storage room. We know that Denise's ghost fingered Brittany in the murder."

I sighed. "That's a lot of suspects. That might not even be all of them. How are we supposed to narrow all of that down?"

"We're gonna need to go pound the pavement tomorrow and talk to some of these people," said Alba.

Sweets shook her head. "I can't in the morning. I have my internship at the bakery until noon."

"I'm sure classes will resume tomorrow anyway," said Holly, looking at her fingernails. By her tone, I could tell she was still bristling over the fact that we had accused her of flirting with Aaron.

"Fine. We'll all go to class in the morning and Sweets can go to her internship, but at lunch, we're going to go investigate the murder," said Alba.

We heard a noise behind us. I turned around to see Tori Decker standing right behind us. She released a choked breath. "Uh. You're still investigating the murder? Why? They already arrested Brittany Hobbs for the murder."

I turned back around, ignoring her.

Alba couldn't do it, though. "It's really none of your business now is it?" she asked, swiveling around in her seat completely.

"Like the murder is any of *your* business?" Tori retorted, giving Alba a snotty face.

"As a matter of fact, it *is* our business. This is what we do," said Alba. "You've only been at this school for two days. I don't even think you *belong* here. So why don't you just go back to where ever you came from," Alba suggested. She swept the air towards Tori as if to shoo her along.

Tori put a hand on one hip and shifted all of her weight onto one leg. "Oh, I'm not going anywhere. Now that that dead lady is gone, how about we finish up that fight we started."

Alba stood up.

Oh, it's on now! That dead lady? How dare she? My skin prickled with heat as adrenaline surged through my body. I stood up too. Holly, Jax, and Sweets followed Alba and me to our feet.

"How about you show a little respect, Tori," I spat at her angrily.

Tori laughed. "Respect for *what*? A *lunch lady?*"

Alba had heard enough. With one flick of her finger, she sent Tori reeling backwards like she was an ant. The bottom row of the bleachers took out Tori's legs, and she flipped backwards into the wooden rows like a ragdoll. Alba took a step forward. She wanted to teach Tori a little more respect.

"That's enough, Alba," I whispered. "No more. She deserves it, but we can't risk getting Stone after us."

Alba turned and looked at me. Her head and body were erect, and her fists balled by her sides. "You're either in this fight, or you're out of it, Red."

In the split second that Alba had her back to Tori, Tori was on her feet and rushing towards Alba.

"Alba!" I hollered, pointing behind her.

Tori's face was that of a madwoman as she launched herself onto Alba's back. Alba spun around in a circle with Tori clenched onto her shoulders. Tori climbed her. Wrapping her slender limbs around Alba's neck, she began choking her out.

"Oh my gosh, what do we do?" Jax hollered.

"Get her off!" Alba yelled back as she wrestled with the weight of the girl on her back.

Together, Holly, Sweets, Jax, and I circled the two writhing girls. I bounced back and forth on the balls of my feet, just waiting for the perfect moment to jump in and grab Tori.

"What are you waiting for?" Alba yelped. "She's choking me!"

Before I could even make a move, Jax lurched forward and jumped on Tori's back like a spider monkey. Alba's face was now beet red as she carried both the weight of Tori *and* Jax.

"Help me!" Alba screeched at me as she spun around to face me again. Tori's grasp tightened as she got a hold of the arm lodged under Alba's chin and pulled it harder. Jax worked to weave her own stick arms between Alba and Tori, but Alba's feet were moving too fast.

I stepped forward and got a hold of a handful of Tori's hair and pulled. The girl yelped in pain but managed to hang on to Alba's neck. Jax pulled on her shoulders trying to get her to loosen her grasp on Alba, but it only served to choke Alba tighter. I pulled harder on Tori's hair and moved with them as they danced about.

The sounds of whoops and hollers reverberated off the gym walls as the girls from other tables circled the fight.

Then, out of nowhere, this enormous stream of energy engulfed the group of us. It paralyzed my arms and legs, and I crumpled to the floor. The energy caused Alba to crumple under the weight of both girls. Tori's grasp around Alba's neck loosened and I could hear Alba sucking in air in quick gasps.

I struggled to look up, my head felt like a bowling ball on a pipe cleaner neck. My limbs felt as if they were chained to cinder blocks. Only my eyes moved, and through a tiny pinhole, I managed to see Sorceress Stone's face as she held the energy stream on us. Her gaze was that of pure vitriol. I cursed in my mind. This wasn't going to be good.

~

NEARLY A HALF HOUR LATER, THE FOUR OF US SAT IN FRONT OF Sorceress Stone in her office. Her contempt filled face shone down on us like the sun on a sweltering day. I wondered what she was going to do to us.

"The four of you do realize I'm running a school for *advanced* students here, correct?"

We all nodded somberly.

"This isn't a school for children," she spat. "You were acting like children in there. It's an embarrassment quite honestly. You should all be ashamed of yourselves."

Jax lowered her head. Out of the corner of my eye, I saw her biting the side of her lip hard. That was an expression I was sure that she'd picked up from me. I did it to keep from crying. The pain I felt in my lip seemed to balance the need to cry. Was Jax near tears?

"Now. Let's hear it. What was so important that you felt the need to fight *in my school* once again?" she asked.

Jax glared at Tori. "She referred to Denise as *that dead lady*."

Sorceress Stone nodded. "I see. And you took offense to that because…?"

Jax looked offended. "Because it was rude and heartless! Denise just died," she managed to choke out.

Sorceress Stone looked down her long thin nose at her daughter. "And yet what she said was true. You got into a physical altercation with another student because she uttered a true statement?"

I raised my head in time to see the smirk on Tori's face.

She was gloating because Sorceress Stone appeared to be siding with her. I wanted to groan out loud, but I knew that would only serve to infuriate Stone even more.

Sorceress Stone looked down at the papers on her desk. "I really should punish the four of you for fighting on school property, but I have too much on my plate right now to supervise your punishment. I have no lunch lady. I have no cafeteria and no food. I have no secretary. And I have an ongoing murder investigation that I'm trying to deal with. This is just unacceptable behavior. I'd like to just lock you up in the tower, and forget about you, but because I don't have the time to supervise such a thing, your punishment is that you may not leave campus for the next two weeks. No leaving campus. No visitors on campus. You're in lock up. If I find out that you've left campus for any reason whatsoever, you shall be swiftly and harshly punished. Do you understand?"

Alba looked at Tori and narrowed her eyes.

Sorceress Stone caught the glare. "And there will be no retribution!" she roared. "The three of you will stay away from Ms. Decker and Ms. Decker you will stay away from these three girls."

Tori nodded obediently with that annoying smirk still glued to her face.

Sorceress Stone narrowed her eyes and peered at Tori more closely then. "Ms. Decker, You're new here. There were no issues with my students' behaviors prior to your arrival, and now already there have been two instances of fighting on school grounds and you were involved in both. Don't think that I won't be watching you. The Institute doesn't take kindly to things that disrupt the educative process in my school."

The smirk on Tori's face disappeared, and she looked

down at her hands in her lap. She nodded quietly.

"Very well. You all know your punishments. Dismissed." With a nod of her head and a slight wave of her hand, she ordered us out of her office.

I followed Alba and Jax out, with Tori only a step or two behind me. We ignored her as we left the office and headed to our rooms where the rest of the Witch Squad was waiting for us in Holly and Alba's room.

"Well? What happened?" Sweets asked the minute we opened the door.

Holly looked up expectantly. "I'm shocked you're not locked away in the tower."

I tilted my head to the side and let out a breath of air. "I'm shocked too. I thought for sure that would be our punishment, but she said she's too busy with all the murder stuff and being short staffed to have to supervise that punishment, so we got grounded instead."

"Grounded?" Sweets asked.

"We can't leave campus for two weeks," said Jax, falling onto Alba's navy blue quilt on the bottom bunk.

Holly's eyes widened. "How are we supposed to investigate the murder now if you can't leave campus?"

Alba shrugged. "We go anyway. I'm not going to quit fighting for what's right just because we got in a little bit of trouble."

Jax looked around and nervously wrung her hands in front of her. "I don't know if that's such a great idea. My mom could get seriously mad if she finds out we left campus."

Alba shrugged. "You're welcome to stay here, Shorty. Of course, I don't plan on getting caught."

"Me either. We'll be careful, Jax," I assured her.

Jax sighed. "I'll think about it."

CHAPTER 17

SWEETS

The next morning, I walked slowly to breakfast. I had a noticeable limp coming from the calf in my right leg. My entire body was sore and telling me that I was out of shape. But I was also pretty sure that my calf was telling me that I'd pulled something during my morning yoga class. When I'd told Jax that I was sore from yoga yesterday, she told me that sore muscles were good for me and that it would go away, I just needed to push through. I was pretty sure it had only made things worse.

Even moving my arms hurt and I groaned as I pulled my phone out of my back pocket and logged into my Fitbit app. A new badge appeared on my screen cheering for me because I hit my steps yesterday. *Yay!* I cheered silently. *Go me!* I turned it off and shoved it in my back pocket as I entered the gym where boxes of donuts had been set up on the tables once again.

I sighed. How was I supposed to fight the urge for sugary and fatty foods when all we were ever offered was donuts and pizza? But let's be real, it wasn't that I was complaining. I, for one, was a huge fan of sugary donuts and greasy pizza, it just wasn't helping my diet out when that was my only choice.

I grabbed a long john with chocolate frosting and sprinkles and a round, glazed donut, plopped them both onto a paper plate, and then headed to the table where all of my friends were already waiting.

"Good morning," I sang as I sat down next to Holly and across from Mercy.

"Morning, Sweets. What's with the limp?" Mercy asked.

"I pulled a muscle in yoga class," I answered honestly.

"How's that going anyway?" asked Holly.

Jax smiled happily. "It's so fun having Sweets there with me!"

I sighed. I wasn't sure Jax was going to like me telling her I didn't think I should go the next morning. "Honestly, I'm super sore. My body doesn't know how to stretch like that. I think it's confused about what we're trying to do in there," I said with a giggle.

Jax rolled her eyes. "What did I tell you this morning, Sweets? You just have to push through the sore muscles."

"I don't know, Jax. I think I might have *pushed through* too hard. I really think I pulled something. I might need to give it a few days before I go back."

She stopped eating and looked at me with a frown on her face. "You can't quit now! You just started!"

"Well, I wasn't going to *quit*. I was just going to take a day or two off," I muttered. Jax just didn't get it. She was lean and athletic. Her body understood yoga. Mine didn't. I wasn't sure how to make her cut me a little slack.

"If you take a day or two off then you'll never get started again," she insisted.

"Maybe you should let *her* decide what's best for her body," suggested Alba.

Thank you, Alba, I thought.

Jax shrugged and tried to pretend like she didn't really care, but I knew she did. "Whatever. Do what you want, Sweets. Just don't say I never tried!"

"Can I change the subject?" asked Holly.

"You sure can," I said thankfully.

She sat up straighter in her seat and fidgeted from side to side. "I wanted to tell you all about the dream I had last night."

"Ooh, was it about Aaron?" I asked.

She stared at me blankly. "No, Sweets, it wasn't about Aaron. It wasn't that kind of dream," she retorted.

I'd annoyed her with my suggestion. I frowned. "Oh. Well, what kind of dream was it?"

"It wasn't really a dream, it was more like a vision," she explained.

Mercy flipped her long auburn braid over her shoulder and leaned forward. "A vision? Like a psychic vision? The kind you usually have when you're awake?"

She nodded. "Yeah, sort of like that. I think I was sleep-walking."

Alba looked at Holly curiously. "You had a vision last night while you were sleepwalking and you didn't tell me?"

Holly shrugged and picked off a piece of her donut. "I don't have to tell you everything just because you're my roommate. I wanted to wait until we were all together."

Mercy leaned in closer. "Where did you sleepwalk to?"

"I think I got up to go to the bathroom and then I just had this vision in the hallway. It was really strange. I've never had a vision happen to me in the middle of the night like that. That's why I called it a dream. It *felt* like a dream. It was so surreal."

"Well, what was the vision about?" Jax asked.

"It was about Denise!"

My eyes widened. "What was she doing?"

"Well, she was still dead."

"Did you see who killed her?" asked Mercy.

Holly shook her head. "No. She was already dead when my vision started, but I did see something important." She took a long pause.

"Well, what are you waiting for? Spill!" commanded Alba.

Holly sighed and looked down at her food sadly. "I saw Brittany hovering over her dead body."

My eyes widened. I couldn't believe it! Was Brittany the murderer after all?

"Hovering? What do you mean she was hovering over her body?" Alba asked.

"She was kneeling on the ground, next to the body and she was like leaning over it. And she was glowing. Then she looked back at me, and in my vision, I was standing in the doorway of the storage room. When she saw me, she grinned. Like this really evil grin. My heart is racing just thinking about the look she gave me," said Holly. She trembled as if a shiver had just zipped through her body.

"What do you mean she was glowing? Like how was she glowing?" Alba asked, ignoring the fact that Holly was obviously frightened by her vision. I reached my hand under the table and squeezed Holly's hand.

Holly squeezed back and then looked up at Alba. "She was glowing. She had this green glow around her body."

Alba looked at Mercy. "Just like Denise had a green glow around her body. This is getting interesting."

◞

THE BAKERY WAS RIDICULOUSLY BUSY LATER THAT MORNING. It was much busier than it had been on Monday morning. Mr. Bailey explained to me that on Wednesday mornings he made his special arthritis bread. The combination of eucalyptus oil and his magical potion brought representatives of retirement communities in from far and wide. They picked up the arthritis bread by the crate load to feed their ailing senior citizens.

Instead of helping Mr. Bailey make the bread, however, Louis ordered me to work the front counter. I wanted to complain to him and tell him that I could help with both, but there was no talking to Louis. He didn't seem to want me anywhere near Mr. Bailey's secret herbal potion, and Mr. Bailey was too busy to notice what I was or wasn't doing.

Charlotte Maxwell showed up a little after 10:45. I'd met Char on Thanksgiving when the girls and I discovered that she was holding Alba's husband, Tony, at her house while he recovered from a traumatic head injury. Char, who was also a witch, had done a memory-altering spell on Tony and for a while he thought he was her grandson Arthur Maxwell. But when we came looking for him, she came to her senses and returned him to Alba. In turn, we invited her to spend Thanksgiving with us, where she and Mr. Bailey accidentally ate a matchmaking cake I'd made for Mercy's mother.

Char was a feisty old gal. She matched nicely with Mr. Bailey, as they were both on the shorter end of the height spectrum and both had big personalities that seemed to mesh well together. Char was an avid walker and especially enjoyed taking her dog, Regis, out for long daily walks.

Today, she came in bundled up in a white winter coat with a grey knit stocking cap on over her white hair. Her sunny yellow, polyester pants were tucked into her grey snow boots, and her cheeks were a rosy shade of pink from the cold. Regis, her Chihuahua, was by her side in a red plaid snowsuit, matching red plaid bomber hat, and black doggy snow boots.

"Oh! Char! Regis looks adorable!" I gushed as they came in from the cold.

She looked down at him and smiled. "Oh, well, don't tell him that. He's got an ego the size of Texas. He doesn't need any more compliments. They'll go straight to his head," she quipped.

I smiled at her and nodded. "What can I do for you today, Char?"

"Is Vic here? We need to go over the designs for the wedding cake. The wedding is Sunday, you know. That's only a few days away, and I just have so much to do to finish planning."

"You could have given yourself a few extra weeks, Char."

She smiled at me as if I just didn't get it. "Oh, sweet-heart, at my age, I've learned to seize the day! Carpe diem! No better time than the present. Besides, it's not going to be a big wedding. Just some of our closest friends. Although I am a bit excited..." she said, lowering her voice as if to let me in on a secret. "I've invited all of my old college girl-friends. It's been years since I've seen them. They came for Artie's funeral, and that might have been the last time I saw most of them."

"You went to the Paranormal Institute for Witches too, right?" I asked her.

She nodded. "And Vic went to the Paranormal Institute for Wizards. And he has lived less than a few miles away from me for the last how many years and yet we never met until Thanksgiving at *your* party. Now, how's that for star-crossed lovers?"

"It's your time," I said to her softly. The stars had aligned, and they'd finally made their connection. It was fated to be.

Suddenly Mr. Bailey appeared out of the kitchen. When he saw his bride-to-be, a huge grin sprawled across his face. "Oh! My little cupcake! You've come to see me, how lovely!"

He waddled around the corner and planted a kiss on Char's cheek. "Isn't my bride-to-be radiant?" he asked.

I nodded and let out a little giggle. "She is!" Seeing people so in love and happy made me feel giddy and happy. I needed that positive energy after everything happening at the school lately.

"Vic, I came to sit down and make plans for the wedding cake. We're running out of time," said Char, pulling Regis closer to her on his leash.

Mr. Bailey nodded and then pointed at me. "Did I tell you that I've asked Sweets to make our wedding cake?"

Char looked at me happily and nodded. "Well, that only makes sense," she agreed. "You were the one responsible for putting us together. Can we sit down and talk about this cake?" she asked.

My smile widened as I pulled the pencil out of my hair and a notepad from my apron. "Absolutely! Mr. Bailey, do you have time to join us?"

He shook his head. "It's bread day. There's too much to do in the kitchen. You give my little snookems whatever her heart desires! The sky is the limit!" His arms cut the air above him.

Char chuckled. "Isn't my Vic the best man in the world? And a baker nonetheless! My waistline is never going to thank me for marrying him, but you only live once, right?"

"Absolutely," I agreed. I pointed to a table in the seating area where I could still keep an eye on the counter and said, "How about over there, Char?"

She nodded. "Come on, Regis, follow Mommy."

We took a seat at the table and just as we did Louis came from the back of the kitchen in time to see me taking a seat next to Char. He gave me the evil eye, and then walked over to our table. "I'm sorry, Ms. Maxwell, but Sweets is too busy to sit and visit today. It's Wednesday, and the store's been hopping. I have too much to do in the kitchen to pick up her slack."

My face flushed red. I looked at Louis nervously. He seemed to think he had the right to boss me around, which I understood. He had been there for many years before me, but Mr. Bailey himself had just instructed me to help Char with her cake. I looked between the two of them, unsure of what to do. "I – uh – I," I stuttered.

Char pointed at Louis. "Now, you see here, Sonny. Vic just told her to come and help me with wedding cake plans. So you'll just have to do without her for fifteen minutes. I'm sure you'll survive. You've survived this long without the extra set of hands," she assured Louis.

His anemically pale face prickled with red splotches as if Char had just smacked him across his cheeks. He stared at her in disbelief for a moment and then looked at me. In a huff, he stormed off.

I looked at Char and gave her an appreciative little smile. "Louis doesn't seem to like me much," I told her honestly.

She leaned over and put her hand aside her mouth. "If you can keep a secret, I've never much cared for Louis.

Something about him gives me the creeps. So don't let him get to you. He's wound up tighter than my girdle at an all-you-can-eat pancake feed."

I smiled at her. "Okay. Thanks, Char." Then I looked down at my notebook. "Should we get started?"

"Yes!" she said, throwing a hand in the air for emphasis. "I know exactly what I want, so this shouldn't take long. I want to bring in the tropics with this cake. It's cold and snowy out, but I'd rather it be warm and sunny. So we are going to bring the sunshine inside with this cake. I want each layer to be a different tropical fruit flavor," she began and took the pencil from me and sketched out her idea for the design of the cake.

"Oh, that'll be so lovely!" I said excitedly. "I'm so glad you came today, Char. It's just been a dreadful week at school, and I needed a little cheering up."

She looked at me with concern filled eyes. "Oh, dear. What's going on at school?" she asked and then suddenly the realization hit her. "Oh! I did hear. Your school cafeteria gal, Denise Whiting, was killed. I'm so sorry, dear."

I nodded. "Thank you. My friends and I were very fond of her. It's been hard."

"You poor, poor dear," she said, patting the top of my hand on the table. "I did hear about that. The Whiting's go to my church. Tish Thomas made sure to tell the prayer group at our church to pray for Cal and the kids."

I nodded. "So you know Tish?"

"Yes, she and I both volunteer at our church's food pantry. She's such a sweet little thing," said Char. "She works with Cal, you know, over at his engineering office. Oh, I just feel terrible for him. He's such a nice man and to lose his wife! I bet he's just beside himself."

I nodded. "We met Cal and the kids yesterday. They are pretty devastated," I told her sadly.

From the corner of my eye, I noticed Louis glaring at me from the kitchen. My posture straightened and I took a deep breath and looked up at Char. "Well, now, this week is about you, though. Let's talk some more about this cake!"

CHAPTER 18

"You really think this is going to work?" I asked Holly, as I slowly spun in front of the mirror bolted to the back of Holly and Alba's dorm room door.

"You asked me to make you hot, and I made you hot," she said with a mischievous grin.

The slinky red dress Holly dressed me in had a high neckline, but scooped low in the back, exposing quite a bit of my untanned flesh. She'd gone to great lengths to curl my long red hair and pin tiny tendrils to the crown of my head so that my back was visible.

Jax blinked several times. "With all that makeup on you don't even look like Mercy. Hugh is going to be like, *who are you?* Are you sure you want to go to supper like that?" she asked. "It's just not...you!"

I dotted at the makeup Holly had expertly applied, wiping away a tiny smudge of mascara and then smacked my bright red lips together. "I just want to show Hugh that I can be sexy too," I said. "I think he likes it when I dress up."

Alba shook her head. "You shouldn't want a boyfriend that wants you to be someone you're not."

"I'm not saying he wants me to be someone I'm not," I objected. "I'm just saying that I think every once in a while he wants a *hot* girlfriend."

Sweets took my hand and squeezed it. "Mercy, you're already hot. Don't feel like you need to change to impress him. He likes you just the way you are."

Holly stomped her foot down on their tile floor. "Would you guys quit it? She looks *amazing*. I did a pretty amazing job getting her to look like that!"

"Thanks," I groaned. "I wasn't *that much* of a lost cause before you started."

"Yes, you were. Your idea of couture was wearing a clean hoodie to the cafeteria."

I shrugged and smiled. She was right. I didn't know anything about this fashion stuff, but I did know that I was wearing a red dress, red heels, and red lipstick. What man didn't like red? Hugh was going to have to think I looked sexy in this dress.

"I'm ready to go," I announced. "Are you four ready?"

Alba stood up. "One last time, for what it's worth. I don't think you need to dress like that to impress your boyfriend. You're semi-attractive the way you usually are."

"Aww, thanks, Alba. That's the nicest thing anyone's ever said to me," I said, rolling my eyes.

"Whatever. You're going to do what you want anyway. It doesn't matter what we say," she retorted.

"Let's go," said Jax, rubbing her stomach. "I'm starving."

I took a step forward in Holly's neck-breakingly high heeled stilettos. My ankle turned with the first step. "You girls go on ahead of me. It might take me a while to get there in these heels."

Jax wasted no time in linking arms with Sweets and before I could even blink they were out the door.

"Want us to save you a seat?" Alba asked.

I shook my head. "I'll sit with Hugh. You can save both of us a spot if you want, though."

"Coming, Holly?"

Surprisingly Holly shook her head. "Nah. I'll help Mercy get through the tunnels. Save me a seat too."

I let out a sigh of relief. "Thanks, Holly."

As we walked through the tunnels, I imagined myself gliding into Warner Hall in my seductive red dress and heels. Hugh would see me from across the room and stand up. His eyes would widen, and his jaw would drop for a split second before his mouth curled into an appreciative smile. Wordlessly, I'd remind him that I knew how to be sexy, just like Tori Decker had looked in her dress the other day. Hugh noticing her hadn't gone unseen. Now I wanted him to notice me. Excitement over my plan washed over me as we emerged from the tunnels into the Warner Hall lobby.

With Holly's assistance, walking through the tunnels was a breeze. It was only when she let me loose in the Warner Hall lobby when I began to notice I was having problems.

Hugh sat on one of the couches in the lobby, waiting for me, just as I had imagined. Thankfully, his eyes were glued to his phone, not me as I worked hard to glide gracefully across the stone floor. But instead of walking gracefully as I'd pictured, my feet clomped heavily on the stone floor. And suddenly I felt like a little girl trying to walk in her mother's heels. The stilettos were taller than I'd ever walked in before. I felt myself stiffening.

"Heel toe, Mercy, just like we practiced," Holly hissed at me as she hung back in the shadows of the hallway.

Heel toe, heel toe, I chanted as I walked. I tried. I really did. *Heel first. But these heels are so high*, I thought as they speared me along stiffly. My ankle wobbled, sending a sudden spurt of panic through my body. My hands flattened by my side, wanting to shoot out to help with my balance. I fought to keep them sewn to my sides instead of flailing around on either side of me like my instinct was pleading to do.

Finally, I got into a rhythm of short tight steps. *Heel toe, pause, heel toe, pause.* It was almost like I was walking in them! When Hugh finally looked up, I actually felt confident enough to smile at him. He stood up. It was just as I'd pictured it. An appreciative smile covered his face. *He thinks I look hot!*

And then the unexpected happened. A female voice from the other side of the lobby caught Hugh's attention. "Hugh!"

I watched his head turn. *Toe heel. Wait, that's not right.* In my excitement and overconfidence, my stride lengthened. I turned my head to follow Hugh's gaze and the voice. *Tori!* My eyes narrowed into slits. *Toe heel. Toe heel. Crap.* I stumbled forward. The sight of Tori and the panic over my steps sent an immediate and overwhelming surge of adrenaline flooding through my veins once again. This time it weakened my knees, and I felt them buckle. My right leg tried to catch up to the stride of my front leg to keep me from falling, but the heels spurred me head first. My arms shot out as my eyes bulged.

Oh no! "Agh!" The scream escaped my lips unwillingly. It was high-pitched and shrill.

In a split second, Hugh's eyes were back on me. It had

changed from that of admiration and appreciation to that of terror. He shot forward in his comfortable cowboy boots and Wrangler's to attempt to catch me as I began to fall head first. But he was too far away, and he saw the action begin too late. I sank like the Titanic. My arms reached out, trying to catch me. They jammed into the hard stone floor, buckling my elbows, my face hit next and bounced.

In a humiliating heap on the ground, I could hear the overwhelming sound of laughter. I didn't even have to look up to know whose voice it was. Hot tears burned in the back of my eyes. I swallowed hard as Hugh picked me up off the floor.

"Oh, darlin'! Are you alright?"

I bit the inside of my lip hard. I couldn't let him see me cry. I couldn't let Tori Decker see me cry. I nodded emphatically, but I just couldn't make eye contact with him. "I'm fine," I said, swallowing back the huge lump in my throat.

I limped as he helped me to the couch. The burning sensation in my knees and the heels of my hands told me I'd skinned both up. Without having to touch it, I could feel a goose egg forming on my forehead.

"Well, that was just the funniest thing I've seen all day," cracked Tori from several feet away. "I'd never seen a giraffe walking on stilts before. You did a great impression!"

I wanted Hugh to bark at her, tell her to scram and mind her own business, but he didn't.

Instead, Holly came to my defense. "Get lost, Decker," she said as she rushed to my side.

Hugh crouched in front of me to assess the damage I'd done to my knees. "What were you trying to do?" he asked.

I was trying to impress you, make you notice me *like you noticed* her, I thought. But I couldn't very well say that out loud with Tori Decker standing right there, watching me with those hateful, mocking eyes.

"I – I just wanted to have dinner with you," I stuttered as I struggled to make eye contact. But I couldn't do it. I was just too embarrassed.

"In heels?" he asked lightly.

With my head down, I shrugged.

Before I could speak, Tori's voice rang out, "Aww, do you need me to get you a Band-Aid, Mercy?"

Furious, I glanced up at her. "Don't you have some-where else to be, Decker?" I spat.

Hugh's eyes turned on me. "She's just trying to help," he said patiently.

My face flushed redder than it already was. This time the heat in my cheeks was not from embarrassment, but from anger. I glanced up at Holly. She knew exactly how I was feeling. I sent her a signal with my eyes telling her that I needed to get out of here. Immediately.

That was all it took for her to reach down and help me out of my heels. With the shoes in one hand, she wrapped my right arm around her shoulders and lifted me to my feet. "I've got this, Hugh."

"But—"

"It's fine, Hugh," I said, cutting him off. "Go eat. I'll talk to you later."

~

HOLLY MAY HAVE BEEN ABLE TO BANDAGE MY INJURED KNEES, but my bruised ego wouldn't be so easily disguised.

"I'm telling you, Merc, I totally think Tori caused that fall," said Holly for the tenth time since we'd gotten back to my room.

I shook my head. "My knees locked up," I told her.

"They locked up for a reason. Isn't it a little suspicious that she comes around the corner and bam you're on your face on the floor in front of Hugh?"

Lying on my back on my bed, I covered my face with the crook of my elbow. "Ugh! I can't believe that just happened! I looked like such an idiot!"

The door flew open, and Jax, Sweets, and Alba piled inside.

"We heard about the fall, Mercy. Are you alright?" asked Jax, rushing to my side.

I uncovered my face and looked at her. "What? Does the whole school know?"

"No! Hugh told us. He said we should check on you. Are you hurt?"

I groaned and covered my face up. "Just my pride," I said, trying to hold back a sob.

"It's Tori Decker's fault!" Holly insisted.

"She tripped her?" Alba demanded.

"No! She didn't trip me!"

"She's a witch, Mercy. She caused your fall. I saw her face right before you fell. She nodded at you and then you fell."

"She nodded at Mercy, and that made her fall?" Sweets asked, confused.

"Obviously the head nod was her using her powers."

"It doesn't matter if she made me fall or if I fell all on my own. What matters is, Hugh saw me fall, *and he took up for Tori!* I've had it with that girl!"

Alba narrowed one eye. "I told you. She's evil. We need to get rid of her."

"Get rid of her?!" Jax asked, appalled. "That might be how you do things in New Jersey, but here in Pennsylvania we don't kill people just because we don't like them!"

Alba slapped her forehead with her palm. "Geez, Shorty! You've watched *The Godfather* one too many times. I wasn't talking about *killing her*."

Jax's face sobered. "Oh."

"I just meant we need to get her out of our school."

"Oh. How do we do that?"

"I have no idea," said Alba, shaking her head. "We gotta think of something."

I looked at my red, skinned palms. "At the rate she's going, I don't think we're going to have to do *anything*. The girl's going to get *herself* kicked out."

Alba furrowed her eyebrows. "You know. You're absolutely right. I think we've only scratched the surface of her devious ways. I feel like Tori Decker is involved in Denise's murder. And I'm more determined now, than ever to figure out just what her involvement is."

CHAPTER 19

The stakes were high when we left The Institute Thursday morning. Sorceress Stone had remanded three-fifths of our group to campus. It was Alba's idea to go into town and work on our investigation, but convincing Jax to go was another story.

"Are you scared of your Mom?" Holly asked knowingly.

Jax looked at each of us in turn with her wide crystal blue eyes. "No," she said slowly, shaking her head.

"Liar! You're totally scared of her!" insisted Alba, laughing out loud.

Jax furrowed her eyebrows and stomped her witchy little foot on the ground. "Well, she specifically grounded us! What are we supposed to do?"

Holly looked at Jax questioningly. "Disobey?"

Jax swallowed hard.

"You've disobeyed your mother before, haven't you, Jax?" I asked.

Jax looked over my head, trying not to make eye contact. "Not really," she admitted.

"You're seventeen years old, and you've never disobeyed your mother before?" asked Alba.

Jax shrugged. "Yes."

"You've never snuck out of the house?" asked Alba.

"No," said Jax in a little voice.

"You've never gone out with a boy that she didn't approve of?" Holly asked.

"No."

"You've never had dessert when she told you that you couldn't?" Sweets asked curiously.

Jax looked down at her wiggling toes. "No!"

I pulled my head back. I couldn't believe what I was hearing. "Well. You had to have lied to her at one point or another."

Jax's head bobbed from side to side on her shoulders. "I'm really not a fan of lying."

"But you've done it, right?"

"What?"

"Lie!"

"Oh. No."

"I'm shocked, honestly. You'll steal, but you won't lie to your mother?" I asked.

"Have you met my mother? She's scary!" said Jax incredulously.

Sweets nodded her head. "She's got a point. I don't know if I'd have *ever* lied to my parents if they were as scary as Sorceress Stone."

I took a deep breath and hobbled forward, limping on my sore legs. I cautiously put both of my hands on Jax's tiny shoulders. "Look, Jax, this is important stuff. We're about to start our investigation into Denise's murder. But we can't because we're stuck here. So that means we either can't investigate, Brittany will be sentenced to a life behind bars, and Denise's *real* killer walks away scot-free, *or* we simply sneak out, solve the murder, and don't get caught. Which would you rather do?"

Jax sighed. "Well obviously I'd rather do the thing where we don't get caught, but I'm worried about getting caught. My mother has been keeping an extra close eye on campus since the murder. She's totally going to see us leaving."

"Fine. Then we'll figure out a different way out," said Alba with a shrug.

Then a lightning bolt hit me. "I've got it! We go out through the tunnels!" I suggested.

Holly looked at me like I had a screw loose. "The tunnels? The tunnels are going to take us all the way to Aspen Falls?"

"Well, no, of course not, but they will take us all the way to Warner Hall."

∿

MINUTES LATER THE FIVE OF US WERE STANDING OUTSIDE IN THE men's parking lot next to Hugh's big black truck.

"You're a genius, Red," said Alba with a happy smile on her face. "Now Sweets's car never leaves the parking lot, and Stone will never be the wiser that we left campus!"

"That was very sweet of Hugh to let us use his truck," agreed Jax.

I shrugged. "He wasn't actually *in* his room when I borrowed the keys."

"Mercy!" exclaimed Sweets.

"What? I left a note!" Truthfully, I was thankful that I hadn't had to see him after the incident in the hall the night before. I was still sore at him for not only sticking up for Tori but also for noticing her once again.

I didn't want to dwell on the subject. "Alright, time's wasting, let's go!"

The five of us piled into Hugh's truck, and I drove us into town in the rumbling beast of a truck.

As we got to the first stop sign on the north end of town, I looked around. I didn't even know where we were going. "So. Where do we start?"

"Cal's office, no doubt," said Alba.

We Googled the address and let the GPS on Alba's phone guide us to his office, which was in an old brick train depot on the southeast side of town. The parking lot was empty except one small white car.

"The man's wife just died, he's probably not going to be at work today, right?" asked Sweets as she pulled into the parking spot next to the white car.

"You wouldn't think so. That doesn't mean we can't just ask some questions to whoever is here."

The five of us piled out of the car and tried the front door. I was sure we were going to wind up finding it locked, but when I pulled on it, it opened right up.

"They're open," I said with surprise.

Alba nodded. "They still have a business to run."

Inside, the manly aroma of cedar and suede overtook my senses. A set of old black and white photographs of Aspen Falls in its infancy hung over a long narrow wooden table in the entryway. The lights were all on, but no one was behind the receptionist's desk.

"Hello?" Alba called out, stepping forward towards the low office divider in front of the desk.

A sound coming from another room caught our ear. "I'll be with you in just a second," called a female voice.

"Sounds like Tish," I whispered.

We all stood around, reading the posters on the walls. Jax quietly poked and prodded the papers on the desk.

A minute later, the petite woman we'd met at the Whiting's house came rushing into the receptionist's area.

"Hello, may I help—" she began and then stopped when she recognized who we were. Her head cocked curiously to the right. "Oh! Well hello, girls. What are you doing here today?"

"We were hoping to talk to Cal," I said nervously.

A deep V formed between her eyes. "You were? He's not here right now. I don't expect him in for a while. He's got a lot to deal with right now."

I nodded. "Yeah, we understand."

She sat down on the rolling chair behind her desk. "Is there anything I can help you with?"

Alba looked at the group of us. I could tell she wanted to take the lead. I nodded at her, giving her the go ahead. "We'll just be honest with you, Tish. The girls and I are trying to figure out what really happened to Denise."

Tish nodded. I could tell those words surprised her, but she didn't want to let on that she was surprised. "I see. Well, I was under the impression that the Aspen Falls PD had arrested the murderer. Maybe you should start with her?"

I smiled at her as sweetly as I could. "Oh, yes. We knew someone was arrested. We just don't quite understand *why* the person they arrested would have wanted to kill Denise. We thought maybe Cal would be able to shed a little light on the situation."

Tish sat back in her seat. "Sure, sure. Well, I did ask him if he had any idea what Ms. Hobbs's motive might have been."

"What did he say?" Alba asked.

"He didn't know. He had no idea why she would have wanted to hurt his wife."

I narrowed my eyes and looked at Tish curiously. "There's some talk going on around town that Denise and Cal weren't getting along lately."

Tish's hand flitted to her wrist, where she played absent-mindedly with her watch. It looked like the same fitness tracker Sweets wore. "Oh, umm. Yeah, I wouldn't know anything about that."

I tilted my head to the side, skeptically. "Really? You work in very close quarters with Cal. I heard you were a very close friend of the family. And you didn't know they were having marital problems?"

She fidgeted in her seat. "Well, I..." she began, looking at each of us nervously. "It's really not my place to..."

I raised my eyebrows and patiently waited for her to finish answering.

She swallowed harder. "Cal *might* have mentioned that they had been in a few fights over the last few months."

"Do you know what they were fighting about?" Alba pressed.

Tish shook her head. "Oh, I'd never pry into Cal's personal business."

"So you're saying he never told you why they were fighting?" I clarified.

She looked at us again, nervously as her hand continued to play with the Fitbit on her wrist. "No, I...really. Look – you should probably be asking Cal these questions. It really isn't my place to be discussing his personal life with you."

Jax nodded. "We understand. This must be hard for you too. The kids said you were friends with Denise."

Tish's expression softened. "I *was* friends with Denise.

We were all friends. The Whiting's have been very good to me. Cal gave me a job when I first moved to town, and they were my first friends. Those kids are great, and this is so sad for them. They are much too young to lose their mother."

"Can I ask you another question?" I asked her.

She looked at me nervously. "Umm, sure? I can't promise I can answer it."

I leaned forward on the top of the divider and in a hushed voice I said, "Can you keep a secret?"

Tish's eyes darted around the room uncomfortably. "Umm. A secret? Yeah, sure. I guess."

"We heard through the grapevine that Cal and Denise were talking about getting divorced. Do you know if that was true?"

Tish's jaw dropped. "Divorced? Who said that?"

I waved a hand in front of my face. "Oh, I don't want to rat out any of our sources," I said with a small laugh. "It's just one of those rumors that float around in a small town."

She nodded.

"So can you confirm that?" I asked pointedly.

She blinked several times in quick succession. "Umm, well, no. I can't really – I mean I couldn't say."

Alba who had been wandering around the receptionist area looking at all the posters and photographs on the wall pointed at one poster in particular. "This is an old poster," she said.

Tish nodded as she let out a sigh of relief that Alba had changed the subject. "I've meant to clean-up around here. I really should take that down, that was from the 5k charity run we did this past fall."

Alba nodded. "I see Whiting Engineering and Harding Law sponsored the run."

"Yes, Cal is very philanthropic. He likes to help wherever he can."

"You're a runner, right?" Alba asked, pointing at Tish.

Tish smiled nervously. "Yeah, I help coach track at the high school after I'm off work here."

Jax smiled at her. "Was the 5k your idea?"

"Oh, you know, I don't really remember. It might have been partially my idea. We all like to pitch in with community events."

Alba nodded. "Is Harding Law who Whiting Engineering uses for their law firm?"

Tish shook her head. "Oh, no. We use Mike Erickson. He and Cal went to high school together."

Alba nodded. "I see."

The front door bell chimed, and a cool gust of wind swept us around the ankles. We all turned around and looked up to see Cal Whiting coming in through the front door.

"Cal!" said Tish in surprise. "What on earth are you doing here? You should be at home with the kids," she suggested. Her soft tone implied intimacy that made me sure she was indeed the one having the affair with Cal.

Cal looked at us curiously. "Rachel and Danielle were napping and Aaron went out for a jog. What are you girls doing here?"

Before any of us could speak, Tish spoke up. "They're investigating Denise's murder."

Cal frowned and quirked an eyebrow. "I thought Brittany Hobbs killed her. Detective Whitman said they had her in custody."

"We don't think it was Brittany," said Jax.

Alba and I looked at her quickly. I wasn't sure that that

was something we wanted to be revealed, but now it was out there.

"You don't think Brittany did it?" His voice rose an octave. "Didn't Detective Whitman say that someone at the school talked to Denise's ghost and she said that Brittany did it?"

My stomach flip-flopped. I winced and then met his eyes. "That was me," I admitted.

He looked at me, startled. "You? Well, then why would you think that Brittany didn't do it?"

"I've known Brittany almost my whole life," Jax spoke up. "I just can't believe that she did this."

"We can't either," agreed Sweets. "We think maybe Denise's ghost was confused or something."

"How could my wife's ghost be confused about naming the person who killed her?" Cal demanded. His voice was heavier now.

"She was stabbed in the back. Maybe she didn't actually see the face of the person that did it. Maybe Brittany was the last person she saw before she died and her ghost was confused. I've met lots of ghosts that don't know who killed them and they saw their face. Something about death sometimes just confuses the mind," I explained.

Cal's eyes narrowed as he glared at us. "Does Detective Whitman know that you're snooping around?"

Jax's face went fire engine red. I squeezed her hand. Keep it together Jax, I thought silently.

"Yes, of course he knows. We told him we didn't think Brittany did it."

"And he's alright with you investigating on your own?" Cal asked.

I nodded pleasantly as if everything were perfectly on the up and up.

"Cal, do you have a few minutes to talk?" Alba asked him.

He jiggled the keys in his hand and shifted his weight to his other foot. "I really don't have time. I just came to grab a file, but I wanted to get back to the house before the girls woke up. I really don't feel good about leaving them alone right now."

"It'll only take a minute," I assured him.

On the sly, he tossed Tish a quick glance. It was minor, but I was sure we'd all caught it. "Just a few minutes, we can go in my office," he said and led the way to a thick six-paneled oak door in the corner.

We followed him and when we were all inside, he shut the door behind us and sat in his desk chair. "Okay, what questions do you have for me?"

Alba took a breath. "We know that you need to get going, so we'll just get right to the point. There's a rumor floating around that you and Denise were getting a divorce."

Cal's eyes widened. We watched him as he struggled to remain cool and collected. "Rumors are just that, girls. Rumors. I tell my girls all the time that rumors are great because you learn things about yourself that even *you* didn't know," he punctuated that with what he tried to play off as a light-hearted chuckle. "Especially in a small town, people breathe funny and it's all over town by the afternoon."

Alba furrowed her eyebrows at him. "So you and Denise were not getting a divorce?"

He sat back in his chair, causing it to squeak under the strain. "Absolutely not! Denise and I were just as in love now as we were when we got married."

"How do you think that rumor got started?" I asked him.

He tented his fingers and held them to his temples. "I have no idea honestly. But it's really sad that people would tell you that when I'm just over here trying to grieve for my wife!"

I nodded. He was choking up now. We'd touched a nerve. We hadn't come to point our fingers at him. We'd only come to find out a little bit more about his relationship with his wife. "I'm sorry, Cal. We weren't trying to make you feel bad. Okay, well, we won't take up any more of your time, Cal. Thanks so much for clearing that up for us."

He nodded as he swiped at his eyes with the sleeve of his shirt. "Absolutely. There's nothing I hate more than unfounded rumors. I'm proud of you for coming straight to the source to clear them up instead of asking around town and spreading the lies."

"We appreciate your candidness and your honesty," I assured him. "Let's go, girls."

He stepped forward as if he would open the door for us, but Alba beat him to it. "We'll see ourselves out, thank you."

He nodded and as we left his office, he joined Tish at her desk. They waved at us as we headed out the door.

When we were outside Holly looked at me in surprise. "I can't believe we're just going to go! We know Cal and Denise weren't getting along and we know they were talking about divorce. His own children told us! Why did you let him off the hook so easily?"

"He was never going to tell us. The five of us investigating sounded ridiculous to him. And let's be real, can you blame him? A bunch of college kids show up at your door and say the police have the wrong person and they're going to figure out who really killed your wife? We should have been laughed out the door!"

Alba nodded. "Red's right. It doesn't matter anyway. I have a new plan."

We all got back inside Hugh's truck and I turned the key in the ignition, causing the heavy vehicle to roar to life and music to fill the cab.

"Turn it down, Red. I need to make a phone call," said Alba.

I adjusted the volume and pulled out of our parking spot. "Where am I going?" I asked her.

She looked at the clock on the dash. "Back to campus, we need to get to lunch before we're missed."

I nodded and headed back towards The Institute. While I drove, Alba pulled one of the business cards she'd found in Cal's top drawer out of her pocket and dialed the number on it.

She put the phone on speaker while we waited for someone to pick up.

"Good afternoon, Harding Law," said the professional sounding voice on the other end.

"Hi, this is Cal Whiting's secretary. Mr. Whiting asked me to call you to let you know that his wife passed away this week and that he no longer needs that divorce paperwork filed."

The voice on the other end was silent for a moment. She cleared her throat. "I'm sorry to hear about Mr. Whiting's wife's death, but his grief must have him confused. He called me last week to cancel the divorce paperwork."

My eyes widened as I drove. I clapped a hand over my mouth to keep from making a noise.

Alba was able to keep her composure. "Oh. He did?

Okay, well, yes, like you said. He was probably confused from the grief of the situation. Thank you for your help."

"You're welcome. Please let Mr. Whiting know we are very sorry for his loss."

"I will, thank you," said Alba before hanging up the phone.

"Oh my gosh! He *did* file for divorce!" Holly screamed when the phone was dead.

"And then he canceled the divorce?" asked Jax. "What's up with that?"

"Maybe they worked out their problems," Sweets suggested.

"Maybe he canceled it because he was going to kill her!" I retorted with flared nostrils.

Alba shook her head. "Detective Whitman seemed sure it was a woman that killed her. It wasn't Cal."

"Denise and Cal probably just decided not to go through with the divorce," said Sweets. "It's just strange timing, you know?"

"Yeah, very strange!" I agreed.

"How'd you know that was his divorce lawyer?" I asked Alba.

"I figured that business card in his drawer had to be from either his personal lawyer or his business lawyer and when Tish said they used Mike Erickson and he was an old classmate, I knew the business card was from his personal lawyer. No way Cal would have run his personal family drama through an old classmate."

Sweets's mouth opened wide. "Wow! Good sleuthing Alba! I'm impressed."

I patted Alba's shoulder with one hand while I drove. "Yeah, good sleuthing. You're like Sherlock Holmes."

"I only wish we had more time. I really wanted to visit Midge next," I said.

Jax shook her head insistently. "No way! Tonight is the party and if we're not back in time for lunch and we get caught, we won't be going to that party."

"Ohh, so now you're okay with sneaking off campus to go to the party? Earlier you were *so* worried about disobeying Mommy that we had to practically *beg you* to go investigate with us," I teased.

A slow smile spread across Jax's face. "I can't help it. You four are corrupting me!"

The laughter back to The Institute was a much needed release.

CHAPTER 20

Getting ready for the party later that night was nerve wracking, only because I was supposed to meet Hugh there and I didn't know how I would act around him. I was still mad at him, and yet for someone stupid reason I still wanted to impress him. The internal conflict had eaten at me most of the afternoon.

Originally the plan had been to dress up for the party, but once I discovered how much I sucked at walking in high heels and how sore I still was from falling in them the day before, I quickly changed my mind. Instead, I wore a black t-shirt, jeans, and sneakers, but I added my long cardigan over the top in place of my usual hoodie.

"I'm ready to go," I announced. "Are you four ready?"

I looked around. Everyone else looked cuter than I did – except maybe Alba. She had refused Holly's fashion advice, and while she had agreed to exchange her sweatpants for jeans, she still wore a sweatshirt. She did, however, claim it was an upgrade because it wasn't a Hanes brand sweat-shirt. Sweets wore the new coral blouse her sister Peach had given her for Christmas. Jax wore what she usually wore, and Holly had picked a slinky dress with cut-out shoulders and heels for herself.

Alba stood up and looked at Holly. "You're going to freeze your butt off in that skimpy little dress."

Holly giggled. "The thought of the man I'm going to find tonight will keep me warm."

We all rolled our eyes. Jax, Sweets, and Alba slipped on their winter coats and gloves.

"Aren't you two going to wear a coat?" Jax asked.

I shook my head. "Nah, I'll be fine."

"Ditto. Why would I go to the trouble of wearing my new dress if I'm just going to cover it up with a big ole coat?"

"Whatever," said Alba gruffly. "So we're ready? Let's go."

"Okay. How are we going to pull this off?" I asked. "Sorceress Stone is guaranteed to see us tromping through the school if we go out through the front door."

"How else are we supposed to get to the car?" asked Holly.

"Well. Jax, Alba, and I can't go out through the front door," I said as a plan began to form in my mind. "How about the three of us go through the tunnels to the boy's building, and you two move the car to the Warner Hall parking lot and pick us up there?"

Alba nodded. "It's the only way."

Jax wrung her hands nervously. "I don't feel good about this, girls. We got away with sneaking out the other day, but I feel like our luck can't hold out much longer."

Alba put a hand on Jax's shoulder. "You worry too much, Shorty."

"Yeah, Jax. There's no way Stone's finding out."

Jax shrugged wearily. "Fine," she said slowly.

"What do you think, Sweets? Can you pick us up in the other parking lot?" I asked.

Sweets looked around nervously. "If we get busted does that mean that I'm in trouble for aiding the enemy?"

"The enemy?" Alba asked with a laughed. "Now we're the enemy?"

Sweets sighed. "Fine. I'll pick you up in the other parking lot."

I squeezed Sweets's arms. "Thanks, Sweets. We owe you one!"

"We better get going," said Holly as she grabbed her handbag off the desk. "Before all the hot guys are taken."

"What are we waiting for? Meet you in the Warner Hall parking lot in five minutes!" I said excitedly.

OUR ESCAPE WENT OFF WITHOUT A HITCH, AND BEFORE I KNEW it, we were cruising the back roads of Aspen Falls looking for Darcie Larson's grandpa's old building. If it hadn't been for GPS on our phones, we wouldn't have been able to find the dilapidated barn in the dark.

Pulling down the dark gravel road, we took a right next to a mailbox that clearly read Larson. Once we'd turned into their driveway, we saw the rows of cars lining the road.

"Wow. The whole school turned out for this party," said Jax as we pulled in beside Hugh's truck.

"You don't think Merrick or Sorceress Stone are going to notice the campus is a ghost town tonight?" Sweets asked nervously.

I waved a hand at her, dismissing her concerns. "Sorceress Stone has too much on her plate right now to worry about why there aren't any students in the lobby tonight."

Sweets shrugged and shut off the engine. "If you say so."

We got out of the car and made our way to the source of the booming music. I eyed Holly's smooth perfection in heels with jealousy. She was a natural in them and didn't even seem to notice the snow packed and icy road. I, on the other hand, continued to nurse my skinned knees, limping as I walked the length of the road to the party.

The old barn was hard to see in the dark, but there was a tall pole light out front of it which cast a dull glow in front of the building. There were a handful of wizards outside throwing bolts of energy at a wood pile, trying to ignite a fire. Their laughter and the booming sound of bass from the music inside set the stage for the evening ahead.

"Hey there, girls," said one of them as another one let out a whistle. "Looking good tonight, ladies."

Holly was the only one to pay them any attention before we went inside. "Hey, fellas, having fun?"

"We are now that you're here," one hollered back.

The barn doors were wide open, but the inside wasn't much brighter than the outside, save for the glow of the fire pit in the center of the barn and multiple strings of white Christmas lights which had been strung up around the perimeter of the corrugated metal building. The scent of burning wood and beer filled our nostrils.

We moved about slowly, taking in the scene before we committed to a location. When I saw Libby and Cinder roasting marshmallows on the bonfire, I scooted in closer to them. "Hey, girls, have you guys seen Hugh?"

"Hey, Mercy," said Libby. "I saw him over there last."

She pointed to the other corner of the building where a small bar had been set up.

"Thanks," I hollered back over the music.

The girls and I headed towards the bar and when I saw Hugh seated on a short wooden bench, my heart jumped, and my stomach wrenched nervously. I left the girls next to the bar and walked over to my boyfriend.

"Hi, Hugh," I said stiffly.

"Hey there, Mercy Mae," he said with a smile as he stood to greet me. "How are those knees doing tonight?" he asked with what appeared to be genuine concern.

I gave him a tight smile. I couldn't help but remember him telling me to take it easy on Tori. "They're alright."

"That was a pretty bad tumble you took. I was worried about you."

Just thinking about the fall made my body temperature heat up again. He'd texted me after the fall, to check on me, but I'd been too embarrassed and angry to respond to him with much enthusiasm. "Yeah. Sorry about that."

"You don't have anything to be sorry about. You looked very beautiful," he said sweetly.

"Thanks. I was trying to look nice for you," I admitted.

Hugh wrapped an arm around my waist and pulled me closer to him. "Darlin', you could be wearing a potato sack, and I'd think you looked hot," he assured me, kissing my cheek.

His words immediately made me realize just how foolish I had been to have wanted to dress up to impress him. The girls had warned me, but I hadn't listed. I'd let Tori Decker get in my head. I shivered.

"Are you cold? Where's your winter coat? You look as cold as a banker's heart."

"Y-y-yes," I quivered. "F-f-freezing actually."

He chuckled and sat back down on the bench and pulled me down onto his lap. "I'll keep you warm, Miss Mercy Mae."

With his arms wrapped around me, I relished in his body heat. Leaning my head back on his shoulder, he kissed my forehead.

"Hi, Hugh," said a familiar girl's voice.

My head snapped up to see Tori Decker, dressed in skinny jeans, calf-high fur lined-boots, and a coat with a fur-lined hood standing in front of us with her hands shoved inside her pockets. She looked warm. I groaned inside.

"Hey, lil lady," said Hugh to Tori. The adorable little drawl that I used to find so wonderful was now like nails on a chalkboard.

I stood up, removing myself from Hugh's lap and put a hand on my hip. "What do you want, Tori?"

She pasted a fake "I'm offended" look on her face. "I just wanted to say hello to the two of you and check on how you're feeling after that *unfortunate* fall yesterday." The way she said the word *unfortunate*, made me feel that maybe Holly was right. Maybe Tori *had* engineered my fall.

"I don't need you to check on me," I said snottily.

Alba and the girls approached us. Alba carried a beer in one hand. She took one look at Tori and flicked her index finger at her, shooting her backwards into the person about five feet behind her. "Scram Decker," growled Alba.

Hugh looked up at the group of us in surprise. "Why are you guys being so mean to the new girl?"

I took a deep breath trying to calm myself. If he stuck up for her *one more time*, I was going to scream.

Alba answered for me. "That's the wench that hit me over the back of my head with a lunch tray on Monday."

Holly nodded in agreement. "She's been nothing but rude to us since we met her."

"Huh. I've met her a couple of times, and she's been nothing but super sweet to me," he said, blindly.

I rolled my eyes and harrumphed, crossing my arms across my chest. "That's because she's got a crush on you," I explained to him.

He laughed. "Oh, you think so?"

I slugged his shoulder. "Don't tease about that. I don't like that girl one little bit and the thought of her flirting with you makes my blood boil."

Hugh squeezed the back of my thigh. "Relax, darlin'. I only have eyes for you."

I let out the deep breath I'd been holding and bent over to give him a quick kiss. His lips on mine were the reassurance I needed. I felt a little better.

Holly linked arms with Sweets. "This feels completely ridiculous to say, Sweets, but you and I are the only two singles in the group. We should go scope for boys."

Jax pouted. "Tristan just went outside to do magic with his friends. I want to come, too."

Alba looked at Hugh and me like we had a contagious bacterial disease. "Yeah, I'm coming too. I'm not gonna be left alone with these two love birds," she grumbled.

I smiled at her as I sat back down on Hugh's lap and threw my arms around his neck. "Just give me one more second and then I'll join you," I said to them before I leaned over and whispered in Hugh's ear. "I'm going to go enjoy the party a little bit with my friends. Okay?"

Hugh kissed my cheek. "You go have some fun, darlin'. I'll be right here when you get back," he assured me.

I snuck a peek at Tori. Her friend from The Institute had joined her, and together they were chatting animatedly only ten feet away. When they caught me looking at them, the two of them shot me a set of matching scowls. A tiny part of me felt like I shouldn't leave Hugh unattended, but I didn't want to be that girlfriend that didn't trust her boyfriend. So I gave Hugh a megawatt smile. "Be good, okay?"

He crossed his finger across his chest. "Cross my heart."

CHAPTER 21

The girls were waiting for me at the bar. I pulled my long sweater around myself a little tighter. "I cannot believe I was dumb enough not to wear a real coat to this party," I complained as we began circulating around the barn. I eyed Holly's clingy dress with the cut-out shoulders skeptically. "I'm freezing. Aren't you cold, Holly?"

Alba shook her head. "There's no way she's cold. The thought of the boy she's going to meet is keeping her warm."

Holly giggled. "But first I'm going to find Sweets a cute boy," she announced loudly. Then she pointed at a tall boy in the corner with big beefy arms and wavy brown hair that was parted on the side politely. He was standing by himself holding a beer. "How about him, Sweets?"

Sweets giggled nervously. "He's cute, but there's no way I can talk to him."

Holly looked at her like she was crazy. "Why not?"

Sweets' eyes widened. "I don't know. I'm sort of shy."

Holly waved a hand dismissively at Sweets. "You are not. It's in your head."

185

"Yeah," agreed Sweets. "It *is* in my head. I can't help it. I won't have a thing to say!"

Holly shrugged as her eyes landed on a guy near the entrance that had just walked in. "Fine. Suit yourself. I'm going to go meet a boy then. I'll find you girls in a little bit."

The four of us stopped walking and watched Holly approach the tall, dark, and handsome man that had just come in. She giggled and then linked arms with him. He looked down at her with interest.

Sweets groaned as she watched the voluptuous blonde work her magic. "Why can't I be more like Holly?"

"Because you have *morals* and a *brain*," grumbled Alba.

"Alba! Holly has morals and a brain!" Sweets chastised. "What I meant was, I wish I could be more outgoing with boys like Holly."

"You just have to try," suggested Jax.

"It's too hard for me. Holly makes it look so easy."

I patted Sweets on the back. "She's had a lot of practice, Sweets. You just need to put yourself out there and try."

"I know what you need, Sweets. You need a little liquid courage," suggested Alba holding up her beer.

Sweets's eyes widened. "I'm not twenty-one yet!"

Alba laughed and looked around. "I'm pretty sure I'm one of the few legal people here. Most of these people aren't twenty-one yet either. Haven't you ever been to an underage party in high school?"

Sweets shook her head and swished her mouth off to the side. "Nope."

"Good thing you met me then. Come on. I'll buy you your first beer."

"You're going to turn Sweets into a juvenile delinquent?" Jax asked curiously.

Alba rolled her eyes. "Come on, Shorty. I'll turn you into one too," she said with a laugh.

Jax shook her head determinedly. "No thank you. I don't need to be under the influence to have a good time. I'm naturally high on life."

"Let me guess. You were part of the anti-drinking campaign in your high-school, weren't you?" Alba asked sarcastically.

Jax nodded. "As a matter of fact, I was the President of my school's SADD group for two years running."

"Figures."

Alba led us towards the bar. "You want one too, Red? It'll warm you up."

I thought about Tori flirting with Hugh, and I nodded. "Sure, I'll have one," I said.

We followed Alba to the bar, which was really just two thick pieces of lumber spanning the top of a pair of wooden sawhorses. Two whiz kids were behind the bar offering up cans of beer for two dollars each from an aluminum trough filled with Bud Light and ice. He put three cans on the bar, and she handed him some cash.

"Thanks, Alba," I said as I took my can from the bar and popped the top open. I took a quick sip and then peered through the beer line to discover that the bench I'd left Hugh on a few minutes prior was now empty. I stuck out my bottom lip. "Hugh's gone."

Sweets took a sip of her beer and then looked down at it in disgust. "This stuff is nasty," she croaked. She handed the can to Jax. "You want to try it, Jax?"

Jax pinched her lips between her teeth and shook her head like a toddler who refused to try broccoli. "Uh-uh."

"You'll get used to it," said Alba as she finished off her

first beer and threw the empty can down onto the dirt floor, crunching it with the heel of her shoe.

I took a sip of mine. I'd been to a few house parties like this in Dubbsburg, and I'd even had a few drinks, but the parties were usually busted up by the cops before I had a chance to have too many.

I looked at Sweets. She still had her eye on the boy across the room that Holly had pointed out.

I elbowed her in the side. "Just go talk to him."

"I couldn't," she said nervously, fidgeting with her beer.

"Yes, you can. Just talk to him like you would talk to us."

Sweets guzzled her beer as if she was trying to work up the courage. After she'd swallowed, she let out a deep breath. "What would I say?"

"I don't know. You could ask him about his major and where he's from. You could ask him about his hobbies," I suggested.

"But I don't want to go over there alone," she complained.

Jax linked arms with her. "I'll go with you, Sweets."

"Really? Oh, Jaxie, you're too sweet." Sweets threw her arms around Jax's shoulders and squeezed.

"Come on. If you can't think of something to say, I'll help you out," Jax assured her.

Sweets smiled from ear to ear and let Jax lead her away.

"Good luck, Sweets! Go get him!" I hollered after her.

"Five bucks says she doesn't even talk to him," said Alba with a snicker.

"I'll take that bet," I said with a smile. I was sure that Jax would get Sweets talking.

As the last group of people at the bar walked away, I

had a clear view of the bench where I was supposed to meet Hugh. It was still empty. *Where in the heck did he go?* I didn't have time to dwell on his whereabouts because Holly suddenly came rushing over to us.

"Girls! Oh my God, I totally just had a vision!" she announced.

Alba ignored Holly's statement and pointed at Sweets and Jax. "Check it out, Holl. Shorty took Sweets over to talk to that guy."

With one fingertip clenched between her teeth, Holly turned to look. Then she turned back around again to face Alba and me. "Did you guys hear me? I just had a vision."

"What kind of vision?" I asked nonchalantly as my eyes darted back to the empty bench next to the bar.

"The bad kind. It was about Hugh. He's in trouble!"

My eyes swiveled to Holly immediately as the word Hugh filtered into my brain. "Wait, what? Hugh's in trouble?"

She nodded fearfully. "He was in my vision!"

My body numbed fearfully. "But, I just saw him a few minutes ago," I said, looking back to the bale of hay where he had been sitting. He was still gone.

"We have to go help him right now," she begged.

The blood had all drained from her face. Between her pale face and the desperation in her voice, I was afraid of what she was going to tell us about Hugh. I looked at Alba fearfully.

"Come on, Red. Let's go with Holly. We'll see what we can do to help him," said Alba. I was thankful for her cool, take-charge attitude.

Holly led us out the back door of the barn. The dim glow of a pole light and the moon reflecting off of the snow was the only light available to us out back. Without the bonfire and the collective body heat from the party, I shivered in the cold.

The metal siding dulled the pounding of the music inside, and for a second I was able to hear myself think. "What's going on, Holly? Where's Hugh?" I asked her nervously biting on my lip.

She pointed towards the trees off in the darkness. "There's another barn back there. I saw it in my vision. He's back there."

Our eyes followed Holly's finger, but we were unable to see through much of the inky darkness. "Why would Hugh have gone back there?" Alba asked.

Holly held her hands up next to her raised shoulders. "Three men were holding a knife on him! He looked like he was ready for a fight."

My jaw dropped. "Who were they? Did you recognize them?"

Holly shook her head. "I've never seen them before."

"What else did you see?" I asked. I wasn't sure if someone turned the bass up inside or if it was just my heartbeat thudding heavily in my ears, but the sound around me had suddenly become deafening.

"That's really all that I saw," said Holly nervously as one hand found its way to her mouth where she began nibbling on her fingernails. "One guy pulled a knife on Hugh. All of them had that weird green glow around them again."

"Can you lead us to them?" I asked her, taking two steps into the darkness.

Alba took her phone out of her pocket and turned on her flashlight app. "This should help," she said.

"Good idea," I agreed, pulling my phone out of my pocket.

Holly pounded her fist down on her thigh. "Darn it. I left my phone in the car. I'm pretty sure that barn is back here. I could feel it in my vision," she explained.

Tire tracks in the snow ran parallel to the party barn and led back into the trees. Clinging onto one another, we trekked through the deep ruts and followed the makeshift road into the wilderness. As dark as it was, each step was a mystery, causing my heart to beat faster inside my chest. My chin trembled in the cold, and I feared my trembling was because we were going to discover Hugh's body in a pool of blood.

I threw my head back as my teeth chattered. "Oh, this snow is *so cold*!" I cried as it brushed up against my legs and fell into my shoes.

"Maybe we should go see if we can borrow a truck to drive back there," Holly suggested, holding her arms around her bare shoulders for warmth.

Alba shook her head. "Hugh could be dead by the time we find someone with a truck and drive back there."

"Did they stab him, Holly?" I asked. It was the question I hadn't wanted to ask for fear of what her answer might be, but I had to know.

Holly shook her head earnestly. "I didn't see them stab him," she whispered into the dark sky, her breath puffed out in front of her like a billowing cloud of smoke.

"I'm not sure how much further I can walk in these heels," Holly complained, leaning on Alba and me for support.

"We warned you. You knew this was going to be a party inside of an old barn. Maybe you should have worn sensible shoes," suggested Alba gruffly.

"I didn't know we were going to be playing detective in the snow!" Holly whined defensively.

We came to a little break in the trees, and when I held my phone light up a little higher, I was able to make out the front of an old ramshackle wooden barn. The siding had weathered away to a dark grayish black, and it leaned precariously to one side. By the looks of it, a strong gust of wind could likely knock it over.

Holly pointed with wide eyes. "That's the place in my vision! Hugh's in there!"

Alba held her flashlight up too. "That doesn't look dangerous at all," she said sarcastically.

"It's falling apart!" Worry sank my heart. The thought of Hugh being inside ate at my insides. What if it fell over on him?

"I don't think we should go in there," said Alba.

"I just don't understand why he would be back here," I whispered as we got closer to the rundown structure.

"Maybe those guys with the knife forced him out here," suggested Alba.

With a lump in my throat, I called out into the darkness. "Hugh?"

Alba squeezed my arm and clapped her heavy gloved hand over my mouth. "What the hell, Red?" she hissed. "You *trying* to give the bad guys a chance to find us before we find them?"

"I don't hear anything," I hissed back. "The bad guys are probably long gone by now. Hugh could be in there bleeding to death!"

"Well, then we'll have to go inside and look around for him," said Alba. "We don't have to yell for him."

Standing at the threshold, we scrutinized the entrance nervously. The barn door was barely hanging on to the frame. It hung suspended from one hinge like a loose tooth hanging by a single root. Gripping each other tightly, we stepped over pieces of the barn that had fallen onto the dirt floor.

"Careful, there could be nails sticking up," I warned.

Once inside, we flashed our lights around the dark barn. It was clear that whatever scene Holly had seen earlier was over now. There was no one around.

"Can I call him now?" I asked Alba.

"Yeah, I guess so," she said slowly.

"Hugh!" I called out. My voice echoed off the tin roof as the low rumble of music and laughter from the party rode in on a blast of cold air. My pulse raced at the thought that it might only take a bit of a stronger gust to collapse the building.

Holly joined in. "Hugh!"

"Hugh, are you in here?" I asked.

"He's not in here," said Alba. Her face glowed underneath the light of her flashlight.

"Holly. Are you sure what you saw was happening in here? Maybe it was somewhere else."

Holly shook her head firmly. "No. I recognize this barn from my vision. They were in here. They were over there," she said and pointed towards a fenced in horse stall with a wooden floor.

"Maybe he's in that stall," I suggested. The group of us, still linked at the elbows, moved in unison. The frail floor creaked as we stepped on it.

"This can't be safe," said Holly fearfully as she stretched a foot out to check the strength of the floor before moving further.

Together, we walked towards the fenced in area. "Hugh?" I called out, my voice shaky.

The floor let out a loud creak, an objection to our weight. I was about to suggest that the floor wasn't strong enough to hold all of us, but before I could get the words, the sound of wood splintering filled the air and the wood crumbled beneath our feet, plunging us down into darkness.

CHAPTER 22

SWEETS

"So, you're into fishing?" Jax asked Corey, the cute boy standing in front of us.

I was too nervous to say much besides letting out the occasional giggle. He'd been surprised when we'd come over to talk to him, and he seemed eager enough to have a conversation, but still, talking to a boy intimidated me.

Corey nodded and gave the two of us a small, shy smile. "Yeah. Bass fishing mostly," he said.

Jax's eyebrows rose animatedly. "I see. Have *you* ever been fishing, Sweets?"

My heart lurched nervously, causing me to giggle. "Yeah, I've been fishing lots of times. My dad and I have a stock dam where we like to fish for bass and perch. My mom makes a mighty mean Georgia-style pan fried bass."

Corey's face lit up a little bit. "I'm really good at frying fish too."

Jax put a hand on my arm. "You two have something in common."

"Where are you from, Corey?" I asked, stealing occasional nervous glances up at him.

"I'm from Tuscaloosa," he said.

My eyes widened. "You're from the South too? I'm from southern Georgia," I told him excitedly.

His eyes lit up with interest. He was just about to say something else when Jax tapped me on the shoulder. "Sorry to interrupt," she said and flashed Corey a nervous smile. Then she put her hand on my shoulder and pulled my ear towards her mouth. "Sweets, check out Hugh over there," she whispered in my ear.

I turned to see Hugh directly across from us talking to Tori. Tori had her arm laced through his and was talking animatedly with her free hand. Then she laughed like he'd just said something incredibly hilarious. "This is not good. Mercy's gonna flip when she finds out that Tori's flirting with Hugh. I've got to find her. You stay here."

My heart lurched in my chest nervously as I glanced up at Corey. He gave me a tense little nod and then glanced away. "You can't leave me here all alone!" I hissed into her ear in a panic.

"You'll be fine, Sweets. Just keep doing what you're doing," said Jax.

I wanted to talk to Corey more, but I was too nervous to do it without Jax around. I took hold of Jax's arm and squeezed, holding her solidly next to me. Then I looked at Corey. "It was really nice to meet you, Corey. Maybe we can talk again a little later, but we need to go help one of our friends out right now."

He nodded. I almost thought I saw a look of disappointment cross his face, but if I did, he managed to hide it well with a smile. "No problem. I understand. It was nice to meet you."

As Jax and I walked away, she leaned into me. "You didn't have to leave him!"

"I know, I know. I'm just not ready to talk to him by myself," I said back. The thought of being alone with him had spiked my adrenaline, and I suddenly felt the need to have a snack cake. I had just bought a new pack of them at the grocery store. They were heart shaped with pink icing, and now they were calling my name.

Jax and I approached Hugh and Tori. Immediately Hugh looked at us in relief. "Howdy, ladies," he said with a wide smile as he pulled his arm out of Tori's grasp. "Where's my beautiful girlfriend?"

I wasn't sure, but it seemed like he had emphasized the word *girlfriend* for Tori's benefit.

"I'm pretty sure she thought you were supposed to meet her by the bar a little while ago," said Jax, giving Tori the stink eye.

Tori put one arm on Hugh's shoulder like she'd staked her claim on him. I furrowed my eyebrows at her. Mercy wasn't going to like this one little bit. "Yeah. Maybe we should try and find her," I suggested.

Hugh moved towards us. "That sounds like a terrific idea. It was nice chatting with you, Miss Tori," he said amicably.

Tori visibly pouted. "But we were just getting to know each other," she said.

"I'm sorry, but I promised Mercy we'd meet back up. We'll visit another time," he offered.

I shrank under the vengeful stare Tori shot us as retribution for taking Hugh away from her. Jax linked arms with Hugh and I and pulled us both towards the bar where we had left Alba and Mercy only a few minutes earlier.

"Thank you, ladies," said Hugh as he let out a heavy breath of relief. "That little gal is harder to shake off than a tick on a dog."

"Or like a bad cold you can't get rid of," agreed Jax. "Mercy wondered where you went."

"I was just sitting there when Tori came up to me and asked me if I had a minute because she needed my help," he explained. "I said sure, and she pulled me off of my seat and led me to the fire. I thought she was having a car problem or something, but she just wanted someone to dance with."

We got to the spot where we'd just left Alba and Mercy, but they were gone. "Where'd they go?" Jax asked, looking around her bewildered. "They were literally just here a few minutes ago."

"Maybe they went to find Holly," I suggested. My eyes searched the party carefully, trying to find any sign of the girls. "Look, there's the guy Holly was just talking to."

Jax stood on her tip toes to see over the crowd. "I don't see Holly," she finally said with a frown. "I'll go ask that guy if he knows where she went." Jax pushed her way through the crowd while Hugh and I guarded the spot where the girls were supposed to be.

I looked at Hugh when he shook his head in frustration. "What's the matter, Hugh?"

"I used to go to parties like this back home in Texas. Years ago. When I was in high school," he said. "They just aren't my thing anymore."

"Mercy said they aren't her thing either, but she said she'd go to be with you."

He let a little chuckle escape his lips. "Well, that's my fault then. I thought she might like to go to a party, so I told the fellas I'd go. I wish she would have just told me parties weren't her thing. I'd have taken her out for a nice supper instead."

I giggled. "You didn't know Mercy wasn't a social person?"

He smiled and put a hand on the top of his cowboy hat as he looked down at his feet. "You've got a point there, Sweets."

Jax returned from looking for Holly. "That guy said that Holly left saying she had to go find her friends, something came up."

Hugh's eyebrows furrowed together nervously. "Something came up? Like what?"

"He didn't know," said Jax.

Hugh made a face. "I'm getting kind of a weird vibe right now. I really wish we knew where the girls were."

"Maybe they went outside for some air," I suggested, pointing at the front door.

Hugh nodded. "Come on, let's go find them. I'm ready to go. This party hasn't been that great. Are you girls ready to go?"

I shrugged a shoulder and looked at Corey as the three of us walked to the door we'd come through earlier. He was a wiz kid, so I was sure that I'd bump into him again. The thought of the Valentine's Day snack cakes calling my name beckoned me to get back to The Institute. I nodded. "I'd be happy to go home too," I said.

Jax made a face. "We just got here and already you two want to go home? You guys are a bunch of party poopers!" she exclaimed.

We opened the barn door and stepped outside. No sooner had our feet hit the icy ground than we saw a terrifying sight. The Stones were approaching from up the long lane. Sorceress Stone's long grey dress danced around her ankles and Merrick's long black robe whipped around his legs, prodded by the wind that seemed to have ridden in with them. Their eyes were trained on the group of boys shooting fireballs at the wood pile. They didn't even notice the Stones approaching them as they alternated between laughter and sips of beers.

I sucked in my breath, covering my mouth with my hand, as Merrick drew his long bony finger from the sleeve of his robe and aimed it at the circle of boys. Jax's boyfriend, Tristan, was in the group goofing around. I watched as her face went ashen. She knew what was coming.

"Uncle, no!" she screamed.

The sound of Jax's voice made Sorceress Stone's head snap towards us. Her ice blue eyes widened as she saw her daughter standing in front of the party. "JaclynRose?" she asked, as her hand fluttered to her throat in shock.

But before Jax could utter a single apology to her mother, Merrick unleashed a torrent of electrically charged energy on the group of boys. It encircled them, disempowering them immediately.

"Uncle, no!" Jax screamed again as she watched the energy throw Tristan into the air with the rest of the boys.

"Silence, JaclynRose!" Sorceress Stone hollered. She strode towards the three of us. My mouth went dry as I watched her coming towards us. My heart throbbed in my ears unrelentingly. I'd never been as scared of Sorceress Stone as I was at this exact moment.

Standing directly in front of us, she looked down her nose at her daughter. "I warned you," she spat. "You were punished the other day. How dare you disobey my orders!"

Jax looked down at her hands. "I'm sorry..." she began.

"You must go," she said hastily. "I will deal with you back on campus." She grabbed Jax's tiny wrist. "And deal with you I will, JaclynRose. You will learn never to disobey me again."

Sorceress Stone glanced at me momentarily and then at Hugh. "You two must go also. This party is over. Everyone who is here will be punished," she snapped.

Hugh didn't look afraid. "I didn't know we weren't allowed to attend off-campus parties."

"Underage drinking and improper use of magic are unbecoming of students that attend my Institute," she snapped.

Hugh gave her his best charming smile. "Miss Stone, I'm twenty-three-years old and I didn't perform a single act of magic here tonight. Neither did any of these ladies here. You can hardly punish *everyone* here for being at a party."

She was quiet for a moment, seemingly considerate of Hugh's words. She raised one eyebrow and looked at Jax and then me. I could tell she was debating on what to do with us. Finally, she spoke. "Very well. You will take these two back to campus immediately. JaclynRose, I'll deal with your insubordination when I return to campus. If I find you still here when I've finished clearing out the students, I'll charge you all with insubordination. Do I make myself clear?" she asked.

I nodded my head somberly. I wasn't about to argue with her.

She strode past us into the party. I could hear her thunderous voice booming over the sound of the music.

"Oh my gosh. We have got to get out of here," I said to Hugh and Jax as soon as the coast was clear.

Hugh shook his head determinedly. "We've got to find Mercy and the rest of your friends."

"You heard Sorceress Stone. If we don't go now she's going to charge us all with insubordination," I said nervously. As much as I didn't want to leave Holly, Alba, and Mercy, I was sure they'd find another ride home. We were on a first name basis with most of the girls at the party.

Jax nodded. "I agree with Sweets," said Jax. "I can't stay. My mom's going to kill me."

Hugh dug in his heels. "I'm not leaving here without Mercy."

I tugged on his arm as I moved towards the driveway. Students were beginning to flee the scene now, running in every direction.

"We're never going to find her in this mess. Mercy is resourceful. So is Alba. Libby and Cinder are in there, and they know all the rest of the girls in there, too. They'll find a ride home. Don't worry," I said. "Come on, Hugh. We have to go!"

Jax pulled me towards the driveway as the number of people fleeing increased. "Come on, Sweets. We are never going to get out of here at this rate. We have to go."

"I'll look for them," he hollered over the thickening crowd.

I lost Hugh's arm in the chaos. "Bye, Hugh. See you back at The Institute!" I hollered back.

"Don't worry, Sweets," hollered Jax. "He'll be fine. And I'm sure he'll find the girls. Come on. We have to go now."

IT TOOK SORCERESS STONE LESS THAN AN HOUR TO GET BACK to campus and find Jax in her dorm room. She and I had been holding our collective breaths, waiting for her to arrive. Nervously I'd opened the door when we heard the knock. I'd hoped it would be Mercy, Alba, and Holly coming home, but it wasn't. It was Sorceress Stone.

Without a word, she strode past me into Jax's dorm room. With her usual stiff posture, she raised one eyebrow and looked down at Jax, who was sitting on Mercy's bed, curled up in a ball.

"Hi, Mom," she said with a tiny voice.

"JaclynRose. I'm very disappointed in you. I gave you one order. That was to stay on campus, and you couldn't even follow that one simple punishment. Did you think that I wouldn't find out? Do you think that I'm stupid?" she asked.

"I'm sorry, Mom. I – it was the first party of the year. I didn't want to miss it," she stumbled weakly.

My heart lurched for poor Jax. All she wanted was to please her mother, and she never seemed able to do it. Now not only was she *not pleasing* her, but she was specifically *dis*pleasing her. I looked down at my feet.

"Where's your roommate?" she asked, looking around the room.

Jax peered at me nervously. "Mercy? Oh – she – she's with some other friends," Jax replied vaguely, shaking her hand as if to squash the subject.

"Was she at the party?" asked Sorceress Stone knowingly.

Jax shook her head vigorously. Her widened eyes and vacant expression made her look like a zombie. "No, ma'am."

I let out the breath I was holding. After Jax's admission that she hadn't lied to her mother before, I wasn't sure if she'd be able to keep Mercy's participation in the party under wraps.

Sorceress Stone nodded. "Very well then. Follow me."

Sorceress Stone left the room without another word. Slowly Jax crept off the bed.

My eyes widened. "Where are you going?" I asked.

Jax shrugged her shoulders but didn't say a word. She was too scared to talk. Instead, she quietly followed her mother to the hallway.

"Jax! Where is she taking you?"

I poked my head out the door to find Sorceress Stone leading Jax down the corridor towards the back stairwell. I frowned. Quickly I slipped on the flats I had worn to the party and followed them, leaving Jax's door open so they wouldn't hear it shut behind me.

I followed them to the stairwell. I thought they would be going downstairs to Sorceress Stone's office or something, but when they started heading upstairs, I knew exactly where she was taking Jax. Sorceress Stone was taking Jax to what she called, Purgatory, in the tower.

Oh no. What am I going to do? Girls! Where are you? I didn't know what to do. Jax was being hauled away to witch jail, my friends were missing, and I was alone. I groaned. I had to do something.

Instead of following Jax up the stairwell, I went downstairs. At the bottom of the stairs, I crossed the hall to the basement stairs and took them down to the tunnels. Wordlessly I peered into the shadow-filled corridors. My heart jumped into my throat. I'd never been in the tunnels at night, nor had I ever been in them alone. I sucked in a deep breath. "Buck up, buttercup," I whispered to myself, a phrase my dad had said to me often when I was a kid. Without letting out my breath, I darted into the tunnel and ran as fast as I could through the maze of underground pathways until I reached the basement of Warner Hall. I climbed the stairs and found myself in the lobby. I quickly took the stairs to the second floor and ran down the hallway until I reached Hugh's room. I knocked on the door and prayed silently that he'd answer.

"Mercy Mae?" he asked, pulling the door open quickly. "Oh, Sweets," he sighed sadly. "I was hoping you'd be Mercy."

My hope crumpled, as did my shoulders. "They aren't here? I was hoping you'd tell me they showed up," I said sadly.

"Dammit," he cursed, his arm punched the air out in front of him in frustration. "Where in the hell are they?"

"Maybe they're stranded at the party?" I asked nervously. Suddenly I felt guilty. I had abandoned my best friends. My hand covered my mouth.

He shook his head. "I stayed until the end of the party," he explained. I hid behind the building and waited until the Stones cleared out the party. Once they'd gone and the building was empty, I left. I assumed the girls caught a ride home with another girlfriend or something."

"Maybe they did," I suggested. "Maybe they're in another dorm room."

Hugh shook his head. "No way. Mercy would have made sure to let me know she was alright," he insisted.

I nodded. He was right. "She would have come and told Jax and me, too."

Hugh looked around, poking his head out into the hall-way. "Speaking of Jax, where is that little thing?"

"Sorceress Stone just took her up to the tower as punish-ment," I said, my heart heavy. "I don't know what to do. Jax is in trouble, and the rest of my friends are missing. I'm not usually the one making plans, so now I don't know how to help!"

"We're going to have to go back there," said Hugh determinedly.

"Why? You said you checked the place over and they weren't there."

He shook his head. "Maybe they started walking back? Maybe they're on the road and need me to come for them."

"Why wouldn't they just call for a ride?" I asked. "Have you tried calling them?"

"I've tried Mercy's number about a hundred times. It keeps going to voicemail."

I frowned. "I've had the same problem. I've been trying Mercy and Alba, and they both go to voicemail. Holly left her phone in my car."

"Then that's it. We have no other choice. We're going to have to drive those back roads and see if we can't find them."

My eyes widened. "Hugh, we can't. Sorceress Stone said no one is allowed to leave campus."

CHAPTER 23

"I'm s-s-s-oooo c-c-c-old," Holly complained, her teeth chattering in the darkness.

"I'm cold too, Holl," I agreed, wrapping my sweater tighter around Holly's bare shoulders.

The floor of the old barn we were in had collapsed, and we'd fallen into some kind of pit. In the fall, Alba must have hit her head on something, and she was knocked out cold. Thankfully, she had a strong pulse and was breathing fine.

The room we'd fallen into was some kind of storm cellar or something, but whatever it was, we couldn't find a way out. We'd spent the last half hour trying to figure a way out of the hole, but to no avail. The staircase that led upstairs had been boarded shut at the top of the stairs. It was pitch black above our heads. We couldn't even see high enough to find the ceiling, much less figure out how to crawl out of our dungeon, and we especially couldn't climb out with Alba unconscious.

Holly and I huddled together in the darkness, and together we cradled Alba's head on our lap.

"What if Alba never wakes up?" Holly asked me for the third time since we'd been in the pit.

"She's going to wake up, Holl. She's breathing fine. Her pulse is good. I don't feel any blood."

"But what if she doesn't wake up? We'll be stuck down here forever. It's only going to get colder, you know. We could freeze to death down here."

I was beginning to hear a panic in her voice that hadn't been there before. "We can't freak out. We have to stay calm, okay?"

"If only we had our phones," she whined. "I left mine in the car because I didn't want to carry it around the party. Wasn't that stupid?"

I rubbed the top of my nose with the palm of my hand to keep it from freezing. "At least you'll still have a phone when this is all said and done. Mine broke in the fall, and I can't find Alba's."

"They have to come back looking for us, don't they?"

"The music stopped hours ago. They're all gone."

Holly sniffled, and I felt her arm move like she was wiping away tears. "They wouldn't have just left us! Sweets and Jax wouldn't have driven away without us in the car, would they?"

I shrugged, even though she couldn't see me. "Maybe the party got busted by the cops. The music died down in an awful hurry. It can't be that late. College parties don't end at ten."

Holly sucked in her breath. "Oh my gosh! What if Jax and Sweets got arrested!"

The thought hadn't occurred to me. "Sweets did have a beer," I agreed. "Oh crap. What if they got arrested for underage drinking?" I looked down at Alba in the darkness. I couldn't see her face, but I could feel her dead weight on me. I silently begged her to wake up. We had to get out of the hole we were in.

"Sweets only had one beer. There's no way she's getting arrested for having one beer, right? And Jax wasn't even drinking." The shakiness of her voice told me she was worried. If Jax and Sweets were behind bars, who would ever come looking for us?

"We don't know what the laws are here. Maybe just being at a party where minors are drinking is enough to get arrested," I said.

Holly squeezed my arm tighter. "What are we going to do, Mercy?"

I let out a nervous breath of air and shivered closer to Holly. "Well, there's no way Hugh is going to give up on finding me," I said, taking comfort in that fact.

"Unless he got arrested too," said Holly.

The hole got silent again. The sound of an owl "hoo-hooing" in the distance sent shivers rippling down my legs.

"I don't understand how this happened," I finally said, resting my face on my knuckles. "Hugh wasn't even out here, so how did you see him in your vision?"

"I've been thinking about that, too," agreed Holly. "I don't know what happened. I guess my vision was wrong."

"Do you think maybe all that happened in a different barn?" I asked.

"It was in this building! I know it! I recognized the horse stalls," she said. "It was in here, I swear! It must have just been a bad vision."

"I hope so! Otherwise, that means that Hugh is hurt somewhere else," I said. The thought had been replaying over and over again in my mind since we'd fallen, but I didn't know what I could do about it. "Have you ever had bad visions before?"

Holly shook her head. "No. I still have problems getting visions to show up when I want them to, but when I have them, they're *always* right. I just don't get what's going on. Lately, my visions feel weird."

"What do you mean weird?" I asked her.

"Well, not only was this vision strange, but the last vision I had was of Brittany leaning over Denise's dead body, and we don't feel like Brittany was the murderer. So why would I have a vision that she was leaning over Denise's body?" she explained.

"That *is* weird. That's two questionable visions in a row."

"And then there's the fact that the people in my visions are glowing. I've never had my visions glow before," she said slowly, as if she were trying to piece together what all of that meant.

"Denise's ghost was glowing when Alba and I saw her too. Maybe this has something to do with Denise. Or her killer."

"That doesn't make any sense. What would the vision I had tonight have to do with Denise or her killer?"

I leaned backwards. "Maybe your vision tonight was purely designed to fool us."

"Why would I have a vision like that?"

"I don't know. We go to school with a bunch of witches. Maybe someone was playing a practical joke on us." The thought caused me to take pause. "Could they do that? Could someone make you have a fake vision, Holl?"

Holly thought about it for a second. "I don't know. I suppose anything is possible where witchcraft is concerned. Who would have had something to gain by leading us out here, though?"

"Well, it was a vision about Hugh. Obviously, that

meant that I would go to him," I said. "That gets me specifically out of the picture."

"So Tori could swoop in and talk to him!" said Holly immediately.

I made a face. "You think she'd go to all that trouble just to talk to my boyfriend?"

Holly's nervous laughter filled the dead air around us. "Are you kidding me? She's a horrible girl! She'd do anything to get her way!"

My mouth opened wider. I guess I didn't realize the extent to which she'd go to get alone time with Hugh. "This is just crazy. So you think Tori is responsible for us being down here?"

"Who else would it be?"

My mind drew a blank. "You know, all three things were glowing green. Denise's ghost and your two visions. What if Tori is responsible for all three things we saw?"

"It *would* solve a lot of questions! But why would Tori lead us to believe that Brittany did it?" asked Holly.

"Maybe Tori was trying to frame Brittany," I suggested.

"But why would she do that?" asked Holly.

"Maybe she's the killer."

The hole went quiet again. Once again, the only sound came from the owl above us in the darkness.

"You think *Tori's* the killer?" Holly finally asked, disturbing the quiet.

"I really don't know. I don't think we can put it past her at this point. We need to get out of here. We have to figure out what all of this means!" I said. I jiggled Alba's shoulders. "Wake up, Alba. We need you!"

"You'd think with us being witches and all we'd be able to conjure up something to get us out of here. Think, Merc.

We're witches. We have powers. What can we do to fly out of here?"

I laughed. How had we been so stupid? "Duh. Why didn't we think of that before? We *are* witches, and we *do* know how to fly."

"We don't have our broomsticks, though," said Holly.

"Our broomsticks can come to us! We just have to call them," I said excitedly.

I raised my arms and cupped them to my mouth. "Batman! I need you!" I called up into the solemn night.

"Come here, Handsome!" yelled Holly with a giggle.

"Let's hope that works," I said, wrapping my sweater back around Holly's shoulders. She was the least dressed of us all. "How ya doing, Holl? You okay?"

She leaned her head on my shoulder. "Yeah, thanks for letting me share your body heat with you."

"I'm actually stealing a little of your body heat, too," I said with a chuckle.

We were quiet for several long moments. I broke the silence and asked, "Do you think our broomsticks heard us?"

"They are all the way inside your dorm room," said Holly. "What if they can't get out?"

I hadn't considered that. "Let's hope Jax is in our room, and when the broomsticks go crazy trying to get out, she'll let them out."

"Maybe she'll follow them to us?"

"Doubtful, they'll be flying too fast."

Just then I heard a groan that didn't come from Holly, me, or our stomachs. "Alba?" I asked.

I felt her arm move and go to her head. "Oh, my head is killing me," she said.

"Alba!" squealed Holly happily. "You're alive!"

"Ow, Cosmo, that voice is like nails on a chalkboard in my head."

"Oh, sorry, Alba. We're just so happy you're alive," she whispered.

Alba tried to sit up. "What happened?"

"The floor broke, and we fell into a pit," I told her. "You must have hit your head on something."

"You're not bleeding," Holly assured her. "We checked."

"We need to get you to a hospital," I told her.

"Nah, I'll be fine. I just needed a nap. How long have I been out?"

I shrugged. "Can't be sure. My phone broke, and we can't find yours. I assume it's broken, too because I haven't heard a single call or text. But it has to have been at least two hours."

"Geez, two hours? And no one has come looking for us?" asked Alba.

"The party died down not long after we fell. The music just stopped," I explained.

"We think that maybe Jax and Sweets got arrested," said Holly.

I elbowed her. "We don't think they got arrested. We just think the party got broken up by the cops or something. We're *hoping* no one got arrested, but we *have to* get out of here. You have a coat on and have been in a coma for two hours. Holly and I are freezing. We just called for our broomsticks, but I don't think they heard us."

"Help me up," said Alba, giving me her elbow.

Holly felt her way to the other side of Alba, and together we got her to her feet. "How's your head?" she asked.

"Remember when you were a baby and your parents dropped you on your head? It hurts like that," said Alba tersely.

"Well that was rude," said Holly.

My laughter filled the dead space around us. "Oh, Holly. It just goes to show Alba's alright."

"Alba, you should call your broomstick, just in case ours are on their way," suggested Holly.

"Fine. Uber, I need you!" hollered Alba into the darkness. "Now stand back, I'm going to try something."

We let go of Alba's arms and took a step back in the darkness, careful not to trip over anything behind us.

Without a word, she spun a bright green ball of energy between her hands. It lit up the darkness and provided us a way to see where we were in the pit. The ceiling was about two feet over our heads.

"Stand over there, Holl," said Alba, gesturing with her head to a spot directly underneath the hole we'd fallen through.

Holly moved to the spot. Alba let the green energy dissipate and pointed her finger at Holly and levitated her up through the hole. "Can you feel the floor yet?" Alba asked.

"Yeah! Set me down!" Holly called from up above.

"Your turn, Red."

I moved to the spot that Holly had just been and with Alba's help, I found myself standing next to Holly. My heart thrummed excitedly in my ears. "Now how are we going to get you out?"

I looked down into the hole. Alba was spinning another green ball of energy so she could check out her options. "I don't know. You might have to come back for me."

"Maybe we can pull her out," Holly suggested.

"We could try," I agreed.

"There's no way you two scrawny things are lifting me out of this hole. Go get help!"

"It'll take hours for us to walk into town!" Holly

whined.

A whooshing noise in the distance caught my ear. "What's that sound?"

"What sound?" asked Holly.

"Shh!" I hissed.

"I hear it," said Alba. "It sounds like it's getting closer."

Alba was right. The sound was intensifying. It sounded like it was almost upon us! My adrenaline raced as I tried to ready myself for whatever was coming.

And then just like that, two broomsticks dropped neatly in front of our faces.

"Batman!" I exclaimed excitedly.

"It worked!" Holly cheered.

"Now we just have to wait for Alba's!"

Uber was only two minutes behind Batman and Handsome. It dropped right in front of Alba's face, and she was able to fly out of the hole and join us on the floor of the barn.

"We don't have much time to lose," said Alba when she was next to me. "We've already been out here far too long. We need to get back to The Institute!"

We each mounted our broomstick. "Are you sure you're up to flying, Alba?" I asked.

"I'll be fine," she assured me. "Come on. Let's go!" With a swirling gust of wind, she blew past me and launched herself into the sky.

"Batman, don't let me fall!" I chanted.

"Handsome, don't let me fall."

Up in the air, I leaned forward on my broomstick, careful to hold my knees together for good balance. "Where are we going?" I hollered into the cold starlit sky.

"The Institute," Holly yelled back.

"I know that!" I said with a laugh. "But we can't very

well just go land in front of Winston Hall and walk in. Sorceress Stone could be waiting for us."

Alba shook her head. "Doubtful. She probably doesn't even know we're missing. But to be safe, I think we should go back in through Warner Hall and take the tunnels back to our room."

"Alright, I'll race you!" I said as I threw my head back, sending my long auburn hair whipping back into the wind in a smooth cascade.

Holly giggled as she sped ahead of me, leaning into the wind. "No way, eat my dust!"

Alba, who was not one to be outdone, sped ahead of both of us. I caught the sound of her hearty laughter as she flew past us.

We leap-frogged the rest of the way back to The Institute. When we reached the outer perimeter of campus, we hung like clouds in the night sky.

"Brr! It's so cold!" complained Holly. Her teeth chattered from the frigid ride.

My own body shivered. I didn't know if I'd ever get warm again after that ride. "We need to get inside," I begged as I tried to run a hand through my stiffened hair. But my fingers stopped almost instantly at my temples. My hair was completely twisted and knotted. It would take me an hour to get out all the tangles.

In her puffy winter coat, Alba looked refreshed after the ice-cold ride. "I forgot how much fun flying could be," she said.

Holly and I glared at her. "We need to get inside. Where do we land?" I asked.

"We'll just land in front of Warner Hall," Alba said plainly.

Holly nodded. Then with one quivering finger, she

pointed towards Winston Hall. "Look. The lights are on in the tower!"

"Oh man. Someone got in trouble," I said. "I wonder who it is."

With a devious smile on her face, Alba looked at the two of us. "We could go find out?"

I debated whether my curiosity outweighed my cold-ness and hunger. Finally, I relented. "Yeah, let's do. I'm super curious."

"I'm t-t-too c-c-cold to go l-l-look," chattered Holly.

"It'll be fast," promised Alba.

The three of us lurched forward on our broomsticks, and we flew over the courtyard to the top of Winston Hall. We circled the building before moving in closer so we could hover next to a window. I put one hand over my eyes as I peered inside the glass. I could see someone lying on the bottom bunk of one of the bunk beds.

"C-c-can you see who it is?" Holly asked, peering into the window next to me.

"I can't see her face," I said.

"Is that Jax?" Alba asked. "Those look like her tights."

I peered in closer. They did look like Jax's striped tights. "Oh no. I think it is Jax. She must have gotten busted for leaving campus!"

Holly looked at me with a wrinkled forehead. "What are we going to do?"

"We've got to get her out of there!"

"The room's sealed up tight," said Alba. "Remember the last time we were in there? It's insulated. You can't use magic inside of it."

Suddenly a thought hit me. "What about the attic? Maybe we can get in up there somehow?"

"We've got to let Jax know what we're doing." Alba

pounded on the glass.

Holly and I followed suit until Jax finally looked up from the bed. She spun around when she realized the sound she was hearing was coming from the windows. When she saw it was us pounding, her eyes lit up, and she came running excitedly.

I waved at her, and she waved back.

Alba pointed to the attic. "Go to the attic!" she yelled.

Jax nodded and raced to the closet where the secret stairway to the attic was.

The three of us flew higher until we got to the bell-tower at the very top of Winston Hall. We landed inside of it and looked around. There was an arched wooden door that led inside.

"Stand back," shouted Alba.

Holly and I got behind her. She closed her eyes and collected her energy. In one swift motion, she threw a crackling burst of energy towards the door. It splintered in half sending pieces of the door shooting down the stone staircase inside the building.

Quickly the three of us ran inside and just as we were coming down the stairs, we found Jax in the attic. She came running at me full force. "You saved me!" she squealed as she leapt into my arms.

"How'd you get locked in here, Shorty?" Alba asked her once I'd set her down on the stone floor.

Jax hung her head. "My *mom* locked me in here."

"Well, we figured it wasn't Sweets that put you up here," said Alba sarcastically.

"Oh. Well, Uncle Merrick and Mom broke up the party," said Jax. "Where were you guys? We looked for you!"

"Long story. We'll tell you everything when we get back to the room. We need to eat first. We're cold and starving!"

CHAPTER 24

Friday morning everyone woke up exhausted and ravenous. But because we'd broken Jax out of the tower the night before, she couldn't be seen at breakfast, so Sweets and I made a donut run to the gym for yet another round of stale donuts and cartons of chocolate milk. Once breakfast was finished our plan was to sneak Jax back into the tower before Sorceress Stone realized she was missing.

"This is getting old really fast," Sweets complained as she took a bite of the dry donut. "This tastes like cardboard. It's not even worth the calories."

"Don't you have to work at the bakery this morning?" Jax chirped as she picked at her own donut like a bird. "Why don't you just eat something there?"

Sweets giggled. "Because I'm starving now. Worrying about all of you last night really worked up an appetite!"

I nodded as I licked the chocolate frosting off the top of my roll. "Being stuck in a hole for two hours in the cold and then flying home on our broomsticks made me hungry too."

"I can't believe the night you guys had. I wish I had

been with you. It sounds like so much more fun that having your mom grounding you!" Jax complained.

Alba shook her head as she ate. "You need to stand up to your mom, kid. She's never going to take you seriously if you just crumple whenever she makes a grumpy face. Because let's face it. Her face is always grumpy. You have to learn to stand on your own two feet. You can't be scared of her shadow!"

Jax's head tilted to the side. "I'm not scared of her shadow. But it doesn't matter what I do. She's never going to take me seriously until I become a witch." Jax moved her donut around on her paper plate. "And who knows if that's ever going to happen."

Holly patted Jax on the back. "Don't get down, Jax. You're only seventeen – maybe when you turn eighteen, or – or twenty, you'll get your powers."

Jax shrugged but wouldn't speak after that. We'd all gotten into her head. Sitting cross-legged on top of her desk, she pulled her legs up underneath her tighter.

"We need to talk about our plan," I said quietly. We'd come back to our dorm room the night before and told Jax and Sweets everything we surmised about Tori showing us illusions and fake visions. We'd all been so exhausted after the night's events that'd we'd crashed hard and hadn't gotten around to figuring out what that meant.

"Yeah, where do we go from here?" Holly asked.

I looked at Alba, unsure myself.

Alba shook her head and shrugged. "I really don't know. I guess we have to look more closely at Tori now. She was trying to make us think that Brittany did it. There's only one reason that I can think of for that, and that's that she did it herself and she was trying to frame someone else."

"Why would she want Denise dead? She's a new kid...
she didn't even know Denise!" said Sweets. "That doesn't
make sense."

"Tori *was* super rude to Denise the morning of the
murder," Jax pointed out.

"But was that conflict a motive for murder?" asked
Sweets.

"It seems unlikely," I agreed. I stood up to grab a straw
off of my desk when the light from the window caught hold
in a crystal object on Jax's side of the desk. I'd never seen it
before. I picked it up and showed it to Jax. "What's this
thing?"

Jax's face immediately reddened. "Oh. That," she said
with a nervous titter.

"Jax!" Sweets admonished, taking the large diamond
like object from my hand. "Did you steal something from
someone again?"

Jax looked down uncomfortably. "I didn't really do it on
purpose," she asserted. "It was just so *sparkly*!"

"What is it?" Alba asked, casually looking over the item
in Sweets' hand.

Sweets flipped it over in her palm. "It's like a paperweight or something."

"It's not very big to be a paperweight," said Holly
leaning over to take a look. "It's got something engraved on
it. What does it say?"

Sweets held it closer to her face, squinted, and read the
engraving aloud. "Tish – to the world you may be just one
person, but to one person you may be the world. Thanks for
everything you do, Cal."

My eyes widened. "You stole that from Tish's desk?"

"Jax!" Holly grabbed the paperweight from Sweets's

hand. "I can't believe that's from Ca– " The minute Holly touched the item, her body stiffened.

"Girls, she's having a vision," said Sweets nervously. "Help me before she falls over."

We all rushed around Holly, holding her in an upright position. A tiny moan escaped her lips until finally her body relaxed and she slumped forward.

Alba, who was standing in front of her, caught her as she fell.

"Holly, wake up!" I said to her as Alba lowered her limp body to the ground.

"Holly!" Jax cried, jumping off the desk to be by Holly's side on the ground. "Are you alright? Do you need something to drink?"

As Holly came to, she held her head, rubbing it lightly. "No, I'm fine," she said, trying to sit up. We all helped her back onto her chair.

"Did you have a vision?" Sweets asked her.

She nodded. "Yeah. It wasn't a very big one. I just saw the day that Cal gave Tish the paperweight. They were alone in his office. It was dark. He gave it to her and then he kissed her!"

"What kind of kiss? A quick, friendly peck on the cheek or was it something more?" I asked.

Holly's sighed. "No, it was definitely something more. It was a passionate kiss – the kind you don't want your wife to know about."

Sweets sucked in her breath. "So they *were* having an affair?"

Holly nodded and let a puff of air escape her throat. "Yeah, most definitely."

"Well, we can't say that we didn't already suspect that. We were fairly confident, but it's good to have it confirmed.

I think we need to get back into town today and we need to find out if Tish had an alibi for the day that Denise was killed," said Alba.

"I agree. I think we all meet back here at lunch time and then we go do a little more digging." I stood up and threw my paper plate away. "But first we need to put you back in the tower."

"What if I'm not back out of the tower by lunchtime?" Jax complained miserably.

"You will be. It's your mom. She's not going to let you be up there all day. I bet she'll let you out in time for first-period class," I said, looking down at my watch. "In fact, it's getting kind of late. We probably should get you back up there."

"I think we also need to hide our broomsticks up in the bell tower, in case we ever need to call them again," said Holly.

I nodded. "Good idea. We may need to escape from the tower again someday, too."

As I had predicted, Sorceress Stone released Jax from the tower in time for her first class. At lunch time Sweets texted Holly that she was done with her internship at the bakery and on her way back to campus, the four of us snuck out through the tunnels again and met Sweets in the Warner Hall parking lot. We drove into town and parked in front of Whiting Engineering as we had done a few days prior.

Inside we were immediately greeted by the strawberry blond woman at the front desk. "Well hello, girls, back again?" asked Tish sweetly.

"Hi, Tish," I said nervously.

"What can I help you with today?" she asked. "Did you need to speak with Cal? He just ran home to have lunch with the girls, but he should be back in about an hour."

"He's back at work already?" Alba asked.

Tish nodded. "I tried to get him to take more time off, but he said it was doing him more harm than good just sitting around like that. He's a bit of a workaholic," she admitted. "Actually, we're all a bunch of workaholics."

"Yeah, his children mentioned that when we met them the other day," I said, trying not to let on that we knew *why* he liked to be at work so much.

Alba stepped forward. Her face was grim. "I'll just be honest with you here, Tish. You know we're still investigating Denise's murder," she said matter-of-factly.

Tish nodded, wide-eyed. "I see. Are you having much luck?" she asked.

Alba's head bobbled on her shoulders. "Some. We've narrowed down a few things. We were wondering if perhaps you have a list of the employees that can be accounted for the morning of the murder?"

She nodded and rolled her chair over to her desk. She clicked a few buttons on her computer. "Yes, I typed up a list for Detective Whitman, but you probably already knew that since you're working with him."

"Yes," said Alba as she stared hard at Tish.

Tish shrank under Alba's intense glare. Then a nervous giggle escaped her throat. "Umm, but I can print the same one out for you if that will help?"

"Yeah, that would be great, thanks," said Alba.

I smiled to myself. Alba's cool just dodged us a possible bullet. Seconds later, the printer began making noises and then spit out a single sheet of paper. Tish rolled her chair over to it and pulled it off and handed it to Alba. "Here you go. Is there anything else that I can do to help?"

Alba looked down at the paper. "It says here that you weren't at work that morning?"

I glanced up at her. Her hand was on her wrist, nervously fidgeting with her watch once again. My heart began to race a little faster. We had her!

"Oh, yes. Like I told Detective Whitman, I was home sick. I spent all day Sunday down with the flu. I texted Cal Sunday night and told him I'd be in late Monday morning. I slept until about noon. When I finally looked at my phone a few hours later, I had about a dozen missed messages. Denise had already been killed," she said, her voice low.

We all looked at her skeptically.

She held her smartphone out to Alba. "You're welcome to check my text messages. I really did text Cal. I already showed Detective Whitman the message and Cal vouched for me."

"But did anybody actually see you at home?" I asked her.

"Admittedly, no. I was home alone. I know that looks bad, but I didn't kill Denise. Denise was my friend!" she told us.

"Can we take this with us?" Alba asked, holding the sheet of paper up.

She gave us a tight, nervous smile. "Absolutely. I wish I could help more. I really wish I could."

Unsure of what to do next, I looked at the girls. Alba nodded her head towards the car.

"Thanks, Tish," said Jax as the five of us left the building with the sheet of paper in hand.

Our case against Tish was getting stronger, but before we could go to Detective Whitman, we'd need more proof.

CHAPTER 25

The five of us crowded around the stainless steel island in the kitchen of my family's bed & breakfast. Mom was in the middle of grating carrots for her tossed salads.

"So Tish was home sick the day of Denise's murder," Mom repeated back as she grated.

I picked up a handful of grated carrots and dropped them in my mouth. "Yup. How convenient, right?"

"Kind of sounds like you girls are on to something," she said. "I just hope you're being careful. If Brittany isn't the murderer, then that means that the murderer is still on the loose. I don't want any of you getting hurt."

Alba nodded. "We're always careful," she assured my mother.

Mom turned and looked at Sweets, who was leaning on her elbow on the counter. "How are Mr. Bailey and Char's wedding plans going, Sweets?"

Sweets sighed and stood up. "I'll be thankful when it's over," she admitted.

Mom made a face. "That's surprising to hear. You're

supposed to be the one that's all about the romance and excitement of a wedding!"

Sweets's head fell into her hands. "I know, I know! It's just that my co-worker, Louis, doesn't like the fact that Mr. Bailey and Char have me making their cake. I don't think he liked me before that either, but the fact that Mr. Bailey is showing me a little bit of preferential treatment has him up in a tizzy. He does nothing but constantly berate me for little things. Like if I don't clean up after myself the second I take something out and use it, he barks at me. This morning he gave me all of his prep-work to do, even though he knew the only task Mr. Bailey wanted me to do was to bake the cakes so they are ready for me to decorate tomorrow."

"He doesn't sound very nice, why don't you tell Mr. Bailey what's going on?" Mom asked.

"Mr. Bailey has so many other things on his plate right now. He's trying to get everything ready for the wedding and keep the bakery running smoothly. I just don't want to bother him."

"You need to learn to stick up for yourself, Sweets. You need to find your voice," said Alba.

Sweets sighed. "I know. Mr. Bailey wasn't even at the bakery this morning, anyway. It was just Louis and me, and he yelled at me practically all morning."

Jax patted Sweets's back. "Oh! Why didn't you tell us, Sweets?"

She shrugged. "I didn't want to complain. We have a lot going on too, trying to solve this murder and all. I really wanted to love this internship with Mr. Bailey, but I'm so miserable about how Louis is treating me that I haven't gotten a chance to enjoy it at all. I know I just need to suck it up," she said sadly.

"Maybe we should put a curse on him," Alba suggested. "That'll teach him a lesson."

Sweets gave Alba a half-hearted smile. "I appreciate that, Alba. I don't think we're quite to that point yet. For now, I'll just do what my mother always told me to do – I'll just kill him with kindness. Maybe eventually he'll come around!"

"Hey, ladies," said my brother's voice from the swinging doors to the dining area.

We all turned around to see Reign coming towards us. He looked at me curiously. The last time we'd seen each other I'd been upset about him pushing Mom and Merrick together. While I still didn't feel good about that, I'd had time to cool down considerably.

"Hey, Reign."

The rest of the girls all said hello, while Jax and I took turns giving him a hug.

He threw his arm around my shoulder. "You feeling better today?"

I nodded and looked up at him. "Much better. Still kind of stressed about the murder, but I'll be okay. How are you?"

"I'm good. We've been busy here. Sorry about the other day," he whispered in my ear.

I playfully slugged his rib cage. "Me too."

"Friends again?"

I nodded. I knew I couldn't get mad at Reign for what Mom decided to do.

"Good." He squeezed my shoulder and planted a big-brotherly kiss on my forehead. He looked up at mom. "Mom, someone's here to see you." He let go of me and threw his arm around Jax's shoulder, causing her to beam up at him.

Mom looked up curiously as she finished putting all the carrots she'd just shredded into a big storage container. "Oh? Who is it?"

"It's Detective Whitman."

Mom's eyes lit up. "Mark's here?"

Reign nodded.

Mom looked down at her dirty hands. "Can you invite him to come back here?"

"Will do," he said cheerfully. He pulled the tail of one of Jax's short braids and headed for the dining room.

Mom hurriedly wiped her hands on her apron and used the back of her wrists to brush her bangs out of her face. "Do I look alright?" she asked.

I gave her a once over and then nodded. "You look gorg," I assured her.

"Yeah, Aunt Linda, you look great," chirped Jax.

"Well, hello, ladies," said Detective Whitman as he breezed into the kitchen.

We all greeted him kindly, but Mom was the happiest to see him. "Hi, Mark, it seems like forever since we've seen each other." The lilting tone of her voice told me that perhaps she was a little nervous seeing him.

He shrugged. "You asked for a little bit of space to get settled into the restaurant," he said kindly. "I was just following orders."

Mom smiled at him coyly. "Yes, I guess that was my fault then, wasn't it?"

"No one is at fault. You just say the word when you have time for something other than work," he said, shooting us girls a little wink. "In fact, if you're not busy this Sunday, I thought I might ask if you'd like to go to Vic Bailey and Char Maxwell's wedding with me," he suggested jovially.

My mom's smile immediately vanished, and she frowned. "Oh. The wedding. Yes, about the wedding..." she began hesitantly.

No Mom. Please don't tell him you've decided to go with Merrick! I thought nervously.

She laughed nervously. "I was invited to the wedding earlier in the week. Umm, Merrick asked me to go with him. I hadn't said yes until just this morning," she said.

The deflated, hurt look on Detective Whitman's face made me cringe. His back stiffened. "I see." He nodded at her curtly.

"Please don't be hurt," she begged.

He shook his head. "No. No. I'm not hurt. I'm fine. You have the right to do whatever you want," he said quickly. Then he nodded at all of us. "Well, girls, Linda, I probably better get out of your hair."

Without another word, he made a beeline for the doorway. I was sure he was feeling incredibly foolish right now. I chased after him. "Detective Whitman, wait!"

He didn't stop. Instead, I had to chase him through the dining room to the front door of the restaurant.

In a bit of a huff, he stopped. "Yes, Mercy. What is it? I really have to go."

"I'm sorry about my mom," I said to him. "I didn't think she was going to say yes to him."

He turned around, ignoring my words and pulled the door open and stepped out onto the street.

"Wait!" I called out.

He stopped for a second and looked at me. "I don't want to talk about this, Mercy. I need to get back to work."

"I was just curious if you had any new leads on Denise Whiting's murder investigation."

"We have a few new things. Nothing I can really talk

about," he said curtly. I could tell he just wanted to get in his car and drive away.

"You can't give me anything?" I pleaded. "We've been trying to do what we can to get new information for you. We might have something soon."

His shoulders relaxed slightly. "I hope you're not impeding my investigation."

I shook my head vigorously. "Oh no. We're staying out of your way. But if there is anything you can share, I'd love to hear it."

He sighed and took a pause, looking down at the keys in his hand. Then he looked up at me. "Fine. The knife that was used to kill her didn't come from the school cafeteria."

My jaw dropped. That was huge. If we could find out where it had come from maybe we'd be able to figure out who the killer was! "Do you know where it came from?"

He shook his head. "We're doing some work right now to trace where it came from, but those results might not be back for awhile."

"Okay. Do you have a picture of the knife available? Maybe we'll come up with some ideas!"

"Mercy…" he sighed. "Let the police handle this."

"Oh, we are totally letting the police handle it," I assured him. "We just want to help. Denise was our friend, and we know Brittany didn't do it – we only want to help get her free."

He groaned.

"What harm can we possibly do by having a picture of the knife?" I begged harder. "Holly might see the knife and have a vision or something. I promise to share whatever information we find out!"

"Alright. I'll text you the image file," he relented.

I smiled. "Great! Thanks, Detective!"

～

On our way back to The Institute we stopped at the Chicken Shack to grab a quick bite to eat since we were all tired of pizza and donuts. No sooner had we pulled out of the drive-thru and gotten back onto the main drag towards The Institute than a car sped past us.

"Was that Tori that just passed us?" Jax asked, shoving herself between the front seats to look out the window more closely.

I pulled out another chicken fry and stuck the whole thing in my mouth. "I have no idea, I wasn't paying attention," I said with my mouth full.

Sweets nodded. "It looked like her."

I looked into the front seat at Alba who was riding shotgun. "Did you see her?"

"No, but if it's her I wonder why she's off campus," she said curiously.

"Maybe she's tired of pizza too," Holly suggested with a mouthful of chicken salad.

"You want me to follow her car?" Sweets asked Alba.

Alba nodded as she took a bite of her sandwich. "Might as well. We have an hour before our next class."

When the car in front of us swerved into the turning lane to take a left towards Char Maxwell's neighborhood, Sweets got into the turning lane too.

"Not too close," I said from the backseat. "She'll know we're following her."

"I don't want to lose her in traffic, though."

We all looked out our windows.

"What traffic?" asked Alba.

"Yeah, there's not even another car on the road, Sweets," Holly agreed.

Sweets's head swiveled to the left and then the right, and when she saw no cars, she turned in the direction the car in front of us had turned. "I don't know. I've never been in hot pursuit of a car before."

I laughed from the back seat. "I'm not sure you can consider this hot pursuit. Isn't hot pursuit when you're actually speeding?"

Sweets looked down at her odometer. "I'm going thirty-five in a thirty!" Sweets declared.

"Whoa," I said dramatically.

Suddenly Sweets threw her arms up in the air. "See! You guys made me not pay attention! Now I don't know where she went!" she hollered in frustration.

Alba wiped her mouth with her napkin and then pointed to the side street the car had just turned down. "There she is. She parked in front of that house."

I looked around. The houses in the area looked familiar. "Isn't this the street Char lives on?"

Alba pointed to the little house that we'd found Tony in on the day before Thanksgiving. "Yup. That's Char's right there."

"Park here, Sweets. We don't want to get too close," whispered Jax.

"Why are you whispering?" Alba asked, turning her head slightly to look at Jax, who had stuck her head into the front seat again.

"I don't want her to hear us," said Jax with a broad smile.

"She didn't even get out of her car yet!" Alba said, rolling her eyes.

"She's getting out!" I said, keeping my eyes trained on the car just up the block from where we were parked.

A familiar frame stepped out of the car.

"It *is* Tori!" said Sweets excitedly. "Where's she going?"

"Maybe she has family in town," Alba suggested.

Holly peered out the window. "Is she from Aspen Falls?"

I shook my head, remembering what she had said on the first day of class. "I'm pretty sure she said she was from Iowa."

"Then who in the world could she possibly be going to see in Aspen Falls?" asked Alba.

We watched her walk up to a house across the street and two houses down from Char's house. "I guess we'll find out," I said. I suddenly found myself holding my breath as we waited for someone to answer the door. When the door finally opened, the girls gasped. We all recognized the head that popped out the door!

CHAPTER 26

"It's Midge!" Jax announced with surprise. "Why is Tori going to see Midge?"

I shook my head. "I have no idea, but I guarantee we are going to find out!"

Holly looked at me curiously. "How are we going to find out? You think Tori will tell us if we ask her?"

"No, but Midge will," I said.

"We're going to go ask Midge why Tori came to visit her," Sweets questioned nervously.

"Why not?"

The car went silent.

Finally, Jax sat back in the backseat. "So we just wait out here for Tori to come back outside? And then what?"

"Then we go knock on the door just like she did!" I replied.

Alba took another bite of her sandwich. "Works for me!"

Holly groaned. "We have to sit out here until she comes out? That could take forever!"

"What do you think they're talking about in there?" I asked as I nibbled on another fry.

"Maybe Tori's guilty, and she's trying to get Midge to incriminate Brittany more," Sweets suggested.

"It wouldn't surprise me if Tori is guilty. She's evil, I'm telling you," said Alba.

"Maybe she's not guilty – maybe she's trying to investigate the murder," suggested Holly.

"You think so?" Jax asked. Her eyebrows were drawn up into little peaks on her forehead.

Holly shrugged. "I really don't have any idea."

We speculated on Tori's motives for several more minutes before the door opened and Tori came back outside. She shot Midge a small wave before walking back to her car.

"Pull up in front of Midge's house, Sweets," Alba instructed.

"Okay." Sweets put the car in gear, and as the blue car pulled away from the curb, Sweets took her spot in front of Midge's house.

"Like that wasn't completely obvious that we were waiting for Tori to leave?" I suggested.

"Alba told me to!" argued Sweets.

"I know. I was talking to Alba. Let's hope Tori didn't see us following her."

Alba shoved my worry aside. "You worry too much, Red. She didn't see us."

"Okay. Well, let's get moving. We're running out of time," I said. I opened up my door and climbed out. Seconds later I was knocking on Midge's door, and the girls were all standing behind me like a bunch of girl scouts selling cookies.

"What are you going to say?" whispered Alba.

I shrugged as the door opened. There wasn't any time to dwell on it. "Hi, Midge," I said brightly.

She looked at all of our faces curiously. "Wow, this must be – 'visit your local cafeteria lady day,' huh?"

We all nodded. "We just saw Tori leaving. That was interesting. What did she want?" I asked nonchalantly.

Midge opened the door wider. "Come in. Oh, she just had a few questions for me."

"What kind of questions?" Alba asked.

"Honestly, she wondered why I wasn't at work the morning of Denise's murder," she admitted.

"Did she?" asked Alba suspiciously. "Why did she want to know that?"

Midge shrugged. "It seemed like maybe she was trying to investigate the murder on her own. Is that what you girls are doing? I *have* heard about your reputation for solving murders."

We all smiled. "Yeah, I guess you could say we're trying to solve the mystery too," I said with a nod.

She clucked her tongue at us. "I suspected as much. Well, have a seat. Tell me what you'd like to know, and I'll answer you as best as I can." She strutted to her recliner and sat down while the rest of us found spots on her sofa with Jax and I leaning on the arm rests. "Fire away."

Alba looked at me first. I gave her a little nod of encouragement. "So, why *weren't* you at work that morning?" she began.

"Well. Like I told Brittany when I called in sick that morning, Sorceress Stone when she called me late that afternoon, Detective Whitman when he came to see me two days ago, and Tori just a few minutes ago – I was just getting over a miserable case of the flu, and I really didn't want to pass it on to all you girls. So I decided to stay home one more day and make sure I was all better before I went back to work. I know how germs spread in a school. I had no idea all this was about to go down."

"Can anyone attest to you being at home that morning?" Alba asked.

She shook her head. "No. That's the problem with living alone, I guess. No one to vouch for you when you're accused of murder."

Jax's hand shot out in front of her defensively. "Oh, we're not *accusing* anyone of murder, Midge. We're just trying to eliminate suspects at this point."

Midge shrugged. "It's alright. I understand. I want to know who killed Denise, too. I considered her a friend. No, I don't have anyone to vouch for me, but I can get proof that I saw a doctor for the flu if that helps."

"We believe you," Sweets assured her.

"So, what's the deal with Hobbs?" she asked.

"Do you think she did it?" I asked her.

Midge thought about it for a long second. Then she shook her head. "I know they've got her locked up for it, but I can't picture Hobbs stabbing anyone. She's too nice."

"She could be leading a secret double life," I suggested.

Midge leaned back into her chair and laughed at that notion. "I suppose she could be. Killers would probably have to lead secret double lives to kill someone, wouldn't they?"

"Mm-hmm. Do you have any idea what was going on in Denise's personal life?" Alba asked.

"Her personal life? Like with her husband and kids?" she clarified.

Alba nodded. "Yeah, especially between her and her husband."

Midge's head teetered back and forth on her shoulders.

"I do know something that I actually haven't told anyone else. I suppose I should have told Detective Whitman."

That lead-up piqued our interest. "What is it?" Jax asked.

"Cal asked Denise for a divorce," she revealed.

My eyes widened. She knew about the divorce! "He did? She told you?" I asked.

She nodded. "Yeah. She told me. But she also told me that she wasn't going to give it to him."

This was new information. Alba looked at me curiously and then she looked back at Midge. "If he wanted a divorce, why wouldn't she give him one?"

"Because he was having an affair and she knew it. She didn't want him leaving her for the mistress. She said it was too humiliating."

"Who was he having an affair with?!" I wanted to hear Midge confirm what we already knew.

"His secretary, Tish Thomas," she said matter-of-factly. She leaned over and peered at us a little more closely. "But then, of course, you girls already knew that, didn't you."

I think the smile on Jax and Sweets's face gave that away, so we nodded. "Yeah, we figured that part out. But you didn't tell Detective Whitman? Why not?"

She shrugged and leaned back into her oversized chair. "It wasn't the best-kept secret in Aspen Falls. You girls figured it out. I think it was pretty obvious. I'm sure Whitman has figured it out by now. I didn't want him thinking I was trying to throw suspicion off of myself and onto Tish. I thought it might make *me* look guilty for know-ing," she admitted.

"That makes sense," Jax agreed.

"So do you think Tish could have done something so

evil as to kill one of her closest friends just to get Cal?" I asked her.

"Between you and me, I don't think Denise and Tish were as close as one might believe. I'd heard Denise complain about Tish flirting with her husband plenty of times before it came to light that he was actually having an affair. I think it was a case of – keep your friends close, but your enemies closer."

"What about Tori, Midge?" Alba asked.

Midge looked at us curiously. "What do you mean, 'what about Tori'?"

"We have our suspicions about her, too. She's been acting really strangely since the murder."

Midge shrugged. "I don't even know the girl. Today was the first time I've met her."

"Yeah, she's a new student," Jax pointed out.

"And yet she seems to have an awful big interest in the murder, for a new student," I commented.

Midge nodded. "I *did* think it seemed kind of odd that she was asking me questions about the murder. I mean, you girls, I understand. That makes sense. It's, sort of, become your new *thing*. But why Tori?"

Why Tori indeed! I stood up. "Thanks for talking to us, Midge. When will you be back at The Institute?"

"Whenever they re-open the kitchen. It sounds like I'll be there Monday to get food ordered."

"The sooner, the better! We're getting tired of donuts and pizza," Sweets told her as the rest of the girls stood up too.

"Oh, you poor things!" Midge said with a sad face.

"Will you be taking over full-time for Denise now?" I asked.

"Sorceress Stone asked me to, but I like my current

schedule. I told her I'd go full-time until they can hire someone else for Denise's position."

"Okay, well thanks for all the help, Midge," I said, before following the girls out the door.

"Thanks for stopping by, girls. Holler if I can be of any more help!"

"Thanks, Midge," said Jax.

"Bye, Midge," we all said as we walked out the door and headed back to the car.

When we were back on the road again, we immediately started chatting about the whole thing. "It's really starting to sound more and more like Tish is our killer," said Alba.

"She just seems too nice to have killed Denise!" said Jax sadly.

"Looks can be deceiving," I said wistfully. We learned that the hard way when it came to solving all the other murders.

"I'll drop you girls off at Warner Hall and then go park, okay?" Sweets asked.

I looked down at my watch. "That little stakeout took so much longer than I thought it would. We're probably not going to make it to our next class if we don't just go straight inside. I have to run upstairs to grab my backpack before class."

Holly nodded. "I have to grab mine too. There's no way we'll make it if we have to go all the way through the tunnels and then up to our rooms."

"My next class is with my mom. If I'm late, she's going to know something is up. We *cannot* be late," Jax insisted with wide eyes.

Sweets looked at us in her rearview mirror. "So? We're going to the front door?"

"You'd think by the time we get there Stone would be in class already," I rationalized.

Alba nodded, making the decision final. "We'll take the chance. We'll get out with you in the girls' parking lot, Sweets."

Sweets took the right side of the fork at the big Paranormal Institute sign and followed the long driveway up to our parking lot. The car jerked to a halt in a parking spot and the five us jumped out and ran to the front door as if hell's demons were at our feet.

Wordlessly, Alba threw open the Winston Hall front door. We all shuffled inside, but no sooner had we taken a few steps through the door than we discovered Sorceress Stone standing at the bottom of the stone staircase to our rooms.

Immediately my heart dropped into my stomach, and my feet became glued to the ground. I stopped moving, as did the rest of the girls.

Behind Sorceress Stone on the stairway was Tori Decker. That witch!

CHAPTER 27

"Well, well, well...what do we have here?" Sorceress Stone's sharp voice cackled. "And exactly where have you been, ladies?"

No one spoke.

"They went to town," said Tori haughtily.

I could have wrung her neck.

Sorceress Stone rolled her eyes. "Yes, I *know that*, Miss Decker. I was looking for information from *them*."

Tori's smile faded, but the smug grin on her face told us she was still pleased with herself. I couldn't wait to get my hands on her. There was no doubt in my mind that Alba was thinking the same thing.

"Well, ladies?" Sorceress Stone asked, staring through slitted eyes at the group of us.

"I – we," I began uncomfortably.

"We ran out to get some lunch," said Sweets. "We were all tired of pizza."

That didn't soften her in the least. She raised one snowy eyebrow and looked down her nose at us.

"That doesn't change the fact that you deliberately

disobeyed an order. Now, you leave me no choice, but to sentence you to time in the tower for your insubordination."

My shoulders wilted. This was too much. And it was all because of Tori Decker! I had had it with that girl! She was the one that started the fight that got us in trouble in the first place and now she was the one reporting us for leaving campus.

"Ask Tori how she knows we were off campus!" I demanded. My temper was at a raging boil by now.

Sorceress Stone shook her head. "No need. I already know how she knows," she said.

Tori nodded haughtily. "I had a friend in town who told me."

"That's a lie!" Jax hollered. "We saw Tori off campus!"

Sorceress Stone's hands sliced the air. "Silence!" she shouted. "You will follow me."

Sorceress Stone turned and began the way towards the tower. I stood with my Converse sneakers firmly anchored in place. Why did I have to listen to her? I was an adult. I shouldn't be treated this way!

Shockingly, Alba walked past me without a hint of irritation or concern. "We've got an escape, Red. What's your problem?" she whispered in my ear as she walked by me.

The thought made me smile. In my rage, I had forgotten about that important detail. I worked to suppress my smile and instead I pretended I was upset about having to go back upstairs.

"Tori, you can follow as well," Sorceress Stone called down when she got towards the top of the stairs.

Happy to follow us to the tower to gloat, Tori brought up the rear of the line. Single file we crept up the many hundreds of steps. *This is better than doing squats. My glutes are going to be sore in the morning.* I thought as I walked.

When we reached the top of the stairs, Sorceress Stone unlocked the door and the squad stepped inside willingly. On the other side of the door, Tori crowed gleefully. "Bye, girls. Get some beauty rest while you're in there. *You need it!*"

Sorceress Stone turned towards Tori. "Miss Decker, this is the last stop for you as well."

"What?"

"You heard me. In the room."

"But – why? I wasn't off campus! I told you!"

"Miss Decker. I *know* you were off campus."

Tori shook her head defiantly. "No, I wasn't! You're going to take *their* word for it? That's not fair! You have no proof!"

Sorceress Stone put one hand on her bony hip and extended her other, pointing into the tower room calmly. "I saw you drive back onto campus, Miss Decker. Now must I force you, or will you go on your own?"

"I don't want to be in there with them!" she cried angrily. Her face had quickly filled with blood, and she looked crazed.

Sorceress Stone's steely gaze told us she really didn't care *what* Tori wanted as she continued to point towards the tower room.

Tori turned towards the five of us. We had each taken an offensive stance around the room and had our best death stares plastered on our faces. Prisoners in a murder wing would have looked more welcoming than we did. Grudgingly she followed Stone's orders. "Ugh," she groaned. "This isn't fair."

"Life's not fair, Decker," said Alba as she sidled up to the new girl.

"I'll be back to get you in the morning," sang Sorceress Stone as the door slammed in our faces.

Instinctively the five of us circled wide around Tori. We had all had enough of her antics over the course of the week. She owed us a lot, and her bill was due. Step by step, the five of us made the circle smaller. She held her hands up defensively. "Look, girls, I'm sorry I told Stone on you," she muttered nervously.

No one spoke as we closed in on her. Alba's fist ground into her flattened palm. Jax plunged her fists into her jacket pockets and cocked her head to the side in an effort to look vicious. Had I not been so angry, I might have found the humor in the situation. We probably looked a bit like a gang from *West Side Story*. All that was missing was the music.

"Can't we just get along here?" she begged, her voice caught in her throat as she spoke.

"We didn't start this," I said to her as I finally stood eye to eye with her, with my back arched and my chest extended.

Alba stood shoulder to shoulder with me. She tilted her head to her right and then the left, cracking her neck intimidatingly. "No, we didn't start this. But I think it's about time we finished it!"

Suddenly we heard a cry from the other side of the room. Shocked that we weren't alone in the tower, our heads swiveled to see another girl locked in the room. She was in a heap on the floor, and her face was obscured. A green glow surrounded her body as many of the other visions we'd recently seen had done. It pulled our attention away from Tori just long enough that when we turned back to face her again, she had slunk away from the circle.

She rushed to the side of the crying girl.

"Oh, you poor thing!" Tori cried. "What's the matter? Can we help you?"

I rolled my eyes. We all knew better now. This was just another one of her conjured illusions. The five of us watched her as she pretended to console the apparition.

"You can drop the act, Decker," said Alba snidely. "We know what you're up to."

Tori shook her head from the floor. "I don't know what you're talking about. This girl is obviously injured."

Even Jax had lost her patience with Tori. "Oh stop acting, Tori. We know that you're the one making these fake visions."

"Fake visions? I have no idea what you're talking about."

Alba nodded and then with one tiny flick of her finger, she hurled an energy bolt at the glowing green vision. The glowing figure immediately dissipated into the air like the ghost that it was.

Tori stood up in a huff. Her arms slammed down to her side, and her fake crying halted. A look of bitterness and hatred quickly replaced it. "Oh fine!" she screamed into the air. "Ugh! You people make me sick!"

"Likewise!" I threw back at her. "We're over you, Decker. You're at the wrong school. The Institute isn't a school for the wicked and evil. It's just witch college – for good witches. Not spoiled brats like you."

"You think you're so great, Mercy Habernackle. You and the rest of your Witch Squad. Just because the entire school talks about you like you're *Gods* or something. But you're not! You're just witches like the rest of us. You don't walk on water. I'm smarter than all of you combined, and I'm going to solve Denise Whiting's murder to prove it! Then everyone in school will know what a bunch of phonies your Witch Squad really is!"

Sweets's eyes widened. "Were you looking for clues when you broke into the storage room where Denise was killed?"

"Oh, that was you in the hallway? You're about as subtle as a rhino in a wind chime factory," she mocked.

Sweets furrowed her eyebrows at the girl.

"So that's why you conjured the fake vision of Denise's ghost saying Brittany did it?" I asked, astounded.

"And why you showed me a vision of Brittany leaning over Denise's body," noted Holly.

"Well, duh! Morons! You idiots will buy anything," she scoffed.

Alba rolled her eyes. "We didn't believe your dumb visions for a second! Why do you think we're still investigating?"

Tori laughed as she walked towards Holly, Alba, and me. "Well you three certainly believed my last vision!" she said spitefully. She placed one hand on her chest, and in a mock Holly voice, she teased, "Girls! Hugh needs our help!"

"You witch!" I raged, charging at her then. I was anxious to pound my fist into her ugly face, but Alba beat me to the punch. She flicked her finger again, this time she aimed right at Tori. The blast sent Tori reeling backwards, crashing into the furthest stone wall. Immediately Tori crumpled to the ground.

"What did you do that for?" I challenged, looking at Alba. My pulse thrummed in my ears. My fury demanded to be unleashed. "I wanted to smash her face in myself!"

"I owed her one for the cafeteria. You can have the next one," Alba assured me.

Sweets stepped forward nervously. "Come on you two. I know you don't like Tori, but we can't just spend the day beating her up. We could seriously injure her and that's not the kind of witches that we are!"

Holly nodded. "Yeah. As furious as I am at her for messing with my visions and causing us to be cold in a hole for two hours, she didn't do any permanent damage – so we can't do any permanent damage to her."

Alba rolled her eyes and dramatically sighed. "You've got to be kidding me! Her little *trick* knocked me out cold for two hours!"

"Yeah, and you lived to tell about it," said Holly calmly.

Alba shook her head in frustration. "Why do you guys always have to be such Goody Two- Shoes?"

"It's not about being Goody Two-Shoes, Alba," Jax explained patiently. "It's about being good people. We were good people before Tori got here and we need to be good people despite her. Otherwise, we've allowed her to lower us to her level."

I groaned. Shockingly, Jax had a point. "Ugh. But I want to punch her!" I whined.

"So do I!" agreed Alba.

We all looked over at Tori, who was sprawled out on the floor, holding her head in a daze.

"The girls are right though, Alba. We have to rise above. I know I don't want to be like her. You don't either. Come on. We have a murder to solve. Let's get out of here," I said. "We'll just leave her here to ride out the punishment alone. Tomorrow morning we'll sneak back in and we'll deal with her then."

Alba looked at Tori angrily. "Fine," she growled. "Let's get out of here before she figures out how we escaped."

CHAPTER 28

"**W**e need to regroup!" I said as I wore a path into my dorm room rug.

Alba leaned back in my desk chair. "Yeah. Now that we know what Tori's motive to lie was, I think we can rule her out as the murderer."

Holly looked up sharply. "You think she was telling the truth?"

"Honestly, I never really thought she did it," said Alba. "I just didn't understand her motivation to frame Brittany. I still don't know that I get that part, I mean why Brittany?"

"If her intentions were to show us up, then she needed to frame someone while she bought herself time to find the real killer."

"Yeah, but *why Brittany*?" Holly countered.

"Well, she didn't want us to point our fingers at the real killer, right? Otherwise, we win."

"So she had to frame someone that obviously *didn't* kill Denise," rationalized Sweets.

I nodded. "Exactly. Brittany was the most obvious choice. We all agreed from the beginning that we couldn't see her being the killer. But by pinning it on her, that gave Tori time to nose around before we could. Plus we look like idiots for pointing our fingers at the wrong suspect. This whole thing was about her trying to make us look like a bunch of jerks," I said with frustration. My temperature was starting to rise again. "I should've just punched her when I had the chance."

"It wouldn't have done any good," said Sweets from the bed.

"Yes, it would! It would have made me feel better!" I countered testily.

"Can we not talk about Tori?" Holly asked. "The thought of her just makes me madder. But she's not getting us any close to finding the murderer."

I leaned against Jax's side of the closet and looked at the girls. "Whitman thinks it was a woman, so it can't be Cal. It has to be Tish. We just need to find the proof!"

"We have to find some way to prove that Tish wasn't sick in bed the morning of the murder as she claims," said Sweets.

"But how? That's going to be impossible!" I whined.

"We need to get out of here again," said Alba. "We can't investigate if we're stuck in our dorm room."

"If we go back out into town before Stone lets us out of purgatory tomorrow morning and she finds out...we're dead meat," said Holly with wide eyes.

"Yeah, there is *no way* I'm sneaking off campus again. I can't. She'll send me to normal college. *I can't go to normal college!*" cried Jax, nearly on the verge of tears.

I put a hand on either side of Jax's shoulders and shook her. "Relax, Jax. We'll figure something out."

"So we have to wait until tomorrow when she lets us out of the tower, but then what? We're still not supposed to leave campus," said Alba. "Are you guys all wimping out on me?"

Suddenly Sweets raised her hand up excitedly. "I've got an idea! I think I know exactly how to get her to let us go into town!"

~

THE NEXT MORNING, WE ROSE AT THE CRACK OF DAWN, AND with Jax on the back of my broomstick, the five of us flew up to the bell tower, stashed our broomsticks, moved the brush we'd put in front of the wide open door and descended the stairway.

When we came strutting in through the back of the closet, Tori pounced on us immediately. "There you are!" she bellowed. "How did you get out?"

We simply smiled at her mischievously but didn't say a word.

She crossed her arms across her chest in a huff. "I'm going to tell Stone you snuck out," she promised.

Alba pointed her magic finger at Tori, brandishing it around like a weapon. "You will do no such thing. Do you understand? The jig is up. We know what you've been up to and we know how to deal with you. If you so much as sneeze funny in our direction, I'll blast you so hard you'll forget what normal feels like!"

Tori's eyes widened, and she backed away from Alba. "You wouldn't!" she said angrily.

Alba cocked one eyebrow up. "Try me!"

I nodded. "You see, Tori, I think the six of us need to come to a little understanding – if we're all going to go to school together, I think we need to get along.

Tori's attitude seemed to change, almost instantaneously. "You mean we need to call a truce?" she asked.

We all nodded. "Yes," I agreed. "Like a truce. You leave us alone, and we'll leave you alone."

A smile covered Tori's face, almost too easily. "Sure. Let's call a truce," she agreed.

Jax smiled. "Really?"

Tori smiled back at her. "Really. In fact, I think we could actually all be friends now."

"Are you gonna tell Stone we weren't here last night?" asked Alba.

Tori shook her head. "Oh no, I wouldn't dare tell on my new friends!" she insisted.

Something smelled fishy to me, but before we had time to dwell on it, the large, wooden arched door swung open with a giant creaking noise.

Sorceress Stone stood before us. Seeing the six of us standing in front of the door seemed to surprise her. "Well. Very good. The six of you are all still alive. That must mean you managed to control yourselves overnight."

We all looked at Tori. I was just waiting for her to tell Sorceress Stone that somehow we had managed to sneak out. But shockingly, she kept her word and just smiled and nodded.

"Very well then. You may go," she said and stood to the side to allow us all to pass.

Tori darted down the steps ahead of us, happy to be released. The rest of us managed to dawdle behind until she was safely out of earshot.

Sweets stepped forward first. "Sorceress Stone, I need to leave campus today. I'm responsible for making the cake for Mr. Bailey and Charlotte Maxwell's wedding. I've already made the layers, but I need to go to the bakery and move them to the reception hall where I will finish decorating them."

Sorceress Stone nodded. "Yes, I see. Very well. You may go."

Sweets cleared her throat nervously. "Umm. Actually, I was wondering if you would allow the rest of these girls to go with me. I have a lot of work to do and I could really use the extra help. Otherwise, I don't think I'll get the cake done in time for the wedding tomorrow."

Sorceress Stone let out a sigh. She looked down at us for several long seconds before finally nodding. "Very well. They may go."

We all tried to hold back our excitement over being allowed out of the building.

"Thank you, Sorceress," said Sweets as she walked passed her into the hallway.

Sorceress Stone nodded at each of us as we passed her by and made our way back downstairs.

Jax was the last to pass her mother. She stopped in front of Sorceress Stone, who continued to look down her nose at the group of us. We all waited for her on the stairs. Jax gave her a tight little smile and then impetuously threw her scrawny arms around her mother. "Thanks, Mom!" she said and then promptly let go. "See you later!"

CHAPTER 29

SWEETS

Thirty minutes later we were dressed and ready for the trip into town. We had a lot to do. I hadn't been lying to Sorceress Stone when I said that I needed the girls' help finishing my cake. I was just relieved that I had the cake parts made and only had to focus on assembling it, frosting it, and decorating it, though that could take me hours. I was disappointed that I'd probably have to let the girls do most of their sleuthing without me.

"So where are we going first?" Jax asked as she poked her head into the front seat again as usual.

I turned my head sideways to look at her just over my shoulder. "Do you have your seatbelt on?"

Jax looked back at the empty clasp on the seat. "No."

"Do you mind putting it on?" I asked calmly. Jax had a horrible habit of bouncing around in the car while I was driving. The poor girl just didn't know how to keep still.

"Oh, okay," she said meekly. She sat back down and quietly put on her seatbelt.

I adjusted my rearview mirror to peer at her until I heard the clasp snap into place. "Thank you. Now, what's first is that we need to go to the bakery to get the pieces of the cake that I made yesterday. We're going to take them over to the reception hall so we can start assembling them and then I'll worry about the frosting and the decorations," I explained.

Holly made a face. "So you seriously *do* need our help with your cakes?"

"Of course I do! At least I could use your help getting everything over to the reception hall. Then I can work on it while you guys go do whatever sleuthing you need to do!"

From my rearview mirror, I could see Holly rolling her eyes and looking out the side window. "Fine," she muttered.

I tried to ignore the blatant disdain for manual labor in her voice. "Thank you," I chirped.

I parallel parked my car in front of the bakery instead of parking on the side street like I usually did. That way we had an easier route to carry all the necessary things to my car.

We entered the bakery chatting a mile a minute as usual. The sound of the doorbell chiming brought Louis out of his hiding spot. The pleasant expression on his face faded the second he saw that it was me.

"What are you doing here? It's Saturday. You don't work today," he grumbled.

Alba gave him a curious look as if to say "is this guy for real?"

"I have to pick up the cake for Mr. Bailey's wedding," I told him as I walked around the counter.

He cleared his throat as if he had a response to that, but instead, he held his tongue.

"Come on, girls, this way," I said as I led them around the corner into the kitchen.

Louis stood in the way of them following me. "No non-staff allowed in the kitchen," he stated firmly.

I turned around and looked at him with my eyebrows furrowed. "They're just going to help me carry the cakes out to the car. They aren't going to be baking or anything."

He shrugged, uncaringly. "No non-staff behind the counter. Bakery rules."

"Where's Mr. Bailey?" I asked him, looking back into the kitchen. I was sure he'd let the girls back to help.

Louis rolled his eyes. "Where do you think? His wedding is tomorrow! Would you be working the day before your wedding?"

"Ugh," I groaned. I had had it with Louis. I glanced back at the girls to tell them they could wait for me in the dining area. The looks on their faces told me what they thought of Louis's attitude. "Fine. Girls, I'll bring the cake parts out here."

Without another word, I spun on my heel and turned towards the kitchen, where I'd put the cake I'd made in the walk-in cooler. Louis followed me and stopped when I put my hand on the stainless steel handle.

"Oh, and clean up your mess while you're in there," he said snottily.

"My mess?" I asked curiously. "I didn't leave a mess when I left yesterday."

He lifted one shoulder and walked away. I pulled the cooler door open and was stunned and horrified to find my beautiful layers of cake all on the floor in broken piles.

"Oh no!" I screamed. My heart crumbled in my chest as I realized that all my hard work the day before had been for not! Louis had destroyed Mr. Bailey's wedding cake! I slammed the door shut. "How dare you!"

Louis, who had waltzed over to the sink turned around

and put his hand to his chest in mock surprise. "You really should be more careful with how you store things in the cooler."

"That was not my fault!" I insisted. "I put the cakes safely inside cardboard boxes to make sure that they were safe from getting accidentally bumped."

"Apparently you weren't careful enough. I don't know how they got like that," he claimed.

"You most certainly do know how it happened, because *you did it*! And if I were to venture a guess, I would guess that you did it intentionally!"

Louis shook his head. "Now why would I do a thing like that?"

"Because you don't like me. You haven't liked me for some reason since the day that I set foot in here!"

He scoffed at the notion. "I have no reason not to like you."

I groaned. I would never be able to prove to Mr. Bailey that Louis smashed my cakes intentionally. Instead, I strutted out to the lobby area. "Let's go, girls."

"We heard you hollering," said Jax as I came around the corner. "Is everything alright?"

Hot tears burned in my eyes, but I was too infuriated for them to fall. "No. Everything is not alright. Louis intentionally smashed the wedding cakes!"

"That creep did what?!" Alba asked in surprise, her eyes widening.

"Forget it," I said, leaving the girls' side. I burst out of the glass doors of the bakery and out onto the street where the brisk winter air cooled my overheated face. "We're going to the grocery store, and we're getting new ingredients and then we're going to the reception hall, and I'll make a new cake there. I'm not going to let Louis ruin Mr. Bailey and Char's big day!"

THE RECEPTION HALL WAS UNLOCKED WHEN WE GOT THERE. Mr. Bailey and Char had already begun decorating it. As Char had requested, they were going with a festive Hawaiian theme. The decorations weren't subtle as many weddings were – they were over the top, bright, and colorful with colorful balloons and streamers everywhere, fake banana trees and coconut trees stood in the corners of the room with real fruit and bright tropical flowers as centerpieces.

"Wow," I said, stunned when we entered the big dining area.

"Yeah, wow is right," Mercy agreed, her jaw hanging open.

A sound from the storage room caught our ear, and suddenly Char appeared in her usual high-water pants, white sneakers, and visor.

"Hi, Char," I called out.

"Oh, hello, girls! What do you think of our decorations?" she asked, standing back with her hands on her hips triumphantly.

There was a slight pause while we all collected our thoughts. Finally, Jax nodded. "It's – lovely," she said.

Lovely wasn't the word that came to mind, but I was glad Jax came up with it. It was probably better than the word on the tip of my lips – tacky. I giggled to myself and heaved my bags of groceries towards the kitchen.

"Whatcha got there, girls?" Char asked. "Need any help?"

"No, we've got it, Char. You just focus on your decorations. We are going to work on your wedding cake," I told her. Hoping she wouldn't ask why we were getting such a late start on it. I didn't want to have to complain to her that Louis had ruined her first cake.

"Where's Mr. Bailey?" Mercy asked, looking around.

"Oh, he's picking up his suit from the dry cleaners for the wedding. He'll stop in later and see how decorations are going. Decorating really isn't his thing. He's left it all up to me," Char announced happily.

"Okay, well, we'll just be in the kitchen baking up a storm, don't mind us," I said as I pointed towards the kitchen.

"Hey – what were you girls doing parked in front of my house yesterday? I thought maybe you were coming to see me and then you never came to the door," she said.

"Oh, we were visiting Midge," chirped Jax.

"My neighbor Midge?" Char asked.

Jax nodded. "Mm-hmm. Do you know her?"

"Of course I know her. She's my neighbor. We've known each other for years. She'll be at the wedding. What were you girls doing visiting Midge?"

"We've been working on the Whiting murder, and Midge was her co-worker. We just had a couple of questions to ask her," I said.

Char nodded and then peered at us more closely. "You don't think Midge had anything to do with Denise's murder do you?!"

"She said she was home sick the day of the murder," said Alba. "Which we can't prove, so we can't rule her out. We don't have a motive, though."

Char nodded. "Oh yeah, she was sick last weekend. I remember that. I brought her soup and crackers and a couple of bottles of Sprite. She was having problems keeping things down."

Alba nodded. "That's good to know. Thanks."

I looked down at the time on my Fitbit nervously. "Okay, Char, well we better get baking. Lots to do and not a lot of time to do it."

Char looked at our bags. "You're just getting started on the cake now? I thought Vic was going to give you time yesterday to work on it during your work hours?"

I giggled nervously. "Oh, yeah, hehe. No worries, I'll get it done in time!"

Char nodded. "Okay. Have fun. I'll stay out of your hair."

I rushed the girls into the kitchen. I didn't want Char asking any more questions about why the cake wasn't further along.

"Why didn't you tell her what Louis did?" Alba asked as I flipped the lights on in the kitchen.

I heaved my groceries up onto the counter in the large commercial sized kitchen. "It's the woman's wedding weekend. She shouldn't have to deal with my stress. I'll get it figured out."

Holly looked around as she put her groceries down too. "This is a gigantic kitchen."

"It's huge," Jax agreed. "Way bigger than the kitchen at the b&b."

"Definitely better that we bake it here rather than at the b&b," Mercy agreed.

"Yeah, if we had baked it there I knew we'd be competing for space. This is nice. Now we can all spread out."

Jax pulled open a double set of wooden doors in the

back of the kitchen. "Why do they keep so much food in here?"

As I unpacked my bags, I looked back at Jax. "Oh. Their church does a food pantry here for the less fortunate," I explained. "Char mentioned something about it the other day."

"So. Let's get started. We need to get the cakes made so they can cool and then we can all go do a little more investigating, but first we need to have the cakes done."

"Here are some aprons," said Jax, passing one out to everyone.

Holly took one and pulled it over her head. "Where do we start?"

$\sim$

TWO AND A HALF HOURS AND SIX LAYERS LATER, WE FINISHED step one: baking. After setting the cake layers out to cool, I put myself in charge of washing the dishes and the girls in charge of drying and putting away.

"Where does this go?" Alba asked, holding up a big tin bowl someone had used to mix the batter.

With a dripping finger, I pointed towards the tall metal rack on the right side of the exit door. "On that rack over there."

Standing on the left side of the doorway, Holly groaned.

"What's the matter, Holl?" Jax asked her.

With her back to me, she leaned into a mirror hanging on the wall in front of her. "Look at me! I'm a mess! I've got flour all over my face. Who knew baking could be so messy!" she complained. Using her dish towel, she dusted off her face.

"Where does this go, Sweets?" Mercy asked, holding up a set of beaters.

I pointed to a drawer next to the commercial sized refrigerator. "Umm, I got those out of the top drawer over there."

Mercy nodded and pulled open the drawer to put away the beaters she'd just dried. She paused momentarily, looking down into the drawer. "Girls," she said in a hushed tone. "Check this out!"

I turned around again, to see Mercy holding up a large butcher knife.

"It's a knife," said Jax bluntly.

"Never seen a knife before, Red?" Alba asked with a smirk.

Wide-eyed, Mercy put the knife on the counter top and rushed to the other side of the kitchen. She dug through all of our coats on the counter to find her jacket. She pulled a piece of paper out of her pocket and unfolded it carefully. "Look!" she said. "This is the picture Detective Whitman emailed me. I printed it out. It's the knife that was used to kill Denise!"

Alba dried her hands off on her apron and snatched the picture out of Mercy's hands. "What does that red insignia say?" she asked holding the paper closer to her face.

"What's it say?" I asked.

"The red square is a W with a circle around it. In black next to it, it says Wusthof. That must be the brand."

Mercy rushed to the other side of the kitchen again and retrieved the knife she'd just found in the drawer. "Look. It's a Wusthof knife too."

I pulled my hands out of the tepid water and dried them on my apron. "The knife came from here?" I couldn't believe it!

"The murderer stole it from the church kitchen!" Mercy said excitedly.

Then a small bit of information that Char had told me earlier jumped out at me. "Oh, my gosh. You guys aren't going to believe this!"

"Aren't going to believe what?" asked Jax.

"The other day, Char told me that both she and Tish volunteer here. They work at the food pantry!"

Jax sucked in her breath. "I remember Denise's kids saying that Tish does a lot of volunteer work. Oh my gosh!"

"What do we do now?" I asked. I looked at my cakes. They were cooling nicely on their cooling racks, but I was nervous to leave them. "I have some time before these can be frosted. Should we go to Detective Whitman with what we know?"

Mercy shook her head. "Do you know how many times we've gone to him and been wrong? We have to be absolutely certain about it this time. We've been wrong too many times in the past."

Alba nodded. "Red's right. We need more proof. What we really need is some way of proving that Tish was really at the school when she said she was sleeping."

"Oh! I know exactly how we can prove that," I said excitedly, looking down at my Fitbit. I held it out to show it to the girls. "The Fitbit app on my phone keeps track of my sleep pattern. It's really cool. It shows me when I'm awake, when I'm moving, when I'm restless, and what time I went to bed. Tish wears one, too. I've seen it on her wrist several times. I bet it can tell us exactly when she woke up that morning and what her heart rate was like around the time Denise was murdered!"

Alba's hands flew to either side of her face. "Sweets! You're a genius!" she said excitedly.

I felt myself blushing. "Thanks," I said meekly. No one had ever called me a genius before. I had to admit. It felt pretty good.

"But how are we going to get into her app?" Holly asked. "Don't you need to know her username and password?"

Jax giggled. "Or you could just steal her phone!"

CHAPTER 30

The discovery of the knife was huge for morale. It had been an exhausting week with few clues and finding Mr. Bailey's and Char's wedding cake smashed on the floor had seemingly been the last straw. But with the discovery of the knife in the church kitchen, not only did we now know where the murder weapon had likely come from, but we also knew that Tish had access to the knife! Things were starting to look up!

While waiting for the cakes we'd just made to cool, the five of us raced over to Cal Whiting's engineering office.

"Tish is going to suspect something," Sweets said nervously as she put the car in park and shut off the engine.

"She already knows we're investigating the murder and we've been there twice, so it's not going to come off as a shock to her we're asking more questions," I pointed out.

Alba turned around in her seat to look at Holly and me in the back. "It's going to be up to the four of us to distract her so Jax can grab her phone."

"I only need a few seconds. If you guys can get Tish to turn around or something, I'll grab it and run to the bathroom with it. I'll check the app and return it back to her desk right away. She won't even realize what we did," Jax said proudly.

Sweets sighed nervously. "I don't know about this. What if Tish figures us out! She's a murderer! Who's to say she won't just up and kill us right then and there?"

Holly looked out her window. "There are other cars here, Sweets. She's not going to kill us with other people in the building. Besides, there are five of us and only one of her. Alba can zap her she gets sketchy."

"Zap her? That's what you think I do?"

"I'm sorry, was that not politically correct? What am I supposed to call that thing you do?"

"I don't know. The technical term is electrokinesis."

Holly rolled her eyes. "Fine. Alba can *electrocute* Tish if she gets out of hand."

I groaned and ground the heels of my hands into my temples. Alba and Sweets were right. Tish was going to be on her toes and getting her distracted might not be as easy as we thought it was going to be.

"So what do we say when we go in there?" Alba asked again.

The five of us sat in the car for the next fifteen minutes thinking up an elaborate plan. We decided to tell Tish that Habernackle's Bed, Breakfast, and Beyond was looking to expand, and we needed some new engineering plans drawn up. Of course, the first person we thought of was Cal. While Tish was busy going to Cal's office to explain our needs to him, we would snatch up the phone. Jax and I would rush it to the bathroom where we would find the evidence we needed, we'd screenshot it, email it to ourselves, and then we'd run right over to the police station and show Detective

Whitman the new facts in the case. He'd let Brittany out. We'd drive her back to campus, and then we'd go see the Whiting kids to tell them that it had been Tish all along. Then the five of us would go back to the reception hall where we'd finish frosting the cakes, and we'd be home in time to watch Saturday Night Live in our dorm room with a couple of bowls of Sweets's famous caramel popcorn. We might even grab a few mochaccinos from the coffee shop to celebrate! It was a fabulous plan, and by the time we'd come up with it, we were more than ready to put it into motion.

"Everyone knows the plan?" Alba asked one last time.

With huge smiles on our faces, we all nodded.

"Okay then. Here we go!"

The five of us emerged from the car, and with our hearts beating wildly in our chests we pulled the heavy glass door open and walked into the office.

Surprisingly, Tish wasn't seated at her desk like usual. We all looked at each other curiously. "Now what?" Holly whispered.

Sweets shrugged, and we all looked around nervously, unsure of what to do. The whole office was quiet, but there were a few cars in the parking lot. People had to be in the office somewhere.

"Should we holler for someone?" Holly whispered into the quiet room.

Jax sighed and walked up to the desk where Tish usually sat. Sitting right next to her computer was her phone. Without thinking twice, Jax grabbed the phone off her desk and slunk to the floor in front of the low office divider.

"Jax! Hurry! Someone might come out here!" Sweets hissed.

"This will only take a minute," Jax assured her without looking up from the phone.

My foot tapped anxiously on the office's commercial carpeting while Jax spent all of thirty seconds swiping things left and right. Finally, the look on her face told us we had success, and the sound of a camera clicking told us we had our screenshot.

Alba looked down the side hallway anxiously. "Time's a ticking, Shorty. Someone could come out any second. We gotta go!"

Seconds later, Holly's phone dinged.

Holly looked down at her phone and furrowed her bleach-blond brows. "Huh. I just got a text from a number I don't recognize," she whispered.

From the floor, Jax looked up at her. "That was me, Holly!" Jax hissed back, holding up Tish's phone.

Holly's eyes widened, and she nodded her head sheepishly. "Oh, yeah. Right!"

"We've got what we need?"

Jax nodded from the floor. "Almost. I'm just going to delete the screenshot and the text I just sent Holly - there, all done."

I extended an arm to Jax to pull her up off the ground.

As she sprung to her feet, she smiled exuberantly. "Easy as pie. Come on. Let's go." She placed the phone back down next to Tish's computer in the exact place she'd found it. A fancy gold pen shone proudly on a little notepad next to the mouse. Jax reached for it slyly.

"Jax!" Sweets called to her.

Jax immediately retracted her hand and looked up at Sweets. "Sorry. Old habits die hard," she said with a tiny giggle.

"Come on, let's get out of here before Tish comes back," Alba hissed, leading the way out of the office.

The five of us sprinted to Sweets's car. We didn't even take the time to look at our evidence. We simply pulled out of our spot and took off, with our hearts still racing in our chests.

"What a rush!" Holly squealed.

Jax mirrored Holly's excitement. "Eee! That was so fun!"

Alba leaned back in her seat, letting her head fall against the headrest. "Fun? That was stressful. I think I aged five years in there!"

"So what did we get?" I asked Jax expectantly.

Jax turned to Holly who was sitting in the middle. "I didn't have time to look at the data. I just found the right date and got the picture. Check your phone, Holl."

Holly pulled her phone out of her coat pocket. She opened the picture and using her fingers, enlarged it on the screen. She peered at it closely. "Is this the right day, Jaxie?"

Jax pulled the phone towards her. "Yeah, it should be. Why?" Jax looked at it more closely and then pointed to the top of the screen. "Look, there's the date. That's the right day."

Holly groaned.

"What is it, Holly? Was she not wearing the Fitbit that day?" I asked anxiously. To go through all that and not get the information we needed would be such a letdown.

Holly shook her head and held out the phone to show me. "No. She was wearing it, alright. See, it shows where she was restless during her sleep."

"Right, so what does that mean?" I asked, a bit confused.

Holly pointed to the little lines on the screen. "Those are the times she was restless. See that time right there?"

I looked down. It read *10:19 pm bedtime* and *12:24 pm wake up*.

"So she went to bed a little after ten and got up at midnight?" I asked, nodding. Inside I did a little victory dance – she hadn't slept all day like she'd said!

Holly shook her head. "It says 12:24 pm, Merc. That's *PM*. That means she didn't get up until after noon."

I looked at the screen more closely. Holly was right. The data clearly showed that Tish had gone to bed as she'd said and then not gotten back up again until around lunchtime the next day. It even showed times during the night where she'd been restless and rolled around a bit. There was no denying it. Tish had been telling the truth.

I shoved the phone back towards Holly. "Well that's just great," I snapped.

"Maybe Tish put the Fitbit on someone else that night," Sweets suggested softly.

"Why would've she done that?" I asked bitterly. I was so frustrated; I just about couldn't stand it.

Sweets shrugged. "I don't know. Maybe because she knew the cops might look at the records on it?"

"That's possible," said Jax eagerly.

Alba's head fell into her hands. "Possible, but unlikely."

"Now what?" Holly asked, looking around the car.

No one said a word. We were clueless now. Everything we thought we knew had just gone flying out the window. We were back to square one!

Sweets drove in circles for the next twenty minutes. Either she was too stunned to speak or too scared to ask for the next step. Finally, she pulled over in front of a gas station on the north end of town. "Tell me where to go," she whispered.

Alba looked down at her hands and played with the soft

webbing between her fingers. "I think we need to go tell the Whiting kids that we can't help them. We aren't the super-heroes they thought we were."

As much as I didn't want to admit defeat to them, I felt like we were out of options. Who else had killed Denise? Had Cal hired someone to do it? Was it someone we hadn't thought of – maybe someone else in his office? Was it Tori or Midge after all? Or maybe it actually *was* Brittany! If so, we certainly didn't understand any of their motives. Maybe it was time to admit defeat.

Sweets looked at the three of us in the backseat through her rear view mirror again. "Whiting's?"

I turned my head and looked out my window blindly. I could feel both Jax's and Holly's eyes on me. Swallowing back the lump that was forming in my throat, I nodded silently.

The car lurched forward and then turned down a side street and before I had even regained awareness of where I was, we were sitting in front of Denise Whiting's home.

"Are we all going in?" Holly asked, as she pulled a compact out of her purse and pressed a powder filled pad against her cheeks and forehead.

I turned towards her and eyed her skeptically. "You're primping?"

She snapped the compact shut and shoved it back in her purse. "What? I feel better when I look good."

Trying to ignore the fact that her vanity suddenly annoyed me, I opened my car door. We all met on the front steps of the Whiting house. Quietly I knocked on the door. Having to tell Denise's kids that we were giving up made me feel sick.

Rachel answered the door. She looked surprised to see us but swiftly invited us in.

"Just let me go get Aaron and Danielle. Go sit in the living room," she ordered as she dodged up the stairs to find her siblings.

Alba led the way into the living room and to the faded blue sofa that Midge, Cal, and Tish had all sat on the day we'd been there to visit.

No one sat. Instead, we all milled around the room, looking at pictures on the walls. In every picture, someone in the Whiting family was smiling. In several pictures, Denise stood proudly smiling with her arms wrapped around her children. The sight of her happy, loving face dug into my heart like a knife. We had let her down. We had let her children down.

Thudding on the stairs followed by the sound of a deep male voice caused us to turn around. "Well, what did you find out?"

Aaron, Rachel, and Danielle stood together in the open entryway looking at us expectantly. Hope colored their cheeks and put a glimmer of excitement in their eyes.

"I'm afraid it's not the good news we'd hoped to bring you today," I said slowly.

Their faces fell.

Sweets gestured towards the sofa. "Maybe we should all sit down and talk about this?"

Danielle looked resolute. "Just tell us. No need to sugar coat it. We can take it."

Aaron and Rachel nodded in agreement.

"We thought we knew who it was," Alba admitted, starting the conversation. "In fact, we were very confident. We found where we think the murderer stole the knife from."

Aaron gave us a half smile. "Well, that's something."

"We thought it was, but we just got proof that the person we thought did it had a solid alibi," said Jax.

Aaron's eyebrows furrowed into a deep V. "Well, who did you think did it?"

We all looked at each other. Were we supposed to tell them? Would they laugh us out of their house? Then we'd have to explain to them that Tish and their father had been having an affair. Was that really something that needed to come out?

"Just tell us," he begged.

I winced. "We thought it was Tish."

Their eyes all widened in surprise. "Tish?" the girls sang out in unison.

"What?" Aaron asked. He shook his head staunchly. "There's no way it was Tish!"

"We know that now," agreed Alba.

"Why did you think it was her?" Aaron asked.

I sucked in my bottom lip. This was going to be hard, but I was sure they'd want the truth. "Guys, Tish was having an affair with your dad."

Danielle and Rachel's breath caught in their throats.

Aaron covered his face with his hands. "I should have known," he murmured.

Rachel and Danielle looked at their brother with shock in their eyes. "How?" Danielle asked.

"I don't know. I spent some time working there. I saw some signs, I guess. I just never thought Dad would do that to Mom. I didn't want to believe it," he admitted.

I could see tears shining in his eyes. He reached up and pinched at the corners of his eyes, wiping away the dampness. He cleared his throat. "So. What made you change your mind about Tish?"

"Tish claimed that she was home recovering from the flu

the morning that your mom was killed, but she had no one to back up her alibi. Sweets got the idea that we could check Tish's Fitbit records to see if she was actually asleep when she said she was."

Aaron looked impressed. "That's actually a really smart idea. Tish is a fitness nut. She wears that thing twenty-four-seven."

"That's what we were counting on."

"So she was telling the truth then?" Danielle asked.

"Yeah, the Fitbit said she slept from ten to almost one the next afternoon," I explained. "It couldn't have been her."

"Jeez, that doesn't seem like Tish to sleep so late in the afternoon. I always thought she was an early riser. I know she used to go out for jogs in the morning," noted Rachel.

"She told us that she had the flu. She said she was sick the day before and that she texted your dad before bed to tell him that she was going to be late for work."

Rachel groaned. "We all just got over that flu. It was a nasty bug. Dad had it too. Aaron's the only one of us that didn't get sick."

"So now what are you going to do?" Danielle asked, changing the subject.

I swallowed hard. What could we do?

Alba lowered her head. "We're really sorry that we let you down."

Danielle's eyes widened. "You're giving up?!" she demanded.

"We're stuck! We don't know where else to look! We'll let Detective Whitman know where we think the knife came from and hopefully he'll do some more investigating. Maybe the police will figure something out."

"So you're just going to let the wrong woman be convicted, and you're not even going to keep trying?"

Sweets splayed her hands out in front of her and lifted her shoulders slightly. "We're really sorry. We don't know where else to look."

"If we think of anything, we'll be sure to forward it to Detective Whitman," I said as a lame attempt at covering up our ineptitude.

The sound of our thoughts was the only thing to occupy our minds as we rode in silence back to the reception hall. Our lofty plan for the rest of the day now lay in shambles at our feet. Not figuring out Denise's killer was the most disappointing of all.

CHAPTER 31

When we returned to the reception hall, the sun had already disappeared, and the temperature had dropped, leaving us all feeling cold and miserable inside. We were like robots when we flipped the lights back on in the kitchen. Our steps were succinct and our motions deliberate as we collected bowls and measuring cups. Like a true kitchen boss, Sweets took charge – ordering us around the kitchen, putting Alba and me in charge of mixing up the frosting for two layers, Jax and Holly in charge of two layers, and Sweets took the last two layers. Char had requested a tropical themed cake with each set of layers a different flavor. Sweets made sure that each set of layers had the ideal matching icing.

Once we knew what we were to do, we all worked quietly. The wind had been taken out of our sails. We'd let Denise's kids down, we'd let Brittany down, and ultimately, we'd let ourselves down.

As we plodded along, I allowed myself to think. The knife had very likely come from this kitchen. Who else had access to the kitchen that would want to kill Denise Whiting? Was it a church employee? A church parishioner? Another volunteer worker? Someone entirely different that we hadn't yet thought of?

It just seemed too coincidental that Tish and Cal were having an affair and the knife came from somewhere that Tish had access to. My brain just wouldn't let me get past that. It truly looked like Tish was the murderer. Then a little seed took root inside my mind. What if the killer knew about the affair between Tish and Cal? Armed with that knowledge, they could have been trying to frame Tish by stealing the knife from the church hall and using that as the murder weapon. Eventually, the police would trace it back to the church hall and by then they'd know about the affair.

I stopped smoothing the layer of frosting and looked up at Alba sharply.

She looked up at me too. "What?"

"I just thought of something."

"You're changing your major to cake decorator?" she asked with a small chuckle.

"No, I'm being serious."

"Fine. What did you think of?"

Our voices carried through the rest of the kitchen and the other girls looked up at me. "Hey, girls, what if the person who stole the knife from the kitchen knew about Tish and Cal's affair?" I asked. Just saying the words out loud firmed up my idea.

"What do you mean?" Jax asked, licking off a bit of icing that had smeared on the side of her wrist.

"What if the person who killed Denise, was *trying* to frame Tish?"

"I suppose it's possible," said Alba. "That's a lot of framing. Tori framed Brittany and someone else framed Tish?"

"Fine. Suspend your disbelief just for a second," I begged. I had to get this idea out of my brain before it ate me alive inside.

Alba used her arms to catapult herself into a seated position on the counter. "Alright. Tell us more about this theory, because what I'm hearing so far doesn't get us any closer to finding out who the killer is."

"No, but it might explain why they took the knife from *this kitchen*. They knew about the affair and they knew that Tish volunteered here. They were trying to make it look like she did it. Maybe they even knew that she was sick and would have no way of proving her alibi."

Holly dropped a set of spatulas into the oversized stainless steel sink. They hit the sides with a clank. "Who would have known that Tish was sick?"

"I don't know," I sighed. And who else would want Denise dead? She was such a nice woman.

After an extended pause with only the sound of Char's singing voice floating in through the open doorway, Sweets started moving around again. She moved several dirty bowls into the sink, plugged the drain, and started the water. "It's really too bad The Institute doesn't have security cameras. We wouldn't even have been investigating if there had been cameras. Jax maybe you should tell your mom to install some."

Jax shook her head. "If The Institute had security cameras then we'd never get away with *anything!*"

Alba stopped frosting the last layer and looked up. "Wait a minute! Sweets might be on to something."

Sweets looked up from the dishes she had begun washing. "I might?"

Alba nodded and dropped the long metal frosting spatula onto the counter and walked towards the exit door separating the kitchen from the rest of the hall. I wiped my hands on my apron and stood next to her. She looked up towards the ceiling and then pointed at a black ball just above the exit door.

"Well looky here," she marveled, looking back at the rest of us.

I couldn't believe it! "We have to figure out where this feeds to!"

Jax dried her hands on a towel. "Should we all come with you?"

Alba shook her head. "Mercy and I will go figure it out. You girls finish up the cakes so we can go home."

Jax and Holly groaned, we were all tired of working in the kitchen. Sweets shot them both a megawatt smile. "Thanks for all your help today! We're almost done, I swear!"

Alba and I rushed towards Char, who was putting up the final decorations on the head table.

"Char! There is a security camera in the kitchen. Do you know where that records to?" I hollered at her before we'd gotten very close.

Slowly, she ambled towards us. "Yeah, I think the security system goes into the furnace room."

"Do you have keys to it?" Alba asked.

She nodded. "It's unlocked. They store the tables and chairs in there too."

"We need to go check something out. We'll just be a minute," I hollered at her as Alba rocketed in the direction of Char's pointed finger.

Several paces behind Alba, I found the camera and TV set up tucked away in a little room off of the furnace room. The door was wide open and Alba was already checking out the system.

"The knife might not have been stolen on the day of the murder," I told her.

She nodded. "I know."

"It could have been stolen a week or more before that. We don't know. Are you really going to look through all that footage?" I asked.

She shot me a confident smile. "Most definitely. The only way to find out is to start looking."

NEARLY THREE HOURS LATER, JAX, HOLLY, AND I HELPED Sweets put the finishing touches on Mr. Bailey and Char's wedding cake. It was beautiful. Even though the layers were different flavors, the multi-tiered cake was entirely white and Sweets had tucked in fresh pink flowers in a swirl around the cake. It was quite breathtaking.

When she'd added the last flower and stood back to admire her work, I said, "Sweets, you've outdone yourself."

Her cheeks flushed pink. "You really like it?"

Jax's eyes lit up. "It's beautiful, Sweets."

"Can you do the cake for my wedding?" Holly asked.

"You're getting married?" Sweets asked with a giggle.

"Of course, you're going to have to find me the man first," Holly quipped and then looked at me. "Though I have a few favorites in mind."

"You better not be talking about my brother," I said, moving towards the opposite counter. "Boy, we really made a mess in here."

"Yeah, we did. It's going to take another hour just to wash all these dishes," agreed Sweets.

I looked at the door. "Might as well get started. We're

stuck here anyway. Alba still hasn't found the footage we need to prove who took the knife."

No sooner had I spoken the words than I heard Alba call us from the furnace room. "Girls, get in here!"

We all ran through the kitchen, down the hallway and to the furnace room where Alba was just peeling out of the room. "Come quick!" she hollered. "I found something!" Alba led us to the cozy little workspace she'd set up for herself with a padded rolling chair to sit on and another to kick her feet up onto. She sat back down and rewound the tape.

My heart thudded heavily in my chest in anticipation of what she'd found.

"Now watch right here," she said and pointed to the door from the kitchen to the hallway. We'd passed through that doorway dozens of times today, and I hadn't even thought about that camera catching us on tape every time we passed underneath it. We couldn't see much of the kitchen – just the metal rack to the right of the doorway and the mirror to the left of the doorway with the light switch underneath it. Alba pushed play. Nothing happened for several long seconds. Then out of nowhere, we watched as a woman appeared carrying a knife. Her head was down, and she wore a hat, obscuring her hair. We couldn't see who it was. She stopped in the doorway, wrapped the knife in a towel that she pulled from inside her coat then stashed the knife inside of her coat, looked slightly to the left, flicked off the light switch darkening the kitchen, and then she was gone.

"But we couldn't see her face!" cried Jax.

Alba threw her hands up. "I know! After all of that searching! But at least we know the knife came from this kitchen."

I groaned. "A lot of good that does us. We already knew the knife came from this kitchen."

"We didn't know for sure. Now we know for sure."

"Play it again, Alba," Holly asked.

Alba rewound it once more and pressed play. Holly watched the video closely. "Look at the mirror there. If only it were tilted about two inches to the right," said Holly. "We'd have caught her face in the mirror when she turned her head to flip off the light switch! I was hoping maybe we would have seen it."

Alba looked at Holly with a smirk. "Your obsession with mirrors may finally pay off Holly. I have an idea. It may be a long shot, but I've gotta try."

She pressed rewind, and everything moved in reverse. The light flipped back on, the woman uncovered the knife and then disappeared back into the kitchen. Alba pressed play again. "Watch the mirror," she whispered and then she leaned in closer to the screen. Alba pointed at the mirror and then focusing on it, she curled her finger towards it in a beckoning motion. The mirror tilted ever so slightly to the right. My jaw dropped.

"Holy crap," came out of Alba's mouth as if it rode out on her last breath.

The small room fell dead silent.

"O-M-G!" Jax whispered as her jaw dropped open.

Holly slow clapped. "Whoa. That was awesome."

"So cool," I agreed. "I didn't know you could do that!"

A slow smile spread across Alba's face. She was in shock. "I didn't know I could do it either!"

With our mouths gaped open and our eyes like saucers, our attention swiveled back to the video camera.

The woman appeared in the video again. She paused in the doorway, pulled the towel from her coat, wrapped it around the knife, stashed the knife under her arm and then pulled her coat around her. She looked slightly to the left as her finger sought the light switch and in that brief movement, Alba paused the recording, and there it was – the face of the killer. We knew exactly who it was!

CHAPTER 32

"Midge?!" Jax cried in surprise. "It's Midge!"

Alba nodded vigorously. "I know! Can you believe it! She was the first one I suspected, too!"

Alba was right, but somehow we'd gotten fixated on placing the blame on Tish, and we'd let Midge off the hook. The lack of motive had been the kicker when it came to Midge.

I shook my head in confusion. "I don't get it! Why? Why did Midge kill Denise? Did they not get along at work?"

All the girls shook their heads. They didn't get it either. We were definitely missing something.

"So now what? Do we go to Whitman or Stone with our new evidence?" Sweets asked. Her voice trembled with apprehension. We never knew the right way to handle these things, but there was one thing we did know. If we went to Whitman first, Stone would get mad. There was no alternative. We had to go to Stone first.

"We tell Stone," I said firmly. "We have no other choice."

We waltzed into the school that night feeling on top of the world. We'd figured out who had killed Denise and we'd gotten Sweets's cake done and ready for the wedding the next day. Nothing could squash our spirits now! I couldn't wait to tell Stone and either allow her to share the evidence we'd collected with Detective Whitman or get permission from her for us to tell him. Either way, we were sure Midge would be in police custody by the end of the evening, and Brittany would be a free woman.

Armed with the incriminating footage from the security camera, pictures we'd taken of the matching knives in the church hall kitchen, and proof that Tish had indeed been sick, we strode into Winston Hall and straight towards Sorceress Stone's office. I was worried that since it was so late in the evening, she might not be in there, but as it turned out, my worry was unnecessary.

The sound of her voice stopped us cold at the door. "This is most certainly a surprise!" We heard her gasp.

A heavy male voice saturated the air, speaking quickly after her. "I know it is, SaraLynn, but I had some time to think about it."

My jaw dropped. It was Detective Whitman! I held up a finger in front of my lips, shushing the girls.

"Well, I must say. I'm quite pleased you finally came to your senses. It is, after all, just a wedding. It's not like it's *our* wedding," Sorceress Stone purred, the smooth sound of her voice led into a lilting laugh.

"You're right. I should have looked at it like that from the beginning. So, you'll accept my apology for not accepting your invitation when you asked earlier in the week?"

"Most certainly," she said. We could hear the sound of

almost real pleasure in her voice, and it made me want to vomit.

I couldn't stand it. The thought of Detective Whitman taking Sorceress Stone to Mr. Bailey and Char's wedding made my blood boil. He was only doing this because my mother had accepted an invitation from Merrick. I wondered if Sorceress Stone knew that. I wondered if she realized that she was only a tool Detective Whitman was using to make my mother jealous.

How could this all have gone so wrong so quickly? *He* was supposed to be the man for Mom, not Merrick! Now if he and SaraLynn ended up together, I'd be stuck with Merrick as my stepfather. The thought sickened me to my core.

Without another thought, I spun on my heel and raced towards the stone stairway and ran to my dorm room. I threw the door open in a huff and slammed myself down on my bed.

The girls came rushing in after me. Jax flew to my bedside first. "It's just a date, Mercy. Why are you getting so upset?"

I stared at her, hurt and angry that Detective Whitman had betrayed my mother and me for that matter. Why didn't Jax see that? "Leave me alone, Jax." I rolled over onto my other side.

Alba plopped down in my desk chair. "So Whitman asks Stone out, and now we're not going to tell them that we know who killed Denise?"

"Go away," I hollered.

"This is bigger than your mother's dating life, Red."

"I said go away!" They didn't understand. I'd grown up for years without a father. On occasion, I'd think about my own father. I'd wonder where he was and what he looked like. I thought about how he'd treat me. Things we'd do together. Never once had I thought he would be evil like Merrick Stone. Not once. Over the last few months of getting to know Detective Whitman, he'd grown on me. I could see him fitting into our lives. I could see him marrying my mom in the future. And now everything was just getting all messed up, and I was over it! I wished that my friends got it – that they would just understand so I wouldn't have to explain it to them. I groaned out loud. It wouldn't matter, they didn't care about my family problems.

When the girls didn't move, I forced myself to show them my rational side. I sat up and faced them. "We'll tell them tomorrow," I said. "I'm too mad to tell them today."

I heard my chair squeak as Alba leaned backwards in the seat. "Fine. Just as long as we tell him tomorrow, we can wait. It's getting late anyway."

"I agree," said Holly. "And I need my beauty rest. The wedding is tomorrow, and I want to look nice."

Sweets made a face. "Oh, aren't we watching TV and having caramel popcorn in your room tonight?"

Holly nodded. "Oh, yeah. I'm up for that. Alba?"

"Sure, whatever."

"I'll go change and get the popcorn ready," said Sweets. "I'll be down in a jiff!"

"Jaxie, are you still up for a girls night?"

Jax nodded. "Just let me change into my pj's, and I'll be over."

"You coming over, Merc?" asked Holly.

I shook my head as I placed my head back down on my pillow. "Nah, not tonight. Have fun without me."

Sweets, Alba, and Holly all said goodnight, and before I knew it, only Jax was left in the room with me. Quietly, she sat on the edge of my bed. "Do you want to talk about it, Cuz?"

My voice muffled through the pillow as I yelled at her. "No!"

She stood up, and the mattress bounced back to its usual position. "Okay. That's fine. I'm sorry you're sad," she whispered.

I closed my eyes. After I heard Jax leave, I let out a deep sigh. I felt sorry for myself. I took pleasure in counting the multitude of ways my life was messed up. Then just like that, darkness overtook me.

"MERCY! WAKE UP!" I HEARD A VOICE CALL OUT THROUGH A misty haze and then my bed began to shake. "Mercy! We're late!"

I worked to pull my eyes open, but my intertwined eyelashes made it difficult.

"Mercy!" A set of hands were on my shoulders now, shaking me.

Finally, I managed to wrestle my eyes open. I squinted at the bright light flooding in through the windows. Surprised by the amount of light coming through, I cranked backwards to look at my alarm clock. The red light clearly displayed ten-fifteen.

TEN-FIFTEEN! I shot straight up and looked Jax in the eyes. "We're late!"

"I know!" she said anxiously. "Sweets and I hung out in Alba and Holly's room last night. After Saturday Night Life, we stayed up late watching a movie and then we ended up just crashing in their room. No one set the alarm. We're all just now getting up!"

No wonder I'd slept so soundly. Usually, Jax was up at the butt crack of dawn doing her yoga stuff. She always managed to wake me up earlier than necessary. Today was the first day I'd gotten to sleep in in weeks! "We're going to be late for the wedding," I said, lurching out of bed. "Now we're not going to have time to go talk to Sorceress Stone or Detective Whitman before the wedding!"

Jax scampered around gathering her dress from the closet and her undergarments from her drawer. "Alba said we'll just have to tell him after the wedding. I need to go take a shower, I'm gross," she announced as she left our room.

I groaned as I followed her example and looked for the dress I'd borrowed from Holly. I grabbed the rest of my clothes and headed for the showers as well.

At precisely eleven-thirty, I was fully dressed and made up. I wore the tight pink, long-sleeve dress that Holly had let me borrow. Instead of heels, I slid on a pair of black flats that I'd picked up in town over Christmas break. I knew that the heels looked better, but the embarrassment of trying to walk in them just wasn't worth it.

Tugging on the hem of my dress, I stood up straight and then knocked on the door in front of me. I glanced down at my Batman watch. We still had a half of an hour to get into town for the wedding if we were going to make it on time.

I heard a bit of rattling around, and then the door opened. Hugh stood in front of me, looking as sexy as always. Today, he wore his good jeans and a nice snap down shirt, but no cowboy hat. His sandy blond hair was freshly washed and neatly combed, though I could see his natural curls beginning to pop up around his ears.

"Hey, handsome, are you ready?" I asked, leaning against the door frame.

His look of curiosity quickly turned to a look of anger. Not only had his face flushed red, but his ears had too. "Mercy. What are you doing here?" he asked.

Since when did he just call me Mercy? No darlin'? No Mercy Mae? My smile faded into an expression of puzzlement. "Did you forget? Today is Mr. Bailey and Char's wedding. You're my date, remember?"

He frowned. "I remember we had *planned* to go together. But that was before."

His attitude caught me off guard. "Before what?"

"You know what. I can't believe you're even here."

My mind reeled. "Why wouldn't I be here? I don't understand, Hugh."

"I need to go. Goodbye, Mercy." He began to shut the door in my face.

I put my flattened palm on it and pressed it back towards him. "Wait. Hugh? What's going on? You're mad at me? For what?"

His eyes rested on me coldly, but he didn't say a word.

"Is this about Thursday night?" The last time I'd spoken to him was Thursday night when we'd gotten home from the party. I'd called him on Holly's phone because mine was broken. I'd made sure to tell him that we'd made it home safely and that I'd see him at the wedding on Sunday. I had been so busy since then, and without a working cell phone, I hadn't been able to text him or call him.

"Well, a-course it's about Thursday. What else would it be about?" he asked gruffly.

"Okay. Well, I'm sorry we didn't get to see each other

after I got home. It was late, and the girls and I were starving. We just wanted to get back to our room and get some food and go to bed."

He nodded. "I see."

"Hugh? You're acting so strangely. Is everything alright?"

He looked at me. His eyes blazed more furiously than I'd ever seen before. "No everything is not alright. You ruined things! Now, like I told you in the various messages I sent you that you never replied to, we're over. Goodbye."

My mouth went dry. *Over?* "Messages? Hugh! My phone broke. I don't have a cell phone. It broke the night of the party. I told you that on the phone."

He paused for a moment. "I don't remember you mentioning that."

I nodded wildly. This was all some kind of misunderstanding. "Yeah, I did. That's why I called you on Holly's phone. So if you've been sending me text messages or voicemails, I haven't gotten a single one."

He paused for a moment as if considering. Then he began to shut the door again. "It really doesn't make a difference after what happened. Goodbye, Mercy."

"But, Hugh!" I hollered, trying to catch the door again with my hand. This time he pushed harder, and before I could get another word out, the door slammed shut in my face and locked on the other side.

What had just happened?! My mind raced. I was completely bewildered by what Hugh could be so upset about! I looked down at my watch. It was now eleven-thirty-five, and if I didn't get back to Winston Hall post-haste, I was afraid the girls were going to leave without me.

CHAPTER 33

I barely caught up to the girls in the Winston Hall parking lot before they began to drive away. I was thankful I'd gone with the flats instead of the heels; there was no way I'd have made that sprint through the tunnels in heels. It was eleven-fifty-five when we finally slid into our seats in the church. We'd made it!

Finally able to relax in our seats, I let out the deep breath I'd been carrying and looked around. Bouquets of bright pink and orange tropical flowers hung at every third row, and a white aisle runner lined by flower petals covered the center aisle. A woman in the front of the church was playing the organ as Mr. Bailey stood handsomely at the front of the church in his formal black suit. Louis, the co-worker that Sweets couldn't stand, was standing by his side, also in a suit. I looked over at Sweets. I could tell she was appalled that Mr. Bailey had chosen Louis to be his best man, but she was holding back her shock.

I scanned the rest of the crowd. I saw my mother seated next to Merrick Stone several rows ahead of me. Reign sat next to them. He must have felt my eyes on him because his head turned slightly and our eyes met for a brief moment. He gave me a tiny nod and a half smile. I nodded back and turned my head away from him. Seated on the other side of the church was Detective Whitman with Sorceress Stone. I saw him glimpse across the aisle at my mother, but my mother appeared oblivious to his presence.

Seated two rows behind Detective Whitman was Cal Whiting and Tish. I couldn't believe that he was already making public appearances with his mistress, only days after his poor wife was killed. They hadn't even had her funeral yet and he was dating again in public. *Sad*, I thought.

Another guest slid into the last row on the opposite side of the aisle. She was dressed all in black and wore a black veil over her face. I furrowed my brows at her. *That's not a very appropriate way to come dressed for a wedding*, I thought. I poked Jax's ribs and when she looked at me, I nodded towards the woman in black.

Jax glanced at her and grimaced. Then she nodded to a pew three rows up. I followed her eyes and my breath caught in my throat. I had missed them. He wasn't wearing his cowboy hat, causing him to blend in with the crowd. But Hugh was there, at the wedding, with none other than Tori Decker by his side! My hands webbed out on either side of me and I grabbed hold of both Sweets and Jax for support. My mind spun as I tried to reconcile the fact that not only had Hugh suddenly dumped me, but now he was here with *Tori Decker*. Had they even been *invited* to the wedding? I felt my temperature beginning to rise and suddenly the room started to get hazy.

Sweets squeezed my arm back and then whispered in my ear. "Did you see that Cal and Tish are here?"

I nodded, trying hard to keep it together.

"Midge is here too," Jax whispered across my lap.

I barely had time to catch my breath from the Hugh and Tori sighting when I looked at her in shock. "What? Where?"

Her head nodded towards the middle row, just two rows behind Cal and Tish. My eyes must have burned a hole in the back of Midge's head because she turned just then and caught my eyes staring at her. She must have seen something on my face. Her eyes widened and then she quickly turned away.

Jax whispered out of the side of her mouth at me. "Did you just see Midge look at you?"

I nodded as I let out a deep breath. "Yeah. She totally caught me staring," I said nervously. The look we exchanged made me feel like she suddenly knew that we knew. My pulse quickened.

"She looked skittish," Jax breathed anxiously.

Sweets bent over and whispered towards us both. "What are you guys whispering about?"

"Midge just saw me look at her. We think she knows that we know," I hissed back.

Midge turned around and looked at us again. Sweet and innocent Midge, had been replaced with evil and vile Midge and this time her eyes said more than they had before. This time they clearly said *if you tell, I will kill you.*

Alba leaned over Jax to whisper to us. "Did you just see the look Midge gave us?"

Were we *all* staring at her? No wonder she was getting jumpy. I nodded. I couldn't take it anymore. My head was going to split open. Merrick with Mom. Detective Whitman with Sorceress Stone. Hugh with Tori Decker. Denise's murder. Cal and Tish's affair gone public. And now *Midge* shooting us threatening glances. It was too much!

As the room began to spin around me, the organ at the front of the church fired up again. This time it strummed out the well-known wedding march and the doors to the back of the church parted. There stood Char, wearing a knee-length, cream-colored dress with a matching silk shawl thrown around her shoulders and a pink hibiscus flower pinned in her short white hair.

The moment when the audience rises to greet the incoming bride was quickly approaching and all I could think about was the fact that there was a murderer amongst us. She would sully Mr. Bailey and Char's beautiful wedding day. We couldn't just let her be! What if she ran out after the wedding and escaped before Detective Whitman could arrest her? What if she hurt someone else? The thoughts filed through my head so fast that I didn't have enough time to vet each idea as it came. Instead, I jumped to my feet before anyone else could beat me to it and pointed at Midge. "Murderer!"

CHAPTER 34

The crowd let out a collective gasp as all eyes turned towards me. I felt Jax and Sweets pulling on the hem of my dress, trying to pull me to my seat, but I continued to stand as the swell of eyes on me intensified. *What did I just do? Did I seriously just yell, murderer, in the middle of a wedding?* Mortified, I felt my face growing hot.

Then a strange thing happened. The music stopped, and the entire audience froze – and I don't mean they froze in the figurative sense. They froze in the *literal sense.* My mouth opened wide as I looked back at Char, who was standing mid-walk up the aisle, her arms and legs weren't moving – even her eyes weren't blinking. I looked back at the girls, Jax and Sweets had their hands glued to the hem of my skirt. Holly was staring at Midge across the aisle. Alba had just begun to say something to me – to tell me to sit down, I was sure, but instead she was in a catatonic state as were the rest of the people in the church.

My head swiveled to Midge. Had she done this? Was she a witch? But she was seated, swiveled around in my direction – as was the rest of the crowd. All of them, including Midge, had a look of horror cast upon their faces. I looked around, curious to see if I was the only person that had managed to escape someone's obvious freezer spell. Two heads bobbed in the rows in front of me – my mother and Reign. They stood cautiously and then turned towards me. Their eyes told me that they hadn't cast the spell, but they certainly wondered who had.

That's when the sound of a familiar voice from the back of the church rang out. "Oh for pity's sake – haven't you taught my granddaughter better manners than that?"

I spun around. The short woman who had slid in last, with her black veil and dress was struggling to get out of her seat. When she finally stood, I peered at her closely. I knew I recognized the voice, but until I saw her face, I couldn't be sure.

Slowly she pulled her black veil back, revealing her identity. "What's the matter, Mercy? No hugs for your dear old granny today?" Her laughter filled the church, reverberating off the walls. I remembered that elephant-sized laugh well. She'd had it since I could remember. *Granny?!*

"Mother!" cried my mom, swallowing hard.

Reign's eyes were wide, but he remained silent. He had his own issues with our grandmother that I knew he was just itching to deal with.

"Granny?" I asked, squinting at her. "What in the world are you doing here?"

"Well, *obviously*, I was *invited*!" she crowed.

"You were invited? By whom?!" I demanded.

"Are we really going to get into that right now?" she asked, stepping out of her pew and walking around the back of the church to come back up the center aisle.

"Gran – did you freeze these people?" I asked.

She hobbled up the aisle and placed herself halfway

between my mother, brother, and myself. She shrugged as she pulled the black veil out of her hair, exposing the wiry white bun atop her head. "Well, of course, I froze these people," she cracked like the spitfire she was. "We couldn't very well have had you ruin my old pal Char's wedding now could we?"

"Mom! You know Char?" my mother asked, shocked.

Granny threw a hand up and mockingly smacked herself in the forehead. "Linda. Do you *not* remember me talking about my old friend Charlotte Adams from college? When you were growing up, I talked about her all the time! I've told you countless stories. Was I talking to myself all those years?"

My mother's eyes widened as she turned to look at the bride in the back of the church who was still frozen stiff. *"That's* Charlotte Adams?!"

Granny nodded. "The one and only. She married into the Maxwell name years ago, but she'll always be an Adams in my memory." Granny looked around and nodded at the groom standing at the altar. "Well. Not for long anyway, I suppose. Soon I'll have to get used to calling her Char Bailey."

Mom nodded. "Well, now I know. When we first met, she seemed to know who I was. She never did tell me how she knew me."

Granny nodded with an ear-to-ear grin plastered on her face. "Yeah, old Char wrote me and told me she'd run into you. I figured that would happen eventually with you and my granddaughter living in the same town as my old best friend. What I *hadn't* planned on was you and old Scarface over there hooking back up again."

Go, Gran, I silently cheered.

Reign who had been silent thus far, piped up. "Are we

going to get our answers now as to why you split up my parents?"

"Oh good Lord, Reign. Are we going to start dealing with *that* now? I just got here!" she whined. Then she looked at my mother sternly and with one hand on her hip; she pointed her finger at her. "You and I will address *that situation* later."

"But, Mother—" Mom began hesitantly, looking down at Merrick, frozen in place next to her.

My granny threw both of her hands up in the air and looked down at the ground with her eyes closed. "No more 'but mothers!' I've heard enough of those for a lifetime. Enough about you and *him* for now. We need to address the current situation. And *your daughter* just about ruined my best friend's wedding." She turned her green eyes on me as did both Reign and my mother. "What were you *thinking*, Mercy?"

I sighed. I wanted to tell her that I'd had a tough morning – a tough week, in fact. Instead, I hung my head.

"Whatsamatter, chickadee? Cat got your tongue?" she asked.

"Gran. Our school cook was murdered this week and the girls and I finally figured out who did it. She's sitting right there!" I said in frustration and pointed across the church to Midge.

Gran lifted her arms up by her side and spun around. She pointed at Midge. "This woman?"

I nodded.

"Right here? Her?" she pointed again, getting closer.

I nodded again. "Yeah. Her name's Midge."

Gran made a face. "Huh. She doesn't look like she'd have it in her! You're sure it's her?"

"Positive."

"So your plan was to, what? Scream it out in the middle of a wedding? What were you *thinking,* Mercy?"

I sighed. I suppose I hadn't been thinking. "Sorry, Gran. I just didn't want her to get away."

Gran laughed. "Where was she gonna go? She's at a wedding for crying out loud."

"She might have jumped up and left, or she might have skipped town after the wedding, before I could tell Detective Whitman," I said.

Gran's eyes opened wide with interest. "Detective *Mark* Whitman?"

I nodded. "Yeah. He's right there." I pointed to Detective Whitman.

"Well now. Char's told me quite a bit about Detective Mark Whitman! I must see this hunka-hunka man for myself now." She followed the direction my finger pointed. "Which one is he, Mercy dear?"

I pointed again. "Back one row, Gran. Yeah, there. Third man over. With the mustache," I told her.

She sucked in her breath. "The one sitting next to Sara Smith?"

"It's SaraLynn Stone now, Gran," I told her. "We call her Sorceress Stone. She's the Headmistress of The Institute."

Gran reeled backward on her heels. "Well ain't that just like a Stone! I forgot they were going by their mother's last name now." She got closer to my mother. "I thought *you* and Mr. Hunka-Hunka were an item?"

Reign's angry onyx eyes burned into my grandmother. "Why don't you just stay out of my mother's personal life?"

Gran turned her glowering green eyes on my brother. "I don't think your mother's personal life is much of your business either."

"I'm not trying to make it my business," he asserted, his jaw clenched firmly.

"Her being here with Scarface has nothing to do with you then?"

"His name is Merrick."

"Yeah, yeah. I know his name."

"Mom can date whomever she chooses. Unlike *you*, I stay out of it," he growled.

My mother held up a hand and placed it gently on Reign's chest. "Okay, okay. Enough from both of you." She turned to Reign and looked at him pleadingly. "Reign, sweetheart. Let me deal with my mother. Please?"

While her plea did little to calm the rage brewing inside of my brother, his lips formed a tight line, and he sat back down in the pew.

"Mother. Can we discuss all of this another time?"

"That's what I said from the beginning, isn't it? We just need to sort out this murder mumbo-jumbo." She looked at me again. "Mercy. Let's get this squared away so Char can get married. What do you want to happen?"

I swallowed hard and thought about it. "I want to tell Detective Whitman that Midge is the murderer."

"Okay. Who else that is here should know this?"

"Sorceress Stone should know," I said slowly, thinking about whom else to tell.

Gran pretended to crumple. "Really? You have to tell *her*?"

"She's my teacher, Gran. She'll have a fit if we tell Detective Whitman and not her. The murder happened in her school. Her secretary is in jail right now because of a fake ghost that this new girl showed us." *Fake ghost*! The thought reminded me of my need for Hugh to know the truth about his date. "Oh! I need to tell Hugh about how Tori manipulated so many of the events this week."

"Ohhh, I forgot you've got a young man you're seeing too," she taunted.

"How do you know that?"

"Char told me. She said she really likes him. She said he's a cowboy," she said with a twinkle in her eye.

"Yeah, we broke up," I said sadly.

My mother and Reign both looked at me, shocked to hear the news. "Mercy! You and Hugh broke up? When?" asked my mother.

I shrugged. "Earlier today. Do we have to talk about it? I'd rather not."

"Want me to have a talk with him?" Reign asked, standing up.

"No. I most certainly do not want you to have a talk with Hugh!" I snapped. "I'll deal with my boyfr-, I mean, *Hugh*, on my own."

"Okay, so I'm unfreezing the detective, Sara, Hugh. Who else?" she looked at her watch. "Come on. We need to get this show on the road."

"My friends," I said, turning and pointing at the girls. "And them." I pointed at Cal and Tish across the room.

"These two?" she gestured towards Cal and Tish.

I nodded. "Yup. That's the cafeteria lady's husband and his mistress."

Her eyebrows shot up. "Hey. This is getting juicy," she quipped.

"Gran! This is serious stuff!"

"Fine. Anyone else need to be awake for this?"

I shook my head. "Nope. That should be everyone."

"Very well," she said and in one swift swirling motion of her hands, she'd awoken Detective Whitman, Sorceress

Stone, Midge, Cal, Tish, Hugh, and the rest of the Witch Squad.

Murderer! The last thing I'd said, hung in the air as Detective Whitman and Sorceress Stone spun around in their seats to face me.

CHAPTER 35

I felt the girls tugging harder on my hem as Alba hissed at me. "Red! What are you doing? Sit down!"

From across the room, Midge pretended to be appalled, but I could see the truth below the surface. She was freaking out.

It took a moment for those newly unfrozen to become acclimated to the fact that the others in the room were still stiff as boards. The paranormals in the group didn't seem as shocked as the non-paranormals. Detective Whitman, Cal, Tish, and Midge all looked around as if they were in an alternate universe.

"What is going on here?" rang out Sorceress Stone's shrill, condescending voice from the front of the church.

"Why are all of these people frozen?" Detective Whitman asked, looking around curiously.

"My granny froze them," I explained uncomfortably.

"Your granny?" Jax asked in surprise. "Your granny is here?"

I nodded and pointed at the woman in the center aisle. "My granny."

Granny held up a hand and waved at everyone that was staring at her. "Hello, everyone. Phyllis Habernackle, so lovely to meet you all. My granddaughter, Mercy has something she'd like to share with you all. So, without further ado, I'll turn the floor over to her. Mercy?"

"Thanks, Gran," I sighed. I turned to the girls and motioned for them to stand up. I wasn't about to do this alone. When everyone was on their feet, I ushered them out of our row and into the aisle. I was feeling restless and needed to pace.

"Can someone please tell me what's going on?" Cal Whiting asked.

Alba took a deep breath and thankfully started the conversation. "Cal, we've solved your wife's murder."

Detective Whitman and Sorceress Stone looked on skeptically. It almost looked like Detective Whitman winced. Already, he didn't believe us.

"Have you? I thought we had the killer behind bars, Detective?" Cal asked, turning to look at Detective Whitman.

Detective Whitman crossed his arms and leaned against the pew behind him. "We do have someone in custody, but my office is working on other leads."

"No need," I said. "We figured it out."

"And you decided to tell us now, of all times? You couldn't have waited until after the wedding?" Sorceress Stone sneered haughtily.

"We were going to wait, except, well, we think the murderer figured out we were on to her," I said nervously, casting my eyes towards Midge. Her face lit up like an ember.

"Well, who did it? We're all dying to know," she pressed.

"It was Midge," Jax interjected excitedly.

"Midge?!" Sorceress Stone said with surprise. "Really?"

We all nodded. Midge's face went from red to crimson. Her jaw dropped in a grand display of shock and horror. "Me?!" she demanded. "I didn't kill Denise! I would never!"

"Maybe we should explain our accusation," Alba suggested.

I nodded. "Of course. For starters, our powers were pointing us in the direction of Brittany Hobbs," I said, looking at Hugh pointedly. "But we could all tell that something just wasn't right about that."

"And then we discovered what the problem was," said Holly. "Tori Decker was showing us lies."

"Lies? How so?" Sorceress Stone asked, surprised to hear that.

"It started with Denise Whiting's ghost telling Alba and me that Brittany killed her. Not only was it strange that Alba was able to see the ghost, because as many of you know, I'm the medium, not Alba, but it was also odd that a strange green glow surrounded the ghost. Which is something that's never happened before," I explained.

"Then *I* had a vision of Brittany leaning over Denise's corpse," admitted Holly. "But that vision was also glowing, which was really unusual."

"Don't forget that I saw Tori trying to break into the kitchen storage room the day after the murder," interjected Sweets.

"Yeah, that definitely alerted us to the fact that Tori was involved in all of this in some way," Alba agreed.

"But *then* the night of the barn party, Tori played a practical joke on us that could have killed us," said Holly with a slight shudder at the memory. "She cast an illusion of Hugh in danger."

Hugh's eyes widened. I hadn't told him what had happened when we got separated that night. I'd been too busy, and I hadn't had a phone all week.

Holly continued. "That vision was also glowing, and as it turned out, Hugh wasn't in danger, but the vision led us right into danger."

"We ended up stranded in a pit under an old barn in the country. Alba was knocked out in the fall. She could have had a serious brain injury. Holly and I didn't have coats. We all nearly froze to death! But that was when we put two and two together. All of this was coming from Tori."

Sorceress Stone furrowed her eyebrows at us. "You have no proof it was Tori."

Alba nodded. "The next day, when you locked us in the tower with Tori, she conjured another illusion that glowed green. We told her we knew it was her and we proved that the illusion that she had conjured was fake. That was when she admitted that it was her and told us that we were all idiots for even believing it in the first place."

I looked at Hugh. "She's been lying to all of us since she started school."

Hugh's entire face changed. He looked at Tori angrily. "She showed me a vision Thursday night too. She showed me you with another guy," he admitted. He looked down at his boots. "It was glowing green too, but I didn't know that meant it was fake."

I smiled at Hugh from across the room. "I wasn't with another guy, Hugh."

He looked like he wanted to fall apart. "I get that now."

My heart suddenly felt a million pounds lighter

knowing what had happened to make him break up with me and knowing that now he knew the truth.

Sorceress Stone shook her head. "So Tori Decker is the one that framed Brittany? Why would she do that?"

Alba rose her hand. "Because she wanted to make us look bad. She wanted us to point the finger at Brittany while she investigated and figured out who the *real* murderer was."

Sorceress Stone let out a shrill laugh. "Well, that's simply ridiculous!"

We all nodded.

"It didn't stop us from investigating, though. We knew it wasn't Brittany. At first, we thought it was Tish," I admitted.

"We discovered that Tish and Cal were having an affair," Holly revealed.

I thought I saw Detective Whitman nod slightly. He knew about the affair!

Cal and Tish looked at each other uncomfortably, and Tish looked like she wanted to crawl into a hole.

"And then we found out where the knife used to kill Denise came from," said Sweets.

Detective Whitman's eyebrows shot up when he heard that proclamation. We knew something he didn't know. "You figured out where the knife came from? You promised to tell me!"

"We're telling you now," I said with a shrug. I was still sore at him for coming to the wedding with Sorceress Stone.

"Excellent timing," he said dryly.

Alba rolled her eyes. "It came from the church hall. We were using the kitchen to finish baking the Bailey's wedding cake, and we found a knife that matched the one that was used to kill Denise."

"So you found a match, you don't know *for certain* it came from the church hall, though," he said, nodding his head.

"We're pretty confident," I assured him.

"Yeah, and we knew that Tish volunteers here, so she had access," Sweets explained.

Midge nodded and pointed at Tish. "Exactly! *She* had access. *I didn't* have access so how can you possibly blame me for the murder?"

Alba held a hand out towards Midge. "Settle down, *Edna*. We're getting to it."

I held a hand up to stifle the laugh that wanted to bubble out. Getting all of this out in the open was making me feel so much lighter!

"But before we could prove that Tish was the killer, we felt like we needed to prove that she wasn't home sick the morning of the murder like she said she was, and Sweets came up with a brilliant way to prove that," Alba explained and then pointed at Sweets.

Sweets held out her arm and showed us her fitness tracker. "I got a Fitbit for Christmas," she began shyly.

"Well, good for you," Midge mocked angrily, rolling her eyes.

Sweets's face turned pink, but she kept going. "It tracks a lot of things, but one of the cool things is that I found it tracks my sleep pattern. So it shows me what time I go to bed every night and what time I wake up in the morning. It also shows me how restless I was in the night. It's very interesting."

"And? What does that have to do with anything?" Midge demanded.

Tish held up her wrist. "And I wear a Fitbit!" she announced. She understood where Sweets was going with that explanation. "You can prove that I was asleep when I said I was asleep."

"We actually checked it," Jax admitted sheepishly. "We went into your office yesterday morning, and no one was around."

Tish's eyes widened. "That was you girls?"

"Yup."

"We were all in a meeting in the back. By the time I got to the front office, you were already gone!"

"Well, you left your phone out by your computer, so we got into the Fitbit app on your phone and took a screenshot of the information and sent it to Holly's phone," explained Jax.

Holly held her phone up. "I still have it if anyone wants to see it. It proved that she was sleeping when she said she was. She didn't wake up until after Denise was already killed."

Detective Whitman smiled. "Very smart detective work, girls. I don't know about resorting to looking through her phone, but I suppose since you cleared her using that technique, Tish probably isn't complaining."

Tish smiled and shook her head as she looked up at Cal. "Not at all! I'm thrilled to know that you don't think it was me anymore!"

"So we came back here feeling defeated," I explained. "We finished making the cake for the wedding, and we realized that there's a security camera in the church hall's kitchen. Surely whoever stole the knife would have been caught on camera!"

Alba chuckled. "So I spent three hours going through the security tapes and lo and behold, we caught ourselves a murderer!"

Midge dropped her head into her hands. She knew she was caught at that point.

Cal looked at Midge angrily. "How could you, Midge? Denise was your friend!"

Midge's head snapped up. "Don't you dare condemn me for this, Cal Whiting! This is all your fault," she raged. Her demeanor suddenly became that of a crazy woman.

"My fault?! I didn't kill my wife!"

She shook her head. "I did this for you," she snapped. "Because you told me that Denise said she wasn't going to give you your divorce."

He looked at Tish nervously. "You don't know what you're talking about!"

"If I'm going down for this, so are you. So don't you dare lie about this!"

Cal swallowed hard. Clearly, Midge had shaken him.

"You all want to hear the story? I'll tell you the story," said Midge, looking around the room. "Cal approached me, at The Institute's employee Christmas party in early December. We were drinking, and he came onto me. At first, I pushed him away, but then he pursued me harder until finally after a few too many drinks that night, I gave in. I admit it, I shouldn't have, but I did. We *both did.*"

Tish sucked in her breath. "Cal! How could you?"

Cal bent forward and buried his face in the palms of his hands.

I rolled my eyes. As if what the two of them had been doing was any better? Did she think she had the right to condemn Cal for cheating on her just like they'd done to Denise?

Midge kept talking. "That began a full-fledged affair. Flowers. Candy. Romantic nights on the couch at my place. He put on the full-court press. It kept up for awhile, and by the end of December, he told me that he was leaving Denise for me. He even showed me the divorce papers he had his lawyer draw up, but then he came to me one day and said that Denise had found out about us and she wasn't going to give him the divorce. We were beside ourselves. We didn't know what to do. And Cal told me that the only way we could be together was if Denise ever died!"

"I didn't tell you to kill her!" he shot out.

"You also didn't tell me you were having an affair with Tish," she spat back. "How convenient it was that you found out that Denise wouldn't give you a divorce, so you struck up a new affair with me."

Detective Whitman was watching Cal curiously now. Midge's words were beginning to make sense to everyone. Had Cal Whiting struck up the affair with Midge purely to get her to do his dirty work?

"You used me!" she spat. "The minute that Denise was gone, you turned all of your attention off. You focused all of your energy on Tish. You didn't even try and hide it!"

Tears were streaming down Tish's face by now. She had no idea what kind of a monster she had been in a relationship with. Even though she'd been Cal's mistress, I felt sorry for her. She hadn't played a role in the murder, only the affair.

"I was your pawn!" Midge hollered.

"I didn't tell you to do anything!" Cal insisted, practically spitting his words now as he pulled at his hair. "You're crazy. That's what you are. Absolutely maniacal."

Granny, who had been surprisingly quiet through the whole big reveal, finally stepped forward. "Alright, you're both one bubble off plumb. I'm just being honest. But here's what's going to happen now. My dear friend Char is going to get married, and she's going to have a lovely wedding.

And you nutjobs are going to jail. So, if the nutjobs in the building would kindly follow me to the back of the church, I'm sure Detective Whitman would be happy to give you a ride to your new home."

Cal looked at Detective Whitman. "Detective, you don't seriously think I had anything to do with this, do you?"

Detective Whitman pointed towards the back of the church. "We'll square all of that away down at the station. Now, as the woman said, back of the church."

Sorceress Stone touched the detective's arm. "Can I ride along with you? I'd like to ensure that Brittany is released immediately."

He nodded. "Yes, we'll work on Ms. Hobbs's release as soon as we get to the station." He and Sorceress Stone slid out of their pew.

Hugh raised his hand while looking at Tori. "Excuse me. What am I supposed to do about this one? She's nothing more than a lying witch."

Detective Whitman looked at Sorceress Stone. "She impeded my investigation. I'll take her to the station too."

Sorceress Stone nodded. "Indeed. Of course, it goes without saying she'll be expelled from my school."

I smiled a silent victory. "Gran. She'll need to be unfrozen so she can go with the detective."

Gran nodded and swirled her hand around Tori's head.

Tori unfroze with a startle. She looked up at Hugh curiously.

"You were just headed that way," said Hugh, pointing at Detective Whitman and Sorceress Stone.

"That way, why?" she asked, completely bewildered. "The wedding is about to start."

"We'll explain it when you come with us," said Detective Whitman.

I wanted to let out a cheer as Tori was led away with Cal and Midge, but instead, Hugh caught my eye. Silently he begged for forgiveness for believing Tori's lies. I didn't have time to inhale a deep breath before Gran rushed down the aisle to the back of the room.

"Alright, let's get this show back on the road. Places everyone!" she called out.

The Witch Squad slid back into our pew and took our seats. The rest of the unfrozen people sat down as well. "Now. We'll just do a quick five-second rewind, so no one remembers that unfortunate 'Murderer' comment," she said. She rolled her fingers over each other in a backwards motion causing Char to back her way out of the church. The doors swung shut, and everyone that had been facing me was still facing forward. "There. We should be good. Is everyone ready?"

I looked around. Heads bobbed around the room.

"Very well. Three...two...one!" She swirled her hand around her head and then clapped, releasing everyone from her magical hold and we heard the wedding march start anew.

The doors in the back of the church parted and Char, clutching her colorful bouquet, stepped forward. Everyone in the church stood as the music began. I took a quick peak towards the front of the church. My heart leapt for a brief moment at the sight of Mr. Bailey wiping away a tear as his bride began her journey towards him. *True love at its finest.*

CHAPTER 36

"You looked so beautiful, Char!" Sweets gushed as we each took turns hugging the bride and groom in the reception hall after the wedding.

"You looked pretty hot too, Mr. Bailey," Holly assured him.

Mr. Bailey smiled and patted his chest. "We make a handsome couple, I'll agree to that!"

"Thank you so much for inviting us, it was so fun to see you two get married," said Jax excitedly.

I held my breath, hoping that no one would remember my little outburst before the wedding. Once Detective Whitman and Sorceress Stone hauled Midge, Cal, and Tori away, the wedding had gone off without a hitch.

"Yeah, thanks for the invite," agreed Alba. "We've been eating junk food all week thanks to Midge, and that seafood buffet over there looks amazing!"

Char smiled proudly. "Oh, I'm so glad you could all come. Help yourselves to the food; we've got plenty of it. Have you had a chance to bump into my special guest yet?" she asked, looking at me specifically.

I smiled coyly. "Perhaps."

Char pointed at me. "You have! Well good. That was hard keeping it a secret all this time. I can't believe your mother didn't tell you that your granny and I were old college chums."

"Mom said that she didn't know *you* were Charlotte Adams. We've both heard stories about old Char Adams, but we had no idea she lived in Aspen Falls!"

Char giggled. "Well, it's sure been a hoot keeping up with you and your mother's comings and goings and reporting back to Phyllis. Now that the cat's outta the bag and Vic and I are hitched, I'm not sure what's going to keep me busy!"

Mr. Bailey looked at his wife in astonishment. "Are you kidding me? You're the busiest woman I know! Now you've got me to look after, and I promise to keep you busy, my little sugar pie."

Char patted his arm playfully. "Oh, Vic. You sure will keep me busy, won't you? Alright, girls. We've got to mingle. Go get yourself a plate to eat and have a fun time."

"We will, Char, thank you. Congratulations!" I sighed and plopped down at the table that we'd claimed for ourselves. Behind me, the DJ fired up the tunes. "Oh my gosh, I'm so glad all of that mess is over."

"Me too," agreed Jax, falling into the chair next to me.

One by one the rest of the girls pulled up a seat until we filled the round table with the pineapple centerpiece.

"I can't believe your grandmother showed up today," said Sweets in a hushed voice.

I rolled my eyes. "Leave it to Gran to make a scene."

Alba nearly choked on the dinner mint she'd just popped in her mouth. "Are you kidding me, Red? She saved your tail. You were the one about to make a scene! I can't believe you were just going to blurt that out at the wedding!"

"I'm sorry. But seeing Midge get all worked up when we looked at her and then all of those mismatched couples together, especially seeing Hugh and Tori together just about sent me over the edge. I think I momentarily lost my mind," I admitted.

"I suppose I oughta take responsibility for that one," drawled Hugh from behind me.

I looked at him over my shoulder. His tiny smirk did little to lessen my anger. The fact that he had fallen so easily for Tori's antics infuriated me. Without a word, my head snapped right back around again.

"I take it you're upset with me, darlin'?" he asked.

"What gave that away?" asked Alba with a little chuckle.

"I don't know about you girls, but I'm starving," said Sweets from the other side of the table.

Holly nodded and pushed herself back from the table. "Yeah, me too. Come on, girls; let's get through the buffet line before all of the senior citizens make it over from the church."

Jax giggled but followed Holly and Sweets.

Alba stood next to me protectively as she eyed Hugh. "You better not hurt her," she muttered. "I know where you live."

Hugh nodded. "You've got my word, Alba."

"I'm gonna get some food. Want us to bring you a plate before all the good stuff's gone?" she asked me.

I smiled at her. It felt good to have a friend watching my back. "Yeah, thanks, Alba."

When she'd gone, Hugh sat down in her chair. I refused to make eye contact with him or turn my chair around to face him.

"Oh, darlin'. I know you've got your tail up, but please don't be mad at me," he began. "Tori flat out lied to me. Just like she lied to you."

"Puh," I breathed. "We knew from the beginning something wasn't right. We knew Brittany couldn't have been the killer. Because *we knew her.*" I turned to him then and looked him straight in the eye. "You *know me*, Houston. I would *never* cheat on you. I'm not that kind of person."

He nodded. "You're right. I'm sorry, darlin'. But there you were right in front of me, smoochin' on another fella. I thought I had the evidence right in front of my very eyes. And then I texted you, and you didn't respond, so I thought that was it. We were over."

"I told you when I called that I'd broken my phone," I said.

He wiped his forehead with the back of his hand. "I know you did. You mentioned it in passing, but I clean forgot. I'm sorry. Can you ever forgive me?"

I sighed as I looked at him. He had really hurt me, and I didn't know how to feel better just because he wanted me to. "I don't know, Hugh. Maybe."

He nodded. "A maybe's better than a no. I'll give you time, darlin'," he said. He leaned over and kissed my forehead. "I'll let you enjoy the rest of the wedding with your girlfriends. I'll see you back at school."

I gave him a tight smile. "Bye, Hugh."

"Bye, Mercy Mae," he said and quietly walked away.

"Where's Hugh going?" Jax asked as she came back to the table with a plate full of seafood and fresh fruit.

"He's going back to The Institute," I said sadly.

Suddenly the excitement I felt over having all that stress off my shoulders, dissipated. Left in its place was a dull heartache.

"Did you two break up?" she demanded.

I shook my head. "We didn't have to break up. He broke up with me earlier today."

"Well then did you get back together?!"

"Nope."

Sweets put her plate down on the table. "What? You and Hugh aren't together anymore? I thought he was coming over to apologize."

"He did apologize. I'm just not ready to forgive him yet."

Holly and Alba returned to the table with three plates of food.

Alba put a plate down in front of me, and the girls all sat down.

"Thanks, Alba," I said, plucking a piece of pineapple off the top of the pile and tossing it in my mouth. The sweet taste of the fruit relaxed my shoulders slightly.

"So why aren't you ready to forgive Hugh?" Holly asked. "It was Tori's fault. Not his."

"I know. I just – I just feel weird."

Alba stopped eating and looked up at us. "I think I know what the problem is."

"What?"

"Finish your food, and then I'll tell you."

An hour later the five of us sat in Sweets's car outside the two-story house. It was our third visit that week.

"Are we ready?" Alba asked.

"Might as well get this over with."

We got out of the car and climbed the front steps to the deck. Jax knocked on the door.

Danielle answered. We could tell that she'd been crying. "You're here!" She turned around and hollered into the living room. "It's the Witch Squad!"

"Tell them to come in," said Aaron's voice from the living room.

We followed Danielle through the foyer and into the living room where the other two Whiting kids were snuggled up on the couch.

"We came to tell you that we solved your mother's murder," said Sweets softly.

Rachel nodded. "We already heard."

"Who told you?" I asked, surprised that word had already made it back to them.

"Tish stopped over. She told us everything. She felt horrible about having an affair with our dad," Danielle explained with a sniffle.

"I'm so sorry that your dad was involved in all of it," said Jax sadly.

"Thanks. We're still in shock. It's going to take a while to put this past us," said Aaron, with his arm around Rachel's shoulder.

Rachel looked up at her big brother. "At least we have each other."

Danielle sat down on the other side of Aaron and leaned her head on his shoulder. "Yeah. We'll get through it together."

"Thank you for everything you did to solve our mother's murder. At least we can finally put her to rest," said Aaron with a glimmer of tears in his eyes.

A staticky image suddenly flickered into view behind the sofa. My eyes widened. I elbowed Alba. "Can you see that?"

"See what?" she whispered back.

"The ghost behind the couch!"

She shook her head. "I don't see anything."

"There's a ghost behind our couch?" Rachel asked, practically crawling up her brother's torso.

I smiled softly. "It's your mom."

Denise's kind smile looked down at her three children proudly as they looked up into the air, searching for her face. "Hi, Mercy. Tell the kids I'll miss them," she whispered.

"She said she'll miss you," I said with a choked voice. Tears dampened my eyes.

"Mom! We'll miss you too," cried Danielle.

"We love you so much, Mom," Rachel told the air behind her before breaking into a sob.

"We'll never forget you, Mom," said Aaron, turning around to search for his mother's face.

Denise tried to hold back her sobs as she looked upon them all sadly. "Thank you, Mercy. Tell all of your friends thank you for giving my children peace. They deserve to be at peace. I can go now. Please tell the children I'll forever watch over them."

"I will. Goodbye, Denise, we'll miss you too," I whispered back as I smiled through my own tears at her.

"She's going to leave now. She said she can be at peace," I told the group.

"Don't go, Mom!" cried Danielle.

Denise's face crumpled, and her body shook with sobs. "Shh, Danielle, sweetheart. Tell them that anytime they're feeling an emptiness inside of them, they shouldn't feel sad. Tell them to rejoice in those moments because I'll be right there filling those empty spaces. I'll walk beside them every time they need me."

I nodded and repeated to them what Denise had said. Even though it brought more tears to their eyes, I could see them taking comfort in that. It lifted my heart to see how those words had helped, if only slightly.

"She's going to go now," I whispered.

"No, Mom, no!" said Rachel. "Stay a little longer."

"I have to go," said Denise sadly. "It's my time."

"She has to," I whispered.

"I love you, Mom," Aaron called out.

"Bye, Mom! We all love you," said Rachel as Danielle sobbed on her shoulder.

The girls all waved at her too and when everyone said their goodbyes and just as suddenly as she had appeared – she disappeared.

"She's gone," I whispered. "She said she'd watch over you forever."

"I know she will," whispered Aaron, hugging his sisters close to him. "Thank you all for helping us get closure. It's what we needed."

THE RIDE HOME WAS QUIET BUT CATHARTIC. JAX WENT WITH the rest of the girls to get a coffee at the coffee shop. I just went back to our dorm room. I wanted a little quiet. Sneaks was waiting for me when I got there.

"Mom, what are you doing in here?" I sighed, falling onto the bed.

"I was just checking on you. That was quite the wedding," she said softly.

"Yeah, it was quite the day," I admitted.

"Are you alright?"

"I will be."

"How are things between you and Hugh?"

I shrugged. "Too soon to tell." Laying on my back, I raised my legs above my head and stuffed my toes into the springs of Jax's bed. "How was your date with *Merrick*?"

"It wasn't much of a date, Mercy. He left after the wedding to go down to the police station."

"I bet Gran's happy about that," I whispered under my breath.

"It was her fault we were ever separated in the first place."

"Thank God for Gran," I snapped angrily.

"Mercy! She ruined your brother's life and much of mine. If she hadn't done what she did…"

"Merrick would have probably been my father. I know, Mom. Like I said, *thank God for Gran*."

Sneaks lowered her head, and mom's voice came out softened. "He was a different man then."

"He's a different man *now*, Mom. I wish you could see that."

"I see more than you think, Mercy. I'm not blind. I'll make a good decision."

"Well, you better make it fast. Detective Whitman only accepted the date with Sorceress Stone because you went with Merrick to the wedding. But they used to date. They could get back together now."

Mom laughed softly. "I told you, Mercy. I'm not blind. I know that's what happened."

"So what are we going to do about Gran?"

"We're going to figure it out, Merc. Together. Whatever she has to say, we'll be there to hear it… together."

"Promise?"

"I promise, Mercy."

ALSO BY M.Z. ANDREWS

Other Books Set in Aspen Falls in Reading Order

The Mystic Snow Globe Mystery Series

The Witch Island Series

ABOUT THE AUTHOR

Hello! I'm M. I live in the Midwest. I enjoy my house full of family, including my wonderfully amazing husband, four beautiful daughters, two handsome sons, and an amazing sidekick cat, who keeps me company all day while I dream up my crazy and exciting stories!

I love writing, gardening, football games, and DIY projects. I love chatting with fans, so feel free catch up with me on Facebook or Twitter.

If you'd like to be the first notified when the next Witch Squad Cozy Mystery comes out, you can sign up for my newsletter. Finally, if you enjoyed the book, **I would really appreciate you leaving a review!**

All the best,

XOXO - M

For more information:
www.mzandrews.com
mzandrews@mzandrews.com

Made in the USA
Las Vegas, NV
24 February 2021

18536770R00198